UNTAMED

SHORE

UNTAMED

SHORE

Silvia Moreno-Garcia

The following is a work of fiction. Names, characters, places, events and incidents are either the product of the author's imagination or used in an entirely fictitious manner. Any resemblance to actual persons, living or dead, is entirely coincidental.

ISBN 978-1-951709-28-0
eISBN: 978-1-951709-00-6
Library of Congress Control Number: 2019956576

First trade paperback edition January 2021
by Agora Books
An imprint of Polis Books, LLC
44 Brookview Lane
Aberdeen, NJ 07747
PolisBooks.com

Novels by Silvia Moreno-Garcia

Signal to Noise
Certain Dark Things
The Beautiful Ones
Gods of Jade and Shadow
Mexican Gothic

Chapter 1

The beach smelled of death. Half a dozen sharks lay under the sun, waiting to be salted. Whenever Viridiana saw them, glistening belly up in the midday heat, they reminded her of dominoes set upon a table before the game begins.

An angry shark can bite through tin and metal, the locals said; it could cut through the boats they took out to sea. And looking at the jaws hanging from the wooden rack, Viridiana might concur. But she liked the sharks, she even liked the stench of their liver roasting on a fire. It was a bitter, foul smell, but she had pleasant memories of her father cooking it, attempting to extract oil out of the liver. He'd done things like that when she was young, trying to make himself comfortable in Desengaño, to leave his city roots behind. He eventually stopped. It was obvious he was a city boy, with his books and his diploma from the university under his arm, and no amount of shoving a shark's liver across a pan was going to make him a fisherman. Besides, there was no point in trying to master the nets and the boats, anyway, since sharks were almost worthless.

Once upon a time, during World War II, fishermen could make a fortune selling shark livers, and many a fool in search of quick cash had steered his boat towards Baja California. Synthetic vitamins had killed that business. In Desengaño, stubborn fishermen still dragged the sharks out of the water, but many

1

others dedicated themselves to hauling shrimp or an assortment of fish. The ones left chasing sharks sold them to merchants who inevitably passed them off as valuable "cod" fillets. No one would pay more than a pittance for shark meat, but shark meat wrapped in plastic and advertised as "genuine Norwegian cod" was worth the effort. Not that this helped the fishermen, since they sold the meat for a peso while the merchant sold it for fifteen in the city.

But people had to make a living.

The shark's skin was sold to make boots, and the fishermen hung the shark's large jaws from a wooden rack, hoping tourists might purchase one, or else they might sell shark teeth dangling from strings.

There were not many tourists. The highway now brought Americans in their cars, pulling their boats behind them, dollars stuffed in their pockets, but Desengaño was out of the way. There was one hotel with two dozen rooms. The owner had a brother in Mexico City who owned a travel agency, and he convinced foreigners to take a trip to scenic Baja and funnelled them into the hotel.

Desengaño was really nothing at all.

Viridiana stared at the sea, at the sharks. Reynier had asked for her to stop by, but The Dutchman never woke before noon. She should have waited until later to leave home, but her mother had popped out another kid and it wailed day and night—a colicky monster.

Viridiana scratched her leg and looked at the shadows traced by the sun. She wasn't wearing a watch, but there was no need for that here. You could figure the time by observing what the fishermen were doing by the seashore, or paying attention to the noises of the town. The church bell clanged early every morning and every evening to further mark the day. At nine Don

Tito opened his tiendita, and everyone else followed suit, doors banging open or metal curtains going up. Around noon the doors banged shut again. They didn't bother lowering the curtains, all the locals knew it was time for a nap. The bar in the hotel didn't open until seven, but the cantina welcomed everyone at four even if the fishermen wouldn't get there until eight. The bar catered to whatever foreigners were passing by and the more moneyed townspeople; the cantina took in fishermen, tradesmen—the local alcoholics who could spare the cash. By eleven, the pharmacy turned its sign off and the drunks stumbled past it, and stumbled home. Desengaño plunged into silence.

The shadows cast by the shark's jaw indicated it was time to get on her way. The few foreigners who had built permanent vacation houses lived outside the town proper. All of them except for Reynier, who was located a few streets from the town square. He had a large yellow house, which distinguished itself from the houses of the wealthier Mexicans in town—the doctor, the pharmacist—by its relative simplicity. It was neither faux-colonial nor boldly modern. Instead, it was made of wood—an oddity in a place where everything was stone, cement, or adobe—and had a gable roof, making it easy to spot. The Dutchman's house, a landmark which you could use to map your steps.

Reynier didn't bother locking the front door, and she let herself in, heading directly to his office. Reynier kept books in three different languages in the office, but they also spilled throughout the house. She had learned to speak English, French and Dutch thanks to these books.

Reynier sat in his big burgundy chair, dressed in one of his prim charcoal suits. He never succumbed to the desire for casual fashions; the 1970s, with their polyester and flared trousers, had not been acknowledged in his home. Reynier's white beard was neatly trimmed, face tanned and streaked with wrinkles. Since she was a child he had always been old, weathered like a tree trunk, but around the house, black and white photos testified to a blond youth.

She sat on the slim, elegant gray couch opposite him. The shades were drawn and a fan whirled above their heads. It was not quite cool inside his office, but it was as good as it got without air conditioning. Some of the foreigners outside of Desengaño partook in that luxury. Reynier did not. In this, too, he was old fashioned.

"I have a job for you," Reynier said, with that deep, soothing voice. "There are people coming to stay at Milton's house and they don't speak a word of Spanish."

Milton had been a long-time visitor to Desengaño. He came every spring, since before they finished the highway in '72, seven years ago. But Milton passed away over Christmas.

"His kids?" she asked.

"No. They're renting the house to friends. They'll be here in two days. I'll hand them the keys. I already sent Delfina and her daughter to clean the place up and air it out."

All the regular visitors knew each other, and they all knew Reynier. He kept an eye on their houses for most of them: Reynier was the only one who stayed all year long. It wasn't difficult, since the regulars had only half a dozen homes. Although Narciso Ferrer, the hotel owner, was always talking about how tourists would one day flow in plentiful numbers through the town, his prophecy had failed to materialize.

"How long will they be staying?"

"A few months. The man I spoke to, Ambrose, has a notion to write a book while he is here. He needs a personal assistant. So it wouldn't be a weekend touring them through the coves. He wants someone to type notes for him and the like."

This was different. When the tourist season was in full swing, Viridiana made a living as a guide. There was another guide in town, Alejandro, four years older than her and the son-in-law of the hotel owner, which meant all business from there was siphoned to him. Viridiana was left to attract the attention of the young people who were camping on the beaches or the sport fishermen who rattled into town with camper in tow. Reynier tried to direct business her way when he could, and he also paid her to stop by once a week and speak to him in Spanish. To improve his language skills, he said, but they spent more time practicing Dutch or English, for her sake, than speaking any Spanish. He didn't need the practice, anyway, he got by well enough. He did it because Viridiana's father had been a friend and Reynier felt responsible for the girl, even if her dad didn't feel responsible for anyone.

Viridiana frowned. Her father's memory had been pleasant before, when she had been thinking about him frying the shark's liver, but that had been a memory of their time together. Now she recalled his abandonment.

"What is it?" Reynier asked.

"It's just, tourist season is around the corner," she lied. She did not talk with Reynier about her father, nor about any personal matters. They discussed books, music and the vegetation of the region. "There will be people going through town. I'd lose business."

"He has money. They pay would be good, I'm certain. If it's not, you could turn it down."

"I wouldn't have time to see you each week if I'm busy with them. And the house is far," Viridiana mused. Milton's house was nicknamed The End for a reason. There was a big stretch of nothing between the town and that property.

"They're expecting you Friday. You should introduce yourself.

If it doesn't suit you, turn it down," Reynier concluded.

"I suppose so," Viridiana said. "The man, then, he's a writer?"

A writer could prove interesting. She'd never met one. He might own a lot of books. She had probably read Reynier's books twice-over. There was no library in town and no bookstore. For fun you could take a dip in the ocean or drive to the lighthouse and contemplate the view. Viridiana did plenty of contemplating.

"I don't know. He has a wife and there is someone else traveling with them, that is all I was told. Get the chess board, please, I'd like to play a round," Reynier said, taking a pair of horn-rimmed glasses from his suit jacket and putting them on.

Viridiana opened the cabinet and took out the chess set, setting it on a circular table. Her father had been so good at chess that he played for money in a park in Mexico City, during his student days. She recalled standing in this very room as a small child, holding onto her father's leg as he spoke with Reynier and moved a chess piece—their conversations also centering on books or music. But there had been something different between those interactions and her gaming sessions with Reynier. Her father exuded a warmth, a joy, which she did not possess. He made many quips. They were not crass jokes, like her stepfather, but witty observations that brightened the room. Her father was charming.

Charming and hopeless and a city man. He withered in the town and when she was six he'd gone off to find employment in Mexico City, promising to send for Viridiana and her mother. He promptly found himself a new family instead.

Viridiana rested her chin against the back of her hand, fixing her eyes on the black and white squares of the board, the beauty of the dark mahogany pieces and the pale figurines carved in bone. The faces of the pawns, the horses' manes, the towers' walls, were exquisitely detailed. Reynier's family had possessed money and although his circumstances had diminished—most of that money had gone to his older brothers—Reynier had bought himself a comfortable life in Mexico.

They played three games and then Viridiana bid Reynier goodbye. On her way home, she ran into Manuel and his mother, Brigida. When Brigida spotted her, she gave Viridiana a venomous look. Manuel had his perpetual, puzzled, slightly lost stare, his mouth trembling. Had Brigida not been there, Viridiana suspected he might have talked to her and the conversation would have awful. More awful than Brigida's contempt.

They had broken up two months before. What would have been an ordinary occurrence in any city took on Hollywoodesque proportions in Desengaño.

The story was both prosaic and expected. Viridiana dated Manuel for two years. They had been pushed together by force of habit and their parents. Viridiana's mother owned a store that sold clothes and makeup. Brigida had a stationery store and was also a money lender. There was a tiny Banamex branch in the town square, but the fishermen would never be able to get credit there, so they all went to Brigida.

Manuel and Viridiana's families thought that if they combined forces, they could both profit handsomely. Brigida believed that if her daughter-in-law manned the counter, she could go to Mexico City with her son to replenish their stock and speak to their suppliers. Normally, Manuel went alone and Brigida thought he couldn't negotiate, that she was better suited for this task. Or else she might take a vacation in Acapulco or Los Angeles, since the running of the store did not allow her any respite. Fanning herself in the noon heat, she had imagined Viridiana breaking the chain which tied her to the counter. She'd said as much to Viridiana's mother, Marta, over coffee.

But Viridiana, rather than marrying Manuel when he proposed, turned him down.

Looking at him Viridiana had read her future in his eyes: the house they would share with his mother, the long hours behind the counter while Manuel went to play dominoes, the three children. She was saving to move to Mexico City and Manuel was talking of tying the knot and settling down. Worst of all, Viridiana was well aware that he was proposing because his mother wanted him to—and because he was plain horny. A man of twenty, he wished to get laid and often. Unfortunately, Desengaño was puritanical. The girls of his age and class kept their legs primly closed. The girls of the lower classes, who readily smiled at tourists or took up with the fishermen, appalled him.

He was a snob. He also dreaded getting one of those women pregnant and then having to pay her off. His mother controlled the purse strings, and if she found out he was frolicking with a hussy, she'd beat him with a frying pan.

Besides, he coveted Viridiana. Years spent staring at her long neck, admiring the blackness of her hair, the eyes which everyone said had a "Moorish" touch, had built up his excitement. He had not seen her naked, small breasts, but he had touched them over her blouse, and the lack of full contact had turned into a sort of frenzy until he told himself he must marry her, sleep with her, possess her.

He thought of this as love.

Viridiana, had she been a bit more like the other girls from "decent" families in Desengaño, might have made the same mistake. But for one reason or another she was suspicious. Of herself, of the world. Viridiana thought Manuel represented more desire than affection, and knew enough about nets and sharks to picture herself tangled in a certain placid mediocrity which terrified her.

Or, like they grumbled in town, she was as stupid as her father.

Brigida walked past Viridiana, rigid as an arrow, her elbow knocking into the girl. Manuel followed his mother, throwing Viridiana one more glance before they turned the corner. Viridiana hurried home. In the living room she found her mother talking with Reina Orozco and was glad. Reina was the town gossip and, with her mother immersed in conversation, Viridiana was able to slip into her room and lock the door, which she was not supposed to do.

She opened the armoire and stood on her tiptoes, bringing down a box and setting it on one of the twin beds. The bedspreads were both pink, unchanged since her childhood. Viridiana's younger sister who shared her room was ten, and perhaps the bedspread was not so outrageous in her case. But Viridiana was a woman. A woman, who if her family had had their way, would have been walking to the altar by year's end. From pink bed to bridal bed, as if maturity were only to be allowed once the priest had officiated a ceremony.

Viridiana lay on the bed and took out the tape recorder and the microphone. Her father sent a card on Christmas, and every two or three years he mailed a birthday present which was both expensive and useless. He never sent alimony.

A few months before he had mailed Viridiana the recorder, with a note saying, "the girls are now keeping audio diaries in these cassette-corders." That was how he wrote it down, "cassette-corder," and included the manual, a leather carrying case, a microphone and a bunch of blank tapes.

Viridiana had not known what to do with the machine. At first, she sat by the seashore and recorded the sound of the waves against the rocks or the cry of the gulls. Then she started speaking into the microphone. It was not an organized diary. She did not record herself every day and sometimes she did not talk for more than a few minutes while others she went on for an hour. Her thoughts were tangled. She spoke about both meaningless and important issues, then carefully noted the date on a sticker or a piece of paper she affixed to each tape. January 1979, February 1979, March 1979. She kept the tapes in order.

She knew not what purpose it achieved, but she found the process oddly comforting.

Viridiana pressed the red button on the recorder. The microphone was much too close to her mouth and there was some popping as she spoke.

"The problem with my technique, Reynier says, is not that I lack talent, but that I persistently deny my blind spots. My technical aptitude is overwhelmed by psychological factors."

Viridiana moved the microphone away a little.

"I need to see movements more clearly and I don't see them because I don't look for them."

Viridiana paused, the microphone resting against her chin for a moment.

"Reynier wants me to meet these Americans who might need an assistant. I'll have to see what they are like."

She stopped the recording.

Chapter 2

The ocean is uncertain in Baja California, as if it wishes to be two things at once; both wild and contemplative. It pounds violently against stark cliffs, then, a couple of kilometers away, sweeps onto gentle beaches. People think Baja California is the desert, and the desert is one single, flat, lonely space. Baja California is mountain ridges, clouds of fog spreading over the land, the salt fields, the shocking sight of a valley shaded by date palms, the orchards where olives grow, the stone missions with sun-dried adobe bricks left to crumble into dust, ancient caves decorated with two-headed serpents, —and yes, the desert dotted with cacti. The weather changes as quickly as the ocean. The sheltered Gulf of California is blazing hot and moist in the summer, while the waters of the Pacific coast remain noticeably cooler. Hurricane season begins in August. Storms are sudden, the rain carpeting the desert with flowers, transforming the land from one day to the next.

Everything changes here and everything stays the same, she thought.

But Viridiana was in motion that day, her feet pedalling with determination, her hat set firmly atop her head. She had that sensation, like when the winds pick up before a storm. Omens, Grandmother used to call it, her toothless mouth grinning.

Milton's house was located on a jagged seaside cliff, up a narrow road, defiant and alone. The End. When you approached it indeed seemed like it was the end of everything, with this house left by itself against the immensity of the sky. Viridiana's grandmother had told her folktales about the days when there were giants walking the peninsula and Viridiana thought it was possible to picture one of those giants bending down and placing the house atop the cliff.

In front of the house, someone had parked a brand new red Cadillac Eldorado, which was dusty from the highway and the unpleasant roads. It was nevertheless a beauty, the sort of car Viridian only saw in magazines or TV. Never up close.

Viridiana rested her battered bicycle against a wall of the white house and took off her hat, dabbing her forehead with a handkerchief as she stared at the car, resisting the impulse to touch it and ensure it was not a mirage. She wasn't car-crazy, like boys were. Driving the family's truck seemed to her pretty much the same as driving anything else, although her stepfather didn't let her drive it that often. But this car. Now this was a car to gawk at.

She straightened her blouse, regretfully eyed her worn tennis shoes and ran a hand over her hair before ringing the bell.

A woman opened the door. She was tall and slim, her blonde hair all layered flicks. Her blue eyeliner matched her eyes and she wore a heavy lapis lazuli necklace around her neck. She looked like she was in her mid-thirties, but Viridiana did not know any woman in her mid-thirties who would wear a tight red jumpsuit like this lady did. She was beautiful enough to be in films. Like the car, she had been transported from a different, parallel reality.

"Hi, I'm Viridiana," she said. "Reynier told me I should stop by."

Viridiana held out her hand.

"Come on in. I'm Daisy," the woman said, but did not offer to shake Viridiana's hand. Instead she started walking and Viridiana followed her.

She had never been inside this house before. The living room was dreadfully large and the shaggy carpet under her feet seemed completely unsuited to such a warm climate. The carpet was white to boot, as was much of the furniture, which would make it extra difficult to clean. There were two couches—white—facing each other, a lone, egg-shaped chair in bright yellow and a matching yellow painting. The stairs leading to the second floor were on the left, and the railing was painted white. Modern, chic and glossy, that was her first impression of this house.

Two men sat in the living room, one on each couch. The one occupying the loveseat was an older man, his brown hair was noticeably thinning, his eyes were small and fanned by numerous wrinkles. He had a painfully receding hairline, a gut which could not be concealed and an expression of utter dissatisfaction.

The second man was much younger. Late twenties, at the most. Like the woman, he was also blond, but a dirty sort of blond, and his eyes were green. If the woman looked like she could be a film star, he looked like he might be a model. His features were chiselled, his mouth generous. He gave the impression of a man who liked to laugh and was, perhaps, in the middle of telling a joke when they had walked in.

"This is my husband, Ambrose, and this is my brother, Gregory," Daisy said.

"I'm Viridiana. Reynier sent me."

"Yes, Reynier, he said you'd come. Where are my smokes?" the older man asked, looking up sharply at the blonde woman.

"You left them in the kitchen," his wife replied.

"Go get them," Ambrose said, making a motion with his hand.

The woman exited. None of them had offered Viridiana a seat, so she stood rigidly in place and slid her hands into her jeans' pockets.

"Did Reynier tell you what I'm looking for?" Ambrose asked.

"He said you want a personal assistant, someone to type notes for you."

"And can you type?"

"Yes. I took a shorthand typing class in high school and I've done work for Reynier and other folks."

"Can you read and write in English?"

"English, Spanish and Dutch," she said. "My French is serviceable, too."

"What do you know," the older man said, looking surprised. "I didn't realize you could study that here."

It always seemed to amaze foreigners that they were not all running around in loincloths, praying to the rain gods.

"You look awfully young," Ambrose said, frowning. "How old are you?"

"Eighteen."

"When Reynier mentioned you, I thought you were older."

"Eighteen or forty, what does it matter?" Daisy said walking back in and handing her husband a packet of cigarettes.

"Kids might get bored here," Ambrose said, he took a cigarette and then, as if considering seating arrangements for the first time, motioned for her to sit down. "Do you want a cigarette?"

"I don't smoke," Viridiana said, and she sat on the same three-piece sofa as the young man, but kept a good deal of space between them. His shoes were two-tone, blue and red, and he had loosely knotted a matching blue and red neckerchief around his throat. It was probably silk. She'd seen such a thing in catalogues.

"It's a good thing. Filthy habit. I'm trying to kick a few of my filthy habits," Ambrose said leaning back on the couch. "The reason why I mention your age is because we'd like to keep you here full time. There's a guest room you could have. But young people, they need bars and movies and excitement, you know? I don't want you complaining that you can't go out all the time."

"There's no cinemas in Desengaño," Viridiana informed him. "But I can come and go, you don't have to offer me a room."

She had never heard of such an arrangement. Only maids lived in a household and Viridiana didn't want them thinking she would scrub their floors, cook their food, wash their clothes, and then also take dictation. They might be trying to get all-in-one servant for cheap. She was not up for that.

"My husband keeps odd hours," Daisy said, sitting down next to Ambrose. "He wakes up at noon and works at midnight. I don't think you can possibly come and go in the dark like that."

"Yes, I'm a night owl," he said, patting his wife's leg. "What would an assistant be worth to me if she's not here when I need her?"

"My rates would have to go up to make up for the inconvenience," Viridiana said.

"Name an amount, I can make it happen."

"Well… "

"Don't be coy."

She blurted an amount twice as much as she had originally thought to ask for. The man smiled and told his wife to bring his checkbook. Which she did. And then in sloppy handwriting he made out a check, which Viridiana carefully inspected.

Ambrose P. Allerton. But more than his name, it said this was a man of great wealth and indifference, whose pen had not faltered for a second as he wrote down the digits. He did not have to worry how much money he spent.

"You understand I'll want you here until the end of the summer," the man said. "I don't want to turn around and discover midway through July that you are off on a vacation or something of the sort."

"I had none planned," she said, setting the check on the wide, low coffee table between them. "But I also haven't said I'll take the job."

"You have to think it over? Think it over. But come back and give me an answer," he concluded. "Take the check. If you don't want the job, return it tomorrow."

He stretched out his hand, holding out the check. She nodded and slid it into her pocket. Then she hesitated, not knowing if this was her cue to leave or if she ought to wait some more. Didn't they have questions? Was that the entire interview?

The younger man, Gregory, stood up. "I'll show you out," he offered.

He walked her to the front entrance. He looked at her placidly, with an appraising eye that was foreign to her. It was the eye of an expert collector.

"It's a good job. Ambrose is lazy. Most days you'll probably do as you please while he waits for inspiration," he said.

He wasn't wearing a jacket and his shirt was tight against his chest. She lingered by the doorway even though she could have taken off with a simple "see ya."

"He wants to write a book?" she asked.

"That's what he says. Between you and me, I don't think he's finished a single page yet."

"Why doesn't he type his own notes, then, if they are so sparse?"

"Ambrose wouldn't know the letter q from the letter p on a typewriter. Besides, I think it makes him feel like he's a 'real' writer if he has a personal assistant. And we don't speak a lick of Spanish. We'll need your help when we run errands in town."

"And you'll really be here until the end of summer?"

"That's the plan. Don't people usually stay for the summer?"

"Some do," she said. "But most folks come for a week or two. Then they're off back home or to see more interesting sights. La Paz, or even Mexico City."

"He wants to stay here. He thinks it'll be quiet. He shipped all kinds of papers and books and things ahead to make sure he'll be comfortable. And he's already asked Reynier to make sure that cleaning woman he sent comes over twice a week."

"Delfina?"

"Yes, that's the name. Like I said, we don't speak a lick of Spanish so you'll have to translate for us even with her. But Reynier assured us she's a hard worker and he said you're reliable," he leaned against the doorway after she finally stepped out, crossing his arms "Is it true they hunt sharks here?"

"When the waters are warm."

"I've never seen a shark."

He smiled. What a smile. Teeth gleaming white, all neat and straight, and the curve of the mouth told her he was used to people noticing the smile, noticing him. The smile almost dared her to stare.

Instead, Viridiana looked down at the hat between her hands and placed it on her head. It had a string, which she tightened, ensuring it would not be blown away by the wind.

"You think you'll take the job?" Gregory asked.

She'd gone to visit them late in the day, but not so late she'd be riding home in the dark. It was folly to take the bicycle in the nighttime. You'd get hit by a car. But now the sky was turning purple and she'd best be off. So she shrugged and rode away.

* * *

Viridiana's mother was not pleased, and she made it known. They sat at the table, Mother, Viridiana and her step-father. Mother lit a cigarette and tapped it against the ashtray, almost violently.

She only smoked when she was angry.

"It's nonsense, that's what it is," Marta said, her voice dipping.

In the next room Viridiana could hear her younger siblings playing and the noise of the TV. *El Chavo del Ocho* was on, the laugh-track punctuating the jokes. There were loud cries, someone was chasing someone. Feet stomped upon the floor. The house was filled with noises from the crack of dawn until the late of night. It was a frenzied nest of activity. Marta's stepfather was decidedly Catholic and he thought each child came into the world with a torta under the arm, hence he approved of his wife's fecundity.

Viridiana's aunt shushed someone, but to no avail, and then the dogs began to bark. They had three, they belonged to her stepfather but he never took care of them. It was Viridiana who had to fill their bowls with leftover rice, bits of chicken, and old tortillas. It was Viridiana who scraped dog shit from the floor, tried to clean the stinking couch where the dogs liked to piss, and threw away the dirty newspapers from the bird cages.

She hated all animals. Except sharks. The sharks were entirely different. She always felt sorry for them, even when she ate their meat.

"It's good money," Viridiana countered, pointing to the check she had set on the table and which her stepfather was examining. "I could save for university."

"University," her mother said.

"Yes."

"And what would you do in your university?"

"Study something," she muttered.

"Study languages. Translate. Charge almost nothing by the page. Mexico City, the university, they're nonsense. You should get married."

Marta had once made the same trek to the city where she'd

met a useless young man who could recite French poems and translate the lyrics of popular American songs. But then he'd gotten her pregnant and translating lyrics never paid the rent. So, she'd journeyed back home, back with a belly full of Viridiana and a husband in tow. It turned out the husband was fool who spent too many afternoons enthused with the contemplation of the sea when what she needed was a man of action, a man who would seize opportunities and save money instead of wasting it on ordering books from the capital.

Marta, made wiser by her brush with mediocrity and misspent dreams, wished tangible rewards for her daughter. A house, a car, vacations in Acapulco and Disneyland. Viridiana could get that if she married. God knew with five brothers and sisters Viridiana could not expect any reliable support from her mother, not in the long run.

"Your mother has a point," her stepfather said. "Besides, we need your help around the house."

Babysitting. Feeding dogs and canaries. That's how they expected her to spend her time.

"I'd give you a portion of my check, of course. A fourth for the family to help with expenses would be fair, don't you think?" Viridiana said. She knew that was what Ignacio wanted to hear. There was enough cash that she was willing to part with a chunk of it. She'd still be left in a good position.

Ignacio pretended to think it through.

"It might do her good," Ignacio told her mother. "It would teach her about real work. She works only an hour or two a day during tourist season, and another hour with the Dutchman."

"I'm aware," her mother replied. "She refuses to sit behind the counter. Putting on airs, that's what she's good at."

Viridiana did not protest. She scratched one of the white flowers printed on the plastic tablecloth. There were yellow plastic flowers in a vase in the middle of the table and a matching arrangement next to the figurine of San Judas Tadeo, who watched them from a corner. Beneath the saint a horseshoe dangled downward from a nail. The horseshoe was wrapped in crimson rayon thread and decorated with gold sequins and a picture of San Martin Caballero. This was an amulet, quite pagan, but of course the inhabitants of the household were all devout Catholics who mixed superstitions and religions with ease.

Once upon a time Viridiana had believed in the mystical powers of the horseshoe and the San Judas Tadeo porcelain figurine with the green robe, but the benevolent, pale saint had not answered her prayers, never brought her father back, and she had long since stopped making the sign of the cross when she passed.

"Let's see how she does having to work for these people every day, each week. It'll teach her to earn her bread. High time, too."

"They're strangers."

"Reynier knows them, mama," Viridiana lied.

Marta looked at the ashtray, brows furrowed, then snapped her head up and stared at her daughter.

"You'd have to come home every Sunday, for mass, and then stay in the evening for supper."

"Sure."

"And you'll have to be polite to Brigida and Manuel Esparza, if they are around," Marta added.

"Why would they stop by?"

"To play dominoes. Like we used to."

Viridiana understood the plan. They'd toss Manuel and her into the same room, hoping to rekindle their relationship. Hoping that Viridiana would get married and move out, solving their space problems in a house that was too crowded now that Marta had a new baby. Six kids, counting Viridiana. If they had a seventh, someone would have to sleep on the couch.

Viridiana had managed to avoid Manuel, but she couldn't avoid him if he was sitting in her living room. Would Brigida object? Perhaps, at first. But Marta must feel pretty sure she'd agree to the plan.

Let Manuel come to visit again, then. Viridiana was capable of polite conversation—or an enduring silence, whichever suited the situation better.

"And you'll behave yourself in that house," Marta said. "No nonsense."

"What nonsense? It's a boring old guy and his family," Viridiana declared. She had not mentioned the family included a man who looked like he had stepped out of the pages of a fashion magazine. No need for that.

She glanced at the figure of San Judas Tadeo and thought that the little statue bore a vague resemblance to Gregory. The hair color, the carefully trimmed beard, most of all the eyes. Although the American's eyes were green and she was certain the statuette had brown eyes, as did the picture on the plastic prayer card everyone carried in their pocket or placed by the nightstand.

Pray for me because I am alone and without help, the prayer card said. This was the real resemblance, the idea rattling in her brain that the American had been sent there to help her, to change her life. She could feel it, like when her Grandma used to read omens, only she'd never taught Viridiana that sort of stuff.

But now, Viridiana thought it was definitely a good omen and that night, when they went to bed she stopped in front of the saint and made the sign of the cross.

Chapter 3

The guest room had white sheets and a white cover. All the walls were white, but the one behind the bed's headboard was painted with red, yellow and brown circles. A curtain with a matching circle pattern hid a closet with built-in shelves, next to which sat a table and a white chair with a red cushion. A large, yellow pendant lamp with a chrome ring hung from the middle of the ceiling.

Viridiana set down her suitcase on the bed and contemplated the room. It looked modern, but sterile, like something out of a science fiction film. She could not imagine anyone living here. Viridiana's room had posters of a couple of Luis Buñuel films which her father had owned before her: *The Exterminating Angel* and *Viridiana*. There were postcards from Paris and Madrid, also leftovers from her father—he had been in Europe for three months before he met Marta. The detritus of his life. And there were other bits she'd collected on her own, from newspapers and magazines. The picture of an actor or a model who struck her as handsome. A hairstyle she'd seen and thought to imitate.

But no one had ever lived in this room, it was an empty shell.

An egg shell, even, since the table was rounded and there were circles on the wall. She imagined herself lying on that bed, on her side, curled up, like the chick inside an egg. Embryonic, lacking a shape.

Viridiana opened her suitcase and took out her clothes and

placed them in the closet. She hadn't brought much, and she was done quickly. Then she unzipped her backpack and pulled out her tape recorder.

Several times she had thought to send the tapes to her father, so that he might hear her voice. But mostly she spoke to an unnamed listener. Like now, as she described the room. On the rare instance when she went to the movies in a nearby town she cut out the ad for the film from a newspaper and glued it into a notebook. She was still at that age when every experience must be catalogued, and she described the room with the vague notion that it might be important one day. That she might be important and her haphazard recollections would be of value to historians.

There was a knock on the door.

"Come in," Viridiana said.

"Hi," Daisy said. "I wanted to see how you're finding the place."

"It's pretty good."

Daisy glanced at the tape recorder and the microphone on the bed and chuckled. "I thought you were talking to yourself for a moment."

"I suppose I was, kind of. It's a sort of journal I keep," Viridiana said, tucking away the recorder in a side table by the bed.

"I kept a journal, too, when I was a girl. But it had pages and I used a pen."

"I had one like that too," Viridiana admitted. "But then my father sent the recorder. He never sends any sensible presents, but all my mother and my stepfather do is give me sensible presents. New shoes, that type of thing, you know?"

"My grandmother used to knit a horrid sweater for me each Christmas," Daisy said, sitting on the bed with her. "She really couldn't knit, so the snowmen were deformed and the reindeer were the wrong color. No matter how much I asked for something else, it was always a sweater. What kind of shoes do they buy you? Are they chunky and horrid?"

"Yes," Viridiana said with a chuckle. "Patent leather, like a little schoolgirl."

"And black? And must you wear them often?"

"Yes, I have to wear them every Sunday."

Daisy smiled. "Then you have it worse. I only had to wear the sweater on Christmas Eve."

Like Gregory, Daisy had a beautiful smile. But it had a different quality. Gregory's smile was self-assured, even vain. Daisy's smile was magnetic. You knew, looking at it, that Daisy had been admired and well-loved wherever she'd been. That when she'd left a town, people had thrown her a party. That she'd promised everyone she'd send postcards, she told them she would be back as soon as summer ended. That she had laughed and raised her glass of wine as others toasted to her. And then they never saw her again.

"I know you've asked only for Sundays off, but if you want Saturday, too, so you can go out with your friends, I can see if Ambrose would agree to that," Daisy said.

Viridiana glanced down at her backpack, tugging at the zipper. "No, there's no need. I don't have many friends these days."

"Oh?"

"I used to. But then my boyfriend and I broke up. You could say they took sides."

"That's sad."

Viridiana thought it was expected. Her ex-boyfriend's family had more money than hers and he was well-liked. She, on the other hand, quickly eroded the patience of the couple of friends who sided with her; she was curt and annoying. She could not help it. She hated how Patricia and Trinidad looked at her with their soft smiles and their hugs, hoping to find her heartbroken, and taken aback when she wasn't. They had been quietly incensed when she finally snapped and told them the simple truth: she could never see herself married to Manuel, she couldn't stomach being tied to this godforsaken town full of mediocre, silly people.

They took that as a personal insult—as ultimate proof that she was a cold-hearted bitch. They took that to mean she was like her father, an outsider cruising through.

"I dunno," Viridiana said.

"Maybe on a Saturday we can go to a spa and have our nails done."

"There are no spas around here. But there's a lady who cuts hair at her home and—"

"Of course there's no spa. I keep forgetting where we are," Daisy said, shaking her head. "We can do our own nails. Let me see those hands. You bite your nails! You shouldn't, it's crass. But, it can be fixed."

Viridiana's hands were indeed rather ugly, her cuticles a mess. She chewed and picked at them. Daisy's hands, on the other hand, seemed perfect and the nails were long, painted a glossy red. They matched the car parked outside.

"I've never really done my nails," Viridiana said.

"You're kidding. I love nails. I have since I was a young girl. The perfect polish can perk up your whole day, like a new pair of earrings. You do have pierced ears, don't you?"

"Yes," Viridiana said, touching her earlobe.

"Good. We'll have fun."

Viridiana didn't normally get this personable with the foreigners she worked for, but Daisy had that special quality which invites others to open their hearts. Within an hour she had decided that she liked the woman very much. She thought they might become best friends, that she could be like one of those lady's maids in old movies. A traveling companion, merrily seeing the world together.

Ambrose, on the other hand, she did not like at all. He had told her to unpack several boxes filled with books and papers, but nothing else. It wasn't hard work, but it was his tone that made her frown. He was used to lording others around.

On Viridiana's third night in the house, Ambrose ordered her to get a notepad and start taking dictation. He had not spoken at all about his book, so it was the first time she was actually asked to do real work.

They sat in the living room. Ambrose was on the couch in front of her, talking about inspiration.

"Don't take notes yet," he snapped, when he saw her grab her pen. "We're chatting right now. I'll let you know when to take notes."

Viridiana placed her hands against the notepad and waited. And listened. And waited.

Daisy came back with two glasses filled with ginger ale and handed one to Ambrose. It had three ice cubes, as he had requested. As far as Viridiana could tell, Daisy's main role around the house was to fetch things for Ambrose. He could never be bothered to stand up and walk to the kitchen.

"What will your book be about?" Viridiana asked, because all through his monologue about the art of writing, Ambrose had given no hints about what he was working on.

"Well... about a lot of things. California, for one. My life in California."

"Then it's autobiographical."

"No, no," Ambrose said, shaking his head and almost spilling his drink. He set it down on the coffee table in front of him. "It'll only be *inspired* by my life. But it'll have a realness to it, real stories, juicy ones. I know a lot of people. Big people. I have a lot of friends in Hollywood."

Ambrose set a hand on Daisy's leg as he spoke. His wife was wearing white shorts and a white t-shirt, but somehow the ensemble managed to look chic and effortless rather than plain.

"I even dated a couple of movie stars."

Daisy let out a little chuckle. "Don't let him fool you. Ambrose, darling, strippers are not movie stars."

It was nothing but a little joke and Viridiana smiled at it. Ambrose did not find it funny. His face went very red, he narrowed his eyes and he lifted the big hand which had been resting on Daisy's leg and brought down with a dry thud. It wasn't a playful slap. It was a mean, harsh blow. Daisy winced and Viridiana opened her mouth, but did not speak.

Even if she had said something, she doubted Ambrose would have heard her because now he was screaming.

"What do you know?!" he yelled. "What the fuck do you know?!"

Daisy did not reply. She clutched her glass of Ginger Ale, her body stiff, her lips pressed together.

"Always with your little digs. You think I don't notice? I notice alright, I notice."

He stood up and walked out, muttering words she did not understand. Once he'd left, Daisy placed her glass on the coffee table and sat back. She did not look at Viridiana, but she also didn't turn her head. She simply seemed to pretend she wasn't there. Viridiana had no idea what to do. Should she stay? Should she leave? Finally she rose, clutching the pen and notepad.

"You should ignore that," Daisy said. "I do."

"I'm... I don't—"

"He's not this bad usually. But he recently stopped drinking and stopped… the other stuff he did, and he's a bit on edge still."

"That's a bit of an edge, for sure," Viridiana said dryly.

Viridiana had seen men mistreat women before. She guessed it didn't matter if you were rich or poor, a local or a foreigner, there were always men wanting to be all-important, making their wives or girlfriend feel like dirt, slapping them around when they got too mouthy. Still, it didn't feel nice to have to witness. It felt like a rerun of those times her aunt's ex-husband came by to make a scene.

Daisy smiled at Viridiana, but the smile was cold. "Go to your room. I don't think he's going to dictate anything tonight."

Daisy stood up and left. Viridiana stared at the two glasses on the coffee table, the ice slowly melting.

Later that evening the couple was laughing, merrily going on with their lives. Daisy had forgotten her husband's cruelties, or pretend to. Viridiana told herself that if a man was ever disparaging to her, she would not forget. She wouldn't sweep it away. She'd hold it in her heart and notch down his cruelties. She'd bite. Hard.

Chapter 4

Daisy was mutable, that Viridiana learned quickly. Her friendliness evaporated the next morning when Viridiana found her in the kitchen, tossing oranges into a fancy juice extractor. Daisy did not acknowledge her when she walked into the kitchen, but she gave her orders all the same.

"You'll need to go town for groceries, we are out of everything," Daisy said. Her hair was wrapped in a turban. The look was effortless and chic, as if it had been thrown together in a second although Viridiana would have never thought of dressing like that in a pinch. "My brother will take you, he has a list of things we need."

"Sure," Viridiana said. She rested a hand against the kitchen table, unsure of what to do. She had intended to make herself breakfast, but Daisy was there, and she did not know if she could fry herself an egg or whether she should wait.

"I'd appreciate it if you didn't discuss my business with anyone when you are in town today, or any other day of the week for that matter," Daisy said.

"I'm sorry?"

Daisy placed the lid on the juice extractor. "My husband. I don't want you telling anyone about Ambrose's little display yesterday."

"I wouldn't."

"I know how people gossip in small towns," Daisy said, opening a cabinet and taking out a glass. She placed it under the juicer's spout. "I come from a small town, myself."

"I'm not like that."

Daisy stared at her. "I don't care what you're like. Keep your mouth shut."

Viridiana nodded slightly and hurried out of the kitchen. Her bedroom was on the ground floor, the other rooms were upstairs, so she climbed the stairs in search of Gregory, but halfway there she bumped into him. He was carrying a camera between his hands and wore hip hugging jeans and a denim jacket. She turned around, he grabbed the car keys which they kept in a blue and yellow Talavera dish atop a table right by the front door, and out they went.

Viridiana got into the car and folded her arms.

"I thought we might stop to take pictures of sharks after we buy the groceries," he told her.

"If you wish," she replied.

"It's an excuse to hang out at the beach."

"We don't hang out at that beach."

"Why not?"

"People work there. And you didn't bring a hat for the sun," she said, looking down at her own hat, which rested on her lap.

"Are you mad about something?"

Viridiana shook her head. She wasn't really *mad*, but she hadn't liked the way Daisy talked to her. As though she was a small child or an idiot. There was contempt in Daisy's voice, in her eyes. She wanted Daisy to like her. Had she already gone down the wrong path with Daisy? Was it impossible for Viridiana to be liked?

They parked by the town square. Viridiana pointed out the businesses. There was the bank, the pharmacy, the tiendita which sold everything from detergent to limes, the butcher. The post office was a narrow little space, and right outside of it sat a letter writer with a typewriter who would, for a few pesos, type letters for the illiterate fishermen. Marta's store was not at the square, but a couple of blocks from there. Viridiana was glad, since she didn't want to introduce Gregory to her mother.

"Most of everything you'll get from Marciano," Viridiana said, and she started to head in, but Gregory steered her away, towards the church.

"Let's go here first. I want to take pictures."

They walked in. Viridiana took off her hat. Gregory took out his camera and snapped a couple of pictures, but seemed disappointed. Not that she could blame him. The church wasn't very grand. The eighteenth century colonial missions that remained around the peninsula, even the ones that had been sorely neglected, had much to show. Some contained precious objects of silver and gold, elaborate furniture, dragged by tired pack mules and deposited in a lonely, harsh strip of land. But this church had not been built until the 1940s and the only notable thing it possessed was a priest, since it was sometimes hard to convince even the most eager seminarist that he should move to a small town like this.

When they stepped out, instead of heading to Marciano's, Gregory asked about the hotel which could be seen from the entrance of the church, it was a mere block away. She walked him there and he seemed more interested in that building. It was two stories high and although its carpets were worn and the walls stained, the exterior was striking enough: it was a pretty colonial-looking stone building. There were new towns and there were old towns in Baja. Most of the new ones were company towns. An American salt company had built Guerrero Negro, a French mining one created Santa Rosalía. Desengaño was never a company town, it did not have a single purpose. It rose, haphazard, chaotically, by the sea, but at one point an American magnate had tried to instill order into it.

The magnate—Taylor was his name—had arrived in Baja California like many men back in the day: by air. Many towns in Baja had an air strip nearby to allow American sportsmen to swoop in on their Cessnas for the weekend, fish, and head back home. Taylor swooped in but he didn't feel like swooping out. He saw potential for a hotel, for tourism, and so had built La Sirena. But while other people got lucky with their dream resorts, La Sirena went nowhere. Ten years after the hotel first opened its doors, Taylor shot himself in the head. He'd lost all his money on this gamble. Narciso Ferrer had picked the property and ran it nowadays. The hotel still had nice furnishings and its faux-mission style packed sufficient charm, but the jet set wasn't exactly dying to stay there.

They walked back to the square and bought the groceries, Gregory wanted to know if there was a liquor store. There was, and Gregory bought three bottles of rum.

"If you want a glass of rum you can come to my room for it," he said as they stuffed their purchases in the trunk. "Just don't tell Ambrose we bought it."

"Why not?"

"Daisy hasn't mentioned it?"

"She mentioned he stopped drinking. Was it really bad?"

Viridiana got into the car. They had parked in the shade of a tree and, although it wasn't noon yet, it was already too warm. That's why Viridiana preferred the bicycle. Cars were stuffy, the plastic sticking to your rear. It was like rolling around in an oven. With a bicycle it would take longer to reach your destination, but if you were smart enough to carry a canteen with water (and when she rode the bicycle, she always did), you could stop by the side of the road, take a sip, admire the yucca or the ash-green pitahaya, and get going after a few minutes. She liked doing that, standing by the road outside town, observing how it stretched towards the horizon.

"Ambrose's pastime was drugs. If he wasn't snorting something, then he was drinking. But he quit a couple of months ago, he was finally afraid for his health, and he's determined to live a clean, healthy life. That's why we're here. To keep him away from all temptations."

"How long have Ambrose and Daisy been married?"

"Less than a year."

Gregory asked her how to get to the beach with the sharks and Viridiana gave him instructions. As the car bumped down a dirt road, she chewed on her lower lip.

"I don't think he treats her well," Viridiana said cautiously. "Have you noticed?"

"I'm not blind," Gregory said. He had both hands gripping the wheel and was frowning.

Viridiana grabbed her hat. It was a dark brown hat with a leather band. It resembled the sort of hats Boy Scout leaders wear. She ran a finger around the rim of the hat.

"I know Ambrose is an asshole," Gregory said. "Daisy knows it, too. But he's her dream man in other ways."

"What ways? He must be twenty years older than her."

"Try twenty-five. Anyway, Daisy has always wanted money, alright? A lot of money. That's what Ambrose has. He can buy her things and keep her happy that way. Daisy thinks it's a fair deal."

"You think it's fair?"

"Daisy would kick me out before she kicks Ambrose out."

"There, to the right," Viridiana said.

The sea came into view and Gregory parked the car. They walked toward the sharks and the fishermen assembled on the beach. She knew all of them. Under a little shack made of tin and wood planks there were three chairs and a radio, plus a folding table on which there lay two Chinese fans, cheap trinkets brought from Mexicali. There, the men played cards or evaded the sun for a few moments. By this impromptu structure the fishermen had set wooden stakes with shark mandibles, which shone under the sun. A boy, no more than thirteen, who had been sitting under the shade of the shack, scrambled to his feet and took out a bunch of necklaces with shark teeth from his pocket.

"Buy a souvenir, mister?" he asked in Spanish. Gregory waved him away.

"Ask again before we leave," Viridiana told the kid, because it was an unspoken pact between them that, should she bring people here, they'd have to buy something. The fishermen were not free performers.

Gregory took out his camera and began snapping pictures. He finally seemed satisfied with his subject. There were three boats by the shore, all of them having seen better days. Half a dozen fishermen stood nearby. They were drying shark meat that day, it hung from clotheslines, like laundry in the wind. The fins were dried flat, on wooden boards. Nearby two fresh carcasses were waiting to be sliced and salted. They fished for other things, of course, but their fathers had hunted sharks and so they hunted them, too. It defined them. It made them into people worthy of notice.

Viridiana wondered how her father defined her, or if, instead, she was supposed to be a carbon copy of her mother.

"How do they catch them?" Gregory asked, looking through the camera's viewfinder.

"They set up lines and the lines have hooks with bait, and then they return the next day. They find the shark there. Some say it 'drowns,' it dies of exhaustion, trying to get the hook out of its jaw. You can also set nets. And some folks—crazy folks—they harpoon them."

"It must be dangerous."

"Most sharks, they leave you alone. They don't swim right here by the shore, there's no killer shark waiting to snap you in two. Whale sharks, they eat plankton. But there's other ones who do have sharp teeth and you can't be an idiot. See that guy there with the checkered shirt?"

Gregory nodded, turning his camera in that direction.

"That's Carlos. He lost a leg."

Gregory slowly put the camera down, eyes narrowing. All the fishermen were wearing trousers, no shorts in sight. You could spot a tourist immediately because they were always in those ultra-short shorts that were in fashion, but the fishermen wouldn't be caught dead like that. Carlos was sitting down and he was wearing trousers, so it was impossible to verify Viridiana's statement.

"He's got a prosthesis now," Viridiana clarified.

"How did he lose it?"

"He was jumping off the cliffs. Sometimes the men do that. That day he cut himself against the rocks during a jump. He should have stayed out of the water after that. But the odds of a shark swimming so close by are slim. He was out of luck, because when he went into the water one last time, a shark came by and snapped his foot off and a chunk of leg."

"Jesus."

"Sharks haven't changed in millions of years. They know how to survive better than we do. And now, I suppose Carlos knows better, too."

Two fishermen were wading in the water, their trousers rolled up to their knees. Gregory ran a hand through his hair.

"Do you want to see the graveyard?" Viridiana asked.

"Sure."

They walked to the far end of the beach, the boy with the necklaces following in the hope of making a sale.

A lump, two became visible. Then, all of them. The corpses.

There lay the sad carcasses of sharks, the bits and pieces the fishermen couldn't sell or were not interested in. It was a festooning mass of flesh, dried by the sun, but still pungent. It reeked ferociously. Fat flies lazily flew by.

"God," Gregory said, pressing a hand against his mouth. "Why do they leave this stuff here? Why not toss it in the ocean?"

"If a shark smells another dead shark it won't swim nearby."

"That doesn't sound right. Really?"

"That's what they say."

"It looks awful."

She thought of the killing of the shark, how they tugged it up that day she convinced some of the fishermen to let her accompany them when she was ten. How the small shark seemed to revive, suddenly biting the sides of the boat, its teeth splintering wood, and down came a heavy club, beating it. First the mouth, then the head, slamming, slamming, slamming, until it lay still. There was no blood, but Viridiana recalled how the shark's gills shivered, softly rippling, how it did not move, but the gills still flexed.

An American once told her you couldn't club a shark to death, that you ought to put a bullet through its head, but he had never met the fishermen. He'd never been on a boat.

You can kill anything if you have enough willpower. Just don't lose your mettle, because the shark always knows. If you weaken, if you falter for a second, it'll strike back.

"They could bury them in the sand," Gregory said.

"It would take too much time and effort."

"It seems barbaric, like something out of prehistory."

Sometimes she thought there was a primordial quality to the land and the water, the sharps cliffs and the gulls flying above, the fiery sun upon the sea. As much as she felt the pull of Mexico City, the need to leave the peninsula behind, there was also the irresistible lure of the ocean.

Perhaps that's why she must go, and soon. Otherwise she would fuse with the land, as easily as the cacti cling to the soil, solid, unmovable. This world, it would swallow her.

Viridiana stared at the carcasses, at the bits left, frayed reminders of mighty beasts. "They say Baja California is the place where time stands still. So, yes, maybe it is barbaric, but it's also Baja California."

"Grim," Gregory said.

Gregory held his camera between his hands but he had snapped no photos of this sight. He seemed intimidated.

He suddenly lost his footing and placed a hand on her shoulder, slumping forward.

"I'm dizzy," he muttered.

Viridiana turned to the boy who had been trailing them. "Get him a drink," she ordered, and the boy ran off, back toward the fishermen.

"What the hell?" Gregory asked, his voice a whisper.

It was the heat, Viridiana thought, the heat and the stench of the shark carcasses. She shouldn't have brought him here. He had no hat, they'd packed no water. A rookie mistake. But he had been adamant about the sharks.

The boy raced back, three fishermen with him, curious to see what all the fuss was about. One of them carried an umbrella under his arm, while the boy produced a can which he handed to Viridiana. She in turn pressed it against Gregory's lips. Gregory sipped and frowned.

"What is that?" he asked.

"Coffee and condensed milk. Cream would spoil in this heat."

He made a face but he drank a bit more. The fisherman with the umbrella opened it and used it to shade Gregory as they walked away from the shark cemetery. When they reached the fishermen's encampment Gregory sat on one of the rickety chairs and tossed his camera on the folding table. Viridiana took off his denim jacket, peeled off his shirt, the undershirt too. The boy, having finally found a way to make himself useful, grabbed one of the cheap Chinese fans and began fanning Gregory.

"You have ice?" she asked one of the fishermen.

"Yeah," he said and he opened a battered white cooler filled with melting ice. Inside there were several bottles of beer and a milk jug filled with water. She handed the fisherman who had given her the cooler a bill and gave the kid another for their troubles. Satisfied, the kid left the fan on the table and ran off. The fisherman thanked her and the other onlookers dispersed, ready to fillet another shark.

Viridiana wrapped ice chips in Gregory's t-shirt and rubbed it against his chest.

"You know, normally you have to buy me dinner first before you get me half undressed," he told her, smiling.

She blushed and glanced down, her hand stilling against his chest. The radio was playing José José, who sang a cover of a Paul Anka song.

"Feeling better?" she asked.

"Yeah."

"I can drive us back."

"Sure. But there's no hurry. Right? Sit down."

Viridiana sat down, handing him the shirt with the ice. She

grabbed the fan and opened it, examining it. A section of it had been ripped and taped together.

"You don't wear dresses."

Viridiana raised her head and looked at Gregory. "What?" she asked.

"I realized, it's very hot every day but you never wear dresses. Daisy wears dresses and heels."

"I wear dresses on Sunday, for church."

"No other day of the week?"

"I would normally be guiding tourists around this time of year. If you're going to be walking around you don't want frilly dresses and high heels. Anyway, why does it matter?" she asked, fanning herself and thinking of her worn jeans and t-shirts. Not exactly the attire for a discotheque.

Gregory leaned in her direction, the shirt pressed against his neck. His chest glistened, slick with sweat, still pale, he had escaped the sun's rays. How would he look after a few more days, skin turned golden by the sun? His eyes were very light and he was smiling like he knew a secret.

"I'm wondering if you have nice legs," he said.

The fishermen had taken out their knives and they were beginning to cut the shark which lay on the beach. She focused her eyes on them, the fan immobile in her right hand and in her throat a nervous little laugh which she was unable to supress.

The fishermen lopped the shark's head off.

* * *

A few days later they had a casino night. That's what Gregory called it. He asked Viridiana to get potato chips and sodas and peanuts, and all manner of snacks that Ambrose liked. Gregory picked through Milton's record collection and assembled a good enough mix of music. Daisy dressed herself in a stunning white dress, and they all gathered in the living room to play poker.

It was obvious, even to Viridiana's untrained eye, that Ambrose was terrible at this game. His face reflected each and every one of his thoughts. It was also obvious that Gregory played well and let Ambrose win on purpose, but he did it with such grace and skill that Ambrose did not realize. If he did, he appreciated the performance.

"You'll wipe me out," Ambrose said, after Gregory had won a couple of hands, although the tide would soon turn.

"Never. But pay attention. I know my brother. He might be hiding a card under that sleeve," Daisy said, smiling.

"There's not a hidden card anywhere," Gregory said. "Viridiana can search me if you want proof."

Gregory smiled at her and Viridiana felt herself blushing. She didn't know how to play and was there to bring them drinks and snacks, to change the records, to be witness to this festivity rather than a participant. She did not mind. It felt like sitting in the front row of a theater and watching a movie.

Okay, maybe she would have liked if they asked her to play *one* hand with them. Maybe she'd have liked to slip into a pretty dress, as pretty as Daisy's, instead of standing there in her jeans, darting in and out of the room when needed. But she was an extra in this film. They were the protagonists.

"That's a good excuse!" Ambrose said, chuckling. "Don't let him get anywhere near you, girl. He's a menace."

Viridiana still didn't like Ambrose, but he was cordial that evening and when he and Daisy retired Viridiana was in the most splendid of moods. While they played Daisy had chatted so amicably with her that Viridiana could not believe the woman had ever been rude to her the other day. She decided it had been an unusual outburst and that it had meant nothing.

Then she wondered if Daisy told herself the same thing when she had a fight with Ambrose, but was not willing to dwell on that.

"Your life is like this all the time, isn't it?" she asked Gregory. He had stayed downstairs, smoking a cigarette and listening to a Diana Ross album while Viridiana lingered near him, with the flimsy excuse that she should tidy up a bit, or Delfina would think them all very dirty and rude when she came to clean next time.

"It's all parties and fun," she said when he looked at her in confusion.

"I can't complain. Let me help you carry those," he said, grabbing a couple of glasses.

They went into the kitchen and dumped the dishes and glasses in the sink. He stood next to her, smiling and smoking. He hadn't mentioned anything else about her legs or any of her other physical attributes. She wondered how he saw her. Whether he thought she was too much, or too little, of something. She wondered whether he noticed how she'd blushed that evening and why he wasn't talking, why they were standing in silence in the kitchen.

Diana Ross was still playing in the living room. Viridiana could hear the muffled notes of her song.

"Feeling exclusive?" she asked him. It was from *A Place in the Sun*, this line she plucked from a movie for the sake of saying something.

"What?" he asked with a chuckle and he gave her a huge smile. His fingers grazed her arm.

"Nothing. I should go to bed," she said quickly. The ghostly sensation of his fingers—if he had even touched her—gave her goosebumps.

Chapter 5

Sunday meant church and seeing her family, but Viridiana stopped by The Dutchman's house before that. She went to borrow a book and to say hi. He had a cold and she offered to make chicken soup for him.

"I have a huge pot of soup already, courtesy of Delfina," Reynier said, sitting in his favorite chair with a blanket on his lap.

"Maybe you want your hot-water bottle, then."

"Don't trouble yourself over me."

She shrugged and browsed the shelfs, sliding a finger against the spines of the books. There was Cortázar, the Argentinian novelist who had moved to France. She wondered what that was like, to simply take up and leave your country, your city behind. Her mother had left her town, but she'd come back.

"How are things at The End?"

Viridiana had wanted him to ask that. It was one reason why she'd come that day, she wanted to talk. She'd been talking a lot to her tape recorder but it wasn't enough. She felt strange, like something inside her was changing.

"Good," she said and slid a book off the shelf. Guy de Maupassant. He'd cut his own throat.

Viridiana opened the book and turned a few pages. "Reynier, do you remember the time you and Dad showed me the serpent stone?"

It was one of the many tiny treasures littering Reynier's house, along with the West Mexican burial effigies sitting in a glass cabinet.

The serpent stone, locals claimed, was miraculous remedy capable of absorbing a snake's venom, but in reality it was nothing more than the burnt horn of a deer or a bezoar, and quite incapable of removing any poison. She remembered her father handing her the little black stone. She had peered curiously at it.

"It is useless," he said, "but pretty."

And then he had explained where it came from and what a bezoar was and she had spent the night with her hand pressed against her stomach, wondering if inside her there lay a secret, odd lump of flesh and hair. If they opened her up, would they find it? Would it be black and tiny and oddly shaped, like the serpent stone? What was beneath her skin, what ran through her veins?

"The serpent stone," Reynier said, wiping his nose with a handkerchief. "Your father procured that for me."

"You still have it?"

"It's around somewhere," Reynier looked at her curiously. "What's on your mind, Viridiana?"

"I don't know. Metaphysical questions, maybe," she said.

Questions about secrets and metamorphosis. About the wild eagerness that lately surged through her limbs. There was a fisherman who once told her a stingray's puncture feels like an electrical shock. She now knew what he meant, because looking at Gregory was like feeling she'd been stung bad and the sting lingered.

But Reynier looked sleepy and old, and what could he know about such stuff? Even if he did, she wasn't going to ask.

"I need to go see my mom. Can I borrow this?" she asked showing him the copy of *Bel Ami* she'd been looking at.

"Sure."

* * *

When she was a little girl, Viridiana loved to collect seashells.

She made bracelets and necklaces with them, proudly placing them around her mother's neck, naming her a queen or an empress, and herself a mermaid princess. Her mother took these offerings with a small laugh. But as the years went by her mother's laugh ebbed, and after she remarried and had more children there was little time to play pretend. To play at royalty. There was always a baby to tend to, and soon, the expectation that Viridiana should serve as a second mother to her siblings, a nurse; that she would stop stringing her seashells together and assist her mother with domestic tasks.

There was always duty. Mind-bogglingly dull duty. Duty without rhyme nor reason. Why, for example, must they go to church on Sunday and then endure the same company, the same food, the same conversation and the same game of dominoes? Week after week, month after month, out came the good tablecloth, the white linen instead of the plastic, and the beer and the snacks. Chicharrones and Japanese peanuts and a bunch of "hello compadre" and "hello comadre" as the people assembled themselves around the table.

Viridiana's mother never played, she was going back and forth from the kitchen to the dining room or minding the children. Her stepfather, on the other hand, always played and had too many beers. So did the pharmacist, who was her godfather, and the town's doctor. The postman, whose brother served as their part-time notary public, preferred a glass of ToniCol—they were from Sinaloa, after all—and the priest, who stopped by once each month, drank sherry. Most of the women did not join the game. They remained in a separate sphere, sitting on the chairs set against the wall, conversing, or at the table but often immersed in their own chatter.

That Sunday was the first one when Manuel and Brigida rejoined the afternoon game. Viridiana kept her promise: she sat at the table, she exchanged a few words with Manuel. But that was it. She was grateful that he didn't want to speak and she didn't try to coax him into conversation.

Once the jingle of dominoes had gone on for about an hour, Viridiana excused herself, thinking she might make a quick escape. But her mother wouldn't have it.

"Come into the kitchen, I want to give you a snack for you to take back," Marta said.

"I'm fine. I didn't bring my backpack anyway."

"I'll get a plastic bag."

Viridiana couldn't make a fuss, and refusing would be futile, anyway. She followed her mother into the cramped kitchen. The refrigerator was plastered with drawings made by her siblings and on a counter sat two bags of Sabritas chips which must go out soon now that the peanuts were beginning to run low.

"What snack?" Viridiana asked.

"Come with me," her mother said brusquely, opening a door and heading out, to the interior patio bordered by bird cages and strewn with laundry set to dry. The canaries chirped noisily while the parrot opened one eye to stare at the women, then slowly closed it.

Viridiana crossed her arms, leaning against the wall. Her bicycle was next to her, hat dangling from one of the handles, and she wished she could jump on it and ride away without a word.

"They saw you the other day in town, with a man. One of the Americans you work for."

"Who saw me?"

"They say he's handsome, that American. That he looked no more than thirty."

They. It could be Memo Medosabal, who tended the register at the tiendita. He had a big mouth. But half a dozen other gossips also came to mind. Viridiana kept her arms crossed and her chin up, shrugging. Her mother would have found out at some point that Gregory existed, that he was indeed a good looking fellow. She had only hoped it might take a while longer.

"I see you, Viridiana. You think I don't, but I do."

"Mama."

Marta placed a hand on Viridiana's head, smoothing her hair back. "I was a lot like you when I was young. I went out with Ignacio in high school."

Viridiana had heard the story before. Childhood sweethearts. An aborted romance which ended when Marta went to university in Mexico City. Then, a relationship rekindled after the divorce papers arrived.

"I had big dreams. I wanted to see the city, to meet people. All kinds of people. Exciting ones. Your father was quite the catch back then. Smart, good looking, charming. He was exactly what I wanted."

"So you married him and it didn't work out. What else?"

"What you want and what you need are two different things," Marta pointed out.

"What are you saying? That we should all marry our high school boyfriends? I'm not interested in Manuel."

Viridiana stepped away from her mother, pretending she was peering at the bird cage which held half a dozen canaries.

"You think you'll be young forever, Viridiana."

"I'm eighteen. Why do I even need to figure this out if I'm eighteen?"

"Because Manuel won't wait for you like a fool."

"Fine."

"It's very easy to ignore what true love really is."

"What is true love? Five kids with Ignacio?" she asked, defiance

46

in her voice.

When she had been small, Viridiana insisted she wanted a sister, but her mother always said small families were better. She remarried and immediately changed her tune. Viridiana suspected her mother had always wanted kids, but not with Viridiana's father. She suspected Marta had recognized the mistake she made and did not wish to add more anchors to her life. She suspected, no, she *knew*, Marta had never wanted Viridiana in the first place. Or if she had, Marta had changed her mind after a few years, just as she had changed her mind about her first husband. He turned out to be a colossal disappointment.

It must have been a relief when Viridiana's father never came back from Mexico City. Marta could finally continue her life.

"Six months ago you were not thinking this way. We were practically discussing wedding dresses, places for nice honeymoons. Here you are now, hating Manuel."

"I don't hate Manuel," Viridiana said. "Besides, I never talked about wedding dresses, you did."

"That's not true."

It was almost entirely true. It was Marta who had bought the magazines with wedding dresses. Viridiana had gone along, nodding when she felt she must nod. She later realized she shouldn't have done this. Marta must have spoken to Brigida, Brigida must in turn have told her son that a proposal would be welcomed. But it was an innocent mistake, she was only playing pretend. It was like dress-up or changing the outfits of a Barbie. A folly of the moment and she had confessed as much to her tape recorder immediately afterwards.

She had not, in any case, accepted the proposal. Why must her family make an extended drama out of that?

"Was it something your father wrote? Did he put ideas in your head? Did he say you could move in with him?"

"No," Viridiana said. At one point her father had mentioned she could live with him and his family if she went to university in Mexico City. To be more precise, Viridiana had suggested this and her father had said okay. But he had never brought it up again.

"Then?"

Viridiana felt flustered, she moved to stand by the parrot cage and picked up a peanut that had fallen on the tiled floor, pressing it between the bars of the cage. The parrot opened its eye again but did not take the peanut. In its water dish there floated bits of soggy Bimbo bread.

"I want to try something different," Viridiana muttered.

"I know. That's what worries me. Hanging out with those people on your own—"

"I'm not doing anything bad," Viridiana protested, turning around, the peanut still in her hand. "They're alright."

"And the man you were walking with the other day, how alright is he?"

Thankfully Viridiana did not flush. If she'd flushed she knew her mother would not have let her be, but she managed to keep her composure, tossed the peanut away and grabbed her bicycle, despite the thumping of her heart. She put on her hat.

"You worry too much, mama."

"I worry enough," her mother said dryly.

Viridiana opened the door which led to the street and mounted the bicycle. She was wearing a simple yellow print dress since it was a church day, but it did not impede her movements, she clutched the hem between her thighs. She was used to this and she rode fast, sweat trickling down her throat. She sped up, breezing out of town, passing the gas station, riding past the road which led to the house on the cliff, riding past the lighthouse where kids sometimes went to drink. Farther yet.

She rode a ways, and then stopped.

The road was empty of cars, empty of anything. It would be dark soon.

She took a deep breath. The desert air kissed her temples; it smelled of salt. Insects buzzed in the brush, there was a soft noise, something stirred awake. Perhaps a snake. But she did not fear snakes. Not even rattlers. Like sharks, it was ridiculous to fear them. They ought to be respected, not feared.

She surveyed the land and waited. For some reason the sun dawdled by her side instead of following its descent. Had she worn a watch, she was sure it would have shown her hours and hours had passed since she'd stopped pedaling.

Before Jesuit missionaries built their vast churches and kindly tried to "civilize" the Cochimí, the indigenous people of central Baja California had measured time by the harvest of the pitahaya. They would say "this ambia" or "three ambias ago." Viridiana did not think this odd. Time dilated in Baja California. It made more sense to speak of ambias than of months or years.

Dreams were different here, too. Or so she thought. Once, someone told her there was a cave in the sierra where all dreams are born. Perhaps it might have been where dreams die, or both. It was, in any case, a land plagued by restless dreams, by dark dreaming, edged by salt and strange cirio trees, which—and here someone else had told her a different story—make evil winds blow if you touch them.

Viridiana dreamt too much. She knew it. Her father had dreamt too. Dreamt himself into pity and exhaustion. When she looked at the land like this, in the purpling dusk, she wondered whether Baja would crush her like it had crushed him, whether that cave was waiting to swallow her every dream. The land was hungry, it had always been a place of hunger. Until the pitahaya season came and the Cochimí feasted and the Jesuits were affronted by their orgiastic joy.

She spoke to her tape recorder so it would save those dreams of hers, but she knew this was only a brief delay.

If the land didn't eat Viridiana's dreams, then her family would.

Chapter 6

Daisy said they should go swimming. Ambrose, Daisy and Gregory had visited the beach a few times already. She had not thought they'd invite her.

She demurred.

"I don't have a bathing suit with me," she told the blonde woman.

"I have an extra," Daisy said.

Viridiana felt this was a bit too personal, too casual. They were supposed to be her employers. The people she guided around the town were never this cordial. She did not know whether it was appropriate to agree.

"You want to spend the afternoon hearing Ambrose snore?" Daisy asked.

Ambrose was indeed snoring in his room, the ceiling fan spinning above his head. Viridiana had planned to lock herself in her room, record a few words for her diary, and spend the evening reading the paperback with a broken spine that she'd borrowed from Reynier and had yet to return.

The beach was an exciting thought, especially because Gregory would be there, frolicking in the water. She did not want to spend her time thinking about a tourist, especially when she was working for his brother-in-law, but he smiled at her too often for Viridiana to ignore him. He smiled and he made jokes and he moved close to her. Nothing obvious and in fact, if you'd asked her, she wouldn't be able to pinpoint what she meant by "close." She merely felt that he was drifting in her direction. That the space between them was rapidly diminishing.

"What's the bathing suit like?" Viridiana asked. Daisy took her by the hand and guided her to her room.

The bathing suit was a white two-piece made of yarn. Daisy wore a yellow bikini and golden sandals. They grabbed some towels and met Gregory downstairs, who bestowed on Viridiana an appreciative smile.

He had with him a striped beach umbrella and a cooler. He had also tucked in there a bottle of rum and three glasses.

"Don't tell Ambrose," he said with a wink, showing them his bounty.

Viridiana carried a towel wrapped around her shoulders. It was a shield, something she could grip as she nervously looked at the ocean while the others opened the umbrella and lay down their towels. Gregory unlocked the cooler and took out the booze, pouring everyone a generous amount of rum.

Daisy held her glass with two fingers, her lipstick leaving a mark on the rim. Gregory was smoking a cigarette and Daisy took it from his lips, smoking for a minute before Gregory snatched it back. Viridiana turned her glass between her fingers.

"Time for a swim," Gregory said when he was done smoking, tossing the stub in his empty glass. "Come on, let's go."

Viridiana slowly put her towel down, smoothing it, but did not move closer to the water.

"What?" Gregory asked.

"I think she's shy," Daisy said.

"Nothing to be shy about."

But she did feel shy. Her bathing suit at home was a one-piece, black, simple, modest. She'd never worn a bikini before. And the bikini, since it was made with yarn, had revealing gaps. It would absorb water quickly. It would sag. It would fall off.

"Come on, Viridiana," Gregory said, unbuttoning his Hawaiian shirt and dumping it on the ground. She'd been right and the days stretched out in the sun had quickly turned his skin golden.

"Leave the kid alone," Daisy said. Viridiana did not like the way she said the word "kid." She spit it out, like you spit a seed and her face seemed suddenly rougher. It was not said in jest.

Very well.

"Fine. Put away your camera," Viridiana said, because Gregory had the camera dangling from around his neck, and he had already taken a snapshot of Daisy.

"Don't want to be immortalized?"

"Not today."

"Alright."

He left the camera under the umbrella and the three of them walked to the water. Gregory splashed Daisy and Daisy shrieked. She sounded like a girl. She sounded very young. It was odd, Viridiana thought, that people that age should be that carefree. After all, her mother already had several children by the time she turned thirty. How old was Daisy? Thirty-five? But no, Daisy was ageless. Daisy had never had to struggle with duty, with a cartload of children, chores and the running of a tiny store.

That might be Viridiana's life one day, too.

She was no Daisy.

"The water is fantastic," Daisy said.

"You're lucky," Viridiana told them. "Not all beaches around here are good for swimming. Some have strong undertows."

"Which ones?"

"Playa Ensueño, a couple of other places. Santa Caridad is the worst."

"There's sharks," Gregory added.

"Don't say that! He's lying, isn't he?" Daisy asked, gripping Viridiana's arm.

Viridiana clasped Daisy's hand, gently. "There's shark hunting, but not this close to land."

Gregory smiled. "What about that man who had his leg chewed off? Or were you telling a tall tale?"

"No. But I didn't tell you the whole tale."

"What's that?"

"They said he deserved what happened to him."

"People deserve to be bitten by sharks?" Daisy asked. Her eyes were luminously *blue, like the sky above their head.*

"They say he killed a pregnant shark. When you catch a shark like that, and you eat the pups, the meat is delicious. But some say it's also bad luck. If you catch a pregnant shark, you need to toss it back in the ocean."

Viridiana wasn't sure if she quite believed that, or if things had really happened the way Carlos told them, but she had sat next to the fishermen at the beach as a kid and listened to their tales, and absorbed some of their superstitions. It might not have been scientific, but who wanted to find out, right? Like the carcasses left on the sand. Some things you didn't probe too deeply.

"Don't say anything else," Daisy frowned and ran her hands through her hair. "You sound like that awful man on the ferry."

"The ferry?"

"Mazatlán to La Paz," Gregory said. "We flew to Mexico City, to see Ambrose's nephew, then went to Mazatlán for a few days."

"Mazatlán was a waste of time."

"We did pick up the car there."

"That silly car! The air conditioning doesn't work, it gave up on us before we got into town. I thought we'd die with this desert heat! But it seems getting anything close to a decent car when you're in a hurry is impossible in this part of the world. And the luxury ferry to La Paz..." Daisy muttered. "The cocktail lounge was a piece of shit and that man sitting next to us kept telling us to watch out for poisonous snakes."

"On the other hand, they did offer pancakes for breakfast," Gregory said.

"There *are* poisonous snakes in the peninsula. Rattlers. Don't stick your hand under rocks." Not that she thought Daisy was the type to take hikes where she might stumble upon a rattler, but it never hurt to mention it.

Daisy frowned, those blue eyes fixing on the horizon.

"It's horrible. This place is horrible," Daisy muttered.

"You're not used to nature," Gregory replied.

"And you are? Going camping twice in your life doesn't count," Daisy said, snappish. "I'm going to work on my tan."

With that, Daisy got out of the water. Viridiana looked at Gregory, who shrugged. Viridiana shrugged back and began to swim. She loved the taste of salt on her lips, the waves whipping against her skin, the wind raking her hair when she bobbed up to the surface. She could not fear the ocean. It had held her in its embrace longer than her mother. Even if she believed Carlos's story of the shark, even if they'd told her the waters by her town were infested with great whites, she wouldn't have feared it.

Great whites. Twenty-four exposed teeth in their mouths. And dozens more growing in rows behind those, hidden, like all things are hidden in Baja California.

Viridiana stepped out of the water and saw that there was no one under the beach umbrella. Gregory stood next to her, water droplets clinging to his chest. Viridiana's bikini was immodest, but his swim trunks were something, too, short and fitted, with the waistband hitting the hip.

His body was amazing.

"Where's Daisy?" Viridiana asked, tearing her eyes from him.

"She must have gone back to the house."

"You think I scared her off?"

"She was probably bored. Daisy gets bored quickly. Want another drink?"

"Okay," she said, even though she did not drink much, except for a sip of sherry sometimes on Sundays. But she remembered the dig Daisy had made about her, the rough-sounding "kid." She didn't want Gregory to think she was a child. After all, in other parts of the world girls her age were regulars at discotheques and bars. They had many drinks and no one batted an eye.

They sat down on the towels, Gregory filled Viridiana's glass. Since he had tossed a cigarette stub into his own glass, he re-filled the glass Daisy had been using. The red mark of Daisy's lipstick was still bright on the rim, like a wax seal.

"Do you take pictures for a living?" Viridiana asked, pointing to the camera that rested by Gregory's feet.

"No, I started taking photos four years ago. But I think I have a knack for it. Maybe someday I'll try to be a professional photographer."

Viridiana nodded. She didn't really like the taste of the rum but she took another sip. Maybe you needed to drink a few times before you developed an affinity for it.

"What do you do back in the States, then?"

"You mean, where do I work? I don't."

"Oh," Viridiana said. She couldn't picture that. Not someone so young. Reynier did nothing but play chess and read, but he was ancient. "Do you have a trust fund?"

"I don't. But Daisy is married to Ambrose and Ambrose is generous."

"But... then what did you do before Ambrose?"

"Nothing interesting," Gregory said stretching out an arm and grabbing his camera. "Business investments together with Daisy. It's very boring."

"Do you live with them in California?"

"No. You kidding me? I have my own apartment. My own life."

"But you came with them on vacation?"

"Ambrose is amused by me, and Daisy always needs help with something. I'm a very handy guy. They wouldn't be able to sort their luggage without me. Honestly, they're both hopeless."

She wondered what it was like to live like that, with no job, no one to answer to. Except maybe Gregory answered to Ambrose. Still, he must be living the high life. The house was rented by Ambrose and the expenses were all paid by the old man. Not that she had a full understanding of his finances or arrangements, but she knew enough that Gregory wasn't putting down his own cash. The checks were signed by Ambrose.

She had fantasized about becoming a traveling companion for Daisy, like in old novels. Now she realized that was Gregory's role. He was a page, talking wittily with Ambrose and ensuring the old man was amused. He'd seen them playing poker, she'd seen Gregory drawing Ambrose into conversation and making jokes, and Ambrose responding with long stories and other jokes in turn. All while Daisy watched them both with a smile on her lips.

"Is there a place where I can have my film developed in town?" he asked.

Viridiana shook her head. "No. You can have it sent somewhere and they'll mail it back."

"How annoying. I might start taking out the Polaroid. Not quite the same, but what the hell."

Gregory scooted closer to her. His knee brushed her knee. She looked at her glass. Half an inch of liquid left. When she spun the glass between her hands, the sun's rays caught in it. She wondered how much the glasses cost. A small fortune, for all she knew.

"Is this the kind of thing you do all year long? Dealing with tourists?" he asked.

Viridiana nodded. "It beats working at my mother's store. It's stuffy in there. Plus, the tourists give good tips. Only problem is, no tourists in the fall or winter."

"Back to the shop, then."

"Yeah."

The shop. The only good thing was she could place a book under the counter and read when it was quiet. But it was dull. Having to make small talk with the customers, like her mother demanded, even when they were assholes. Although, the tourists could be assholes, too. Some felt they owned you. At least with them she was outside, walking around town. She could breathe fresh air, gaze at the sky.

"How many languages do you understand, again?"

"Four. Not perfectly, my Dutch isn't the best and I read French better than I speak it. But I want to get better and learn more. Russian, maybe. Japanese, for sure."

Gregory was amused. "What are you doing here, in this town?" he asked, quick and smooth. Smoother than any boy she'd ever spoken with, the words terribly thrilling even though he'd said nothing special.

"I live here," Viridiana said, blushing, a nervous chuckle escaping her lips.

"Okay, but, come on. Four languages? And I've seen you reading all those books in the library, you're perpetually glued to them. You're smart. You're educated. You're young. Shouldn't you be hanging out somewhere else?"

"Then I wouldn't be hanging out with you."

He laughed. Viridiana smiled and finished her drink. The rum was too warm and so was her skin. Gregory held up his camera, pointing it in her direction.

"Let me take your picture."

"No," Viridiana said, holding up her hand, as if protecting herself.

"Why not?"

"I've been swimming. My hair is a mess."

"Your hair is perfect. Look, it's so damn long and thick," Gregory said admiringly. He extended a hand and touched a lock. "You've got great legs, too. I knew you would."

"How would you know?"

"Sixth sense," he said, tapping his head with his index finger. He set his camera down again. "You're beautiful. People tell you that?"

Viridiana grabbed a corner of the blanket she was sitting on and twisted it. Her glass was now forgotten as she glanced at Gregory and did not know whether she was supposed to smile or not. Her eyes darted away from him.

"Daisy says you used to have a boyfriend. Maybe you dumped him because he didn't mention it enough," Gregory said.

Viridiana felt a little irritated to learn Daisy had told Gregory about that. She had assumed she'd keep her confidence. But she was curious. Had they been talking about her? How did the conversation go?

"Boys should mention that often. Boys should tell you that you are beautiful once in the morning and twice at night."

"Are you drunk?" she asked and again she did not know whether it was okay to smile, but she tried to, tried to make her voice light even though her whole body felt very heavy, like an anchor tossed into the water. She was nervous and licked her lips.

"No. How about you?"

Before she could reply he was reaching for her, planting a kiss on her lips. She had not kissed anyone except for Manuel, and those kisses had always been half-hearted. They tasted of duty and friendship. They were expected. *This* she didn't expect, *this* she wanted. Tongue against her tongue, his hands in her hair.

Manuel was dull, a meal twice reheated, water that never boiled. And Viridiana spent a lot of time reading a myriad of books, yes, and the books promised more, as did the films. Rita Hayworth kissed Glenn Ford. Montgomery Clift embraced Elizabeth Taylor. *I can see you. I can hold you next to me*, they declaimed in glorious black and white.

She'd never thought of swelling music with Manuel. Just the usual beat of her life. Now she thought all sorts of things. Stupid things.

He made her feel too much. She felt like her skin was too tight against her bones, she wished to rake her nails against it until she ripped it all off. He made her so nervous.

It was both insane and exhilarating.

An odd scraping noise made Viridiana push Gregory back and look around, suddenly afraid Daisy had returned. But the noise was nothing, only a seagull which had perched on their beach umbrella. It looked at her quizzically. But it had spooked her thoroughly and when Gregory tried to lop an arm around her shoulders, Viridiana wouldn't allow it.

"What?" he asked.

"It's... I work for you," she said, suddenly remembering that fact and blushing again.

"You work for Ambrose, not for me," he clarified.

"That doesn't make a difference. If... if Ambrose found out I'm sure—"

"How's he going to find out? He's up there, napping," Gregory said, pointing at the cliff, at the distant house perched above it.

"Someone else could come by."

"Here? I don't think this beach is very popular. Anyway, it's *our* beach."

Ambrose's beach, if anything, Viridiana thought wearily. Viridiana tossed her damp hair behind her shoulders and picked up her towel.

"We should head back," she said.

"Hey, look, if you don't like me I'm not going to insist, but I thought…"

"Do you do this often?" she asked, folding the towel.

"What?"

"Women. Do you—"

He grabbed her hand. She froze in place, ceased with her frenetic folding. She stared at him and he stared back at her. He looked better than Montgomery Clift and sounded better than Charles Boyer, and he had a smile genuinely more beautiful than Jorge Negrete's. He had been one of her grandmother's favorite actors. The old woman used to tap her cane against the floor as Viridiana adjusted the rabbit ear antenna to try and get the transmission to look a bit better.

"No, not often. No lady in every port."

"It doesn't matter," she said, placing the glasses and the bottle in the cooler.

Quietly they gathered their things and walked back to the house. A breeze was blowing, but it didn't help. Viridiana's cheeks felt hot and she could barely carry the cooler. It wasn't heavy. It was that when he'd glance at her, she thought she was going to trip. When they were almost at the house's front door, Gregory stopped.

"What are you doing?" she asked.

"Having a cigarette. Put that down for a second," he said.

Viridiana obeyed him. He took out a crumpled pack of cigarettes from the front pocket in his shirt and lit one. Viridiana remembered how Daisy had snatched the cigarette from his lips and for a moment she wished to do the same, even though she didn't smoke.

"I know what you're thinking," he said. "You think I'm a womanizer, don't you?"

"I'm not sure what you are," she said, running her foot along the top of the cooler and looking down.

"I'm not."

"All right."

"But I'm interested in you. That's no sin, is it?"

Viridiana didn't reply because her mother thought everything was a sin. Hypocrite. Everyone knew the only reason she had married the first time was because she'd been pregnant. Viridiana suspected the same story applied to the second marriage, that she'd cinched the deal by telling Ignacio she was going to have a baby.

"What do you want to do?" he asked.

What you *want* and what you *need* are two different things, Viridiana thought, recalling her mother's words.

"I'll tell you what I want to do," he said when she still wouldn't speak. "I want to spend more time with you. I want to have a few more drinks and a few more kisses, a bit of conversation. How about I come downstairs tonight?"

"Tonight?" she repeated.

"After Daisy and Ambrose go to bed. I've got a bottle of rum left. I'll wash the glasses, I promise."

"Rum and kisses and conversation," she said. She didn't even know where that came from.

"Sounds like a perfect evening to me," he said smiling. That winsome smile again. White teeth. As white as the shark teeth which the fishermen sold on the beach.

"Sure," she said, when she ought to have said no. But she'd

thought of the way the sky looked when she stood by the road clutching her bicycle, feeling the immensity of the world, the brittleness of dreams, and she let that sky, that feeling, be her compass. For a moment, at least.

When she went back inside the house Ambrose had woken from his nap and was marching towards his office with a bowl of peanuts.

"There you are," he said. "Right on time. Get changed. I need you to type some letters."

"Yes, sir," she said, hurrying back to her room and grabbing a pair of jeans and a t-shirt.

Ambrose sat on a large leather chair and began dictating to Viridiana, popping a peanut into his mouth every once in a while. When he was done, she sat on a little table with the typewriter while he remained behind the desk, grabbed a pen and busied himself writing.

After checking her work twice, Viridiana gave him the letters and Ambrose signed them. Then he pointed at a cabinet.

"Get me three envelopes, will you?"

She nodded and handed him what he asked. He folded the letters she had typed and stuffed them in the envelopes. He also folded the piece of paper he had been writing on and stuffed it in the third envelope.

"I want these mailed tomorrow morning. And maybe I'll also want a telegram sent to my nephew," Ambrose mused. "He's a brilliant boy, you know? Off in Peru right now."

"What's he doing there?"

"Business matters, but he's also taking pleasure in the vacation. He fiddled with the idea of becoming an archeologist at one point and no doubt is looking at all kinds of ancient ruins and the like."

Ambrose smiled. He had the face of a bulldog but when he

spoke about his nephew he softened up. "What do you want to study, young lady? Are you going to be a translator? You'd have a head start on your classmates."

"I haven't figured it out yet," she said, thinking of her father who had diverged so much from his chosen path.

"That's no big deal. I couldn't figure out anything until I was about twenty-eight. My nephew, now, he's the organized type. He connects the dots real quick. Me, I couldn't tell you what I planned to do when I was your age."

But you had money, she thought. People can take their time when they have money. They can exhaust all roads and partake in all their whims, while people with no cash need to make decisions quickly. They are forced into making those decisions. By their parents, by their neighbours, by the whole town.

"I suppose that's why I'm doing this book thing now," Ambrose mused. "Better late than never, no?"

"I guess."

"Ha! You're a quiet one. It's all right. I talk too much. Too much of everything, that's me. Now, let me think about that telegram," he said, loudly chewing a few peanuts as she put away the carbon copies of the letters.

Chapter 7

On the side table the fan whirred. Normally Viridiana would not have noticed this noise, immersed in her reading, but that night she was nervous, and the drone made her lift her eyes from her book every three minutes. She had tried turning off the fan, but it was too warm in the room, so she'd turned it on again. She tried to speak her thoughts into the tape recorder, but this was also fruitless. She sat in her bed, pensive, fully dressed, waiting.

Then, finally, came the knock at the door. It was loud. Too loud. It made her wince and she thought the whole house would have heard it. She held her breath and stuffed the recorder under the bed, then opened the door slowly.

"Hey there," Gregory said holding up the bottle of rum and two glasses.

"Yes," Viridiana said.

She didn't invite him in, Viridiana simply stepped aside and he walked into the room. There was only one chair. He sat on it and she sat on the bed while he poured each of them a full of glass of rum. They clinked their glasses together and drank in silence. She gulped down the alcohol fast in an attempt to hide her skittishness. She didn't know where to begin.

"You don't have a radio?" he asked eventually.

"No," Viridiana said.

"Ah, too bad."

Yes. Terrible, really. If she'd had thought this through she would have secured one. At least with that they might have distracted themselves listening to the music. Now, Viridiana had to sit in silence, sipping the rum and glancing at Gregory, wondering exactly what he was thinking.

"What are you reading?" he asked, pulling his chair closer to the bed and pointing to the paperback on her bedside table.

"*Bel Ami*," she said. "My French needs work."

"What's that? Is it any good?"

She felt a little disappointed that he did not recognize the title—she might have expected such a thing from Manuel, but assumed more sophistication in others—but, she was grateful that now she had a topic of conversation.

"It's about an ambitious, amoral young man who attempts to climb the heights of Parisian society. He manipulates his way to the top."

"He doesn't sound nice. Is he punished at the end?"

"No. It's not that kind of story."

"Can you read me a line from it?"

"Why?"

"I want a pretty girl to speak to me in French, that's all," he said teasing her and slapping her knee lightly with the book.

She opened the novel and flipped through the pages, coming upon a random passage. "The only certainty is death," she said, and thought this was a terrible line. Instead, she might have picked one of the many pretty phrases in the book. Or she might have grabbed an altogether different book.

But even though she spoke of death he did not understand her. He smiled all the same.

Did it matter what she said, at all?

"How'd you learn all this? French, English," he said, grabbing the book again and looking at the cover. It was an edition of no importance, there was nothing to see.

"My father was a translator," she replied. Her glass was almost empty. Wordless, expertly, Gregory refilled it.

He notices things, she thought. He is attentive.

"He *was*?"

"Yes. He works for an insurance company now. He's in Mexico City."

With his new family. Viridiana wondered if his younger children enjoyed language lessons, if he had them conjugate verbs at the breakfast table and gave them sweets when they could declaim a poem in English. Or if he'd left all of that behind. She knew so little of his life. When they spoke on the phone he was always in a rush. Sometimes she could hear children playing in the background, a dog barking, or his new wife's voice. She'd taken to calling him at his office, though that didn't help either. He was still pressed for time. And he always said the same thing, anyway, "Did you get what I sent?" Meaning her Christmas card or the birthday letter with a couple of bills and the same three lines he scrawled each year.

She didn't even know what he looked like.

"You've been there, right?" she asked.

"Mexico City? Yes, for a couple of days. Ambrose went to see his nephew. Daisy and I took a tour while they had lunch."

"What's it like?" she asked and she lay back on the bed, staring at the ceiling and resting the glass against her stomach.

"It's big. Busy. Full of stuff. A bit like New York in that sense. Then again, I got sick as a dog first afternoon we were there. Can't say I saw much. Moctezuma's curse at work."

"You've also seen New York, then."

"Sure. New York, San Francisco, Los Angeles, Chicago, New Orleans. I've been everywhere around the States. No Paris, though," he said. "I'm terrified of the menu. What if I order snails? Or frog legs?"

She smiled. Her hands rested lightly on the sides of the glass, so the liquid would not spill. "I'm sure you'd be fine."

"You have no idea how stupid I am," he said. "Hey, you should go with me. You can translate and make sure I don't eat crap."

"Sure, I'll go with you to Paris," she chuckled and rubbed a finger against the rim of the glass. Her eyes were closed.

"I mean it."

"Don't joke."

"I'm not joking."

She opened her eyes and turned toward him. He plucked the glass from her hands, placing it on the side table. He also discarded the book and leaned down to plant a sure kiss on her lips.

"What are you doing?" she whispered.

"Drinks, a chat and kisses, we said," he reminded her.

He kissed her expertly, kissed her for a thousand years or maybe more. It was an odd sensation. Manuel didn't kiss well at all, and lately, before they'd broken up, all the kisses were accompanied by pleas that they ought to have sex and get married. When she had said no, he whined like a child.

Gregory talked so differently. He was effusive in his praise. It wasn't only what he said, it was *how* he said it. The words were whispered to her ear, slowly and carefully, each caress punctuated with an absolute certainty she did not experience when Manuel tried to paw her.

"You are the prettiest little thing I've ever set my eyes on," he said. "I could touch you forever."

That was miles away from Manuel's clumsy mumblings.

She closed her eyes and thought of the pale remains of sharks upon the sand. The incongruent image rested behind her eyelids, superimposed. Black on white. Her skin was blistering hot, like nitrate film catching on fire.

Gregory's fingertips raced down her chest, settled on her stomach for a minute, went up to cup a breast, before he changed course and tried to pull down the zipper of her jeans.

She swatted his hand away. Suddenly, this was all very familiar, she had enacted this same play before. Her hand shook as she shoved his fingers away.

"What?" he asked, but he was chuckling. He thought it was a game.

He tried to pull up her shirt, tried to pull it off her, his fingers on the hem, and she tried equally hard to pull it down, to stop him from kissing her exposed midriff.

"Did I tickle you? Are you ticklish?" he asked, smiling against her stomach, his hands busy against the jeans again.

"Stop," she said, squirming against him. "I don't want to... I can't have a baby."

That doused him cold, his smile was gone. He frowned and sat back, and Viridiana sat up, the headboard digging into her back. The room was hot, and her skin covered in a fine film of sweat. The fan whirred, useless, in its corner.

"You're not on the pill?" he asked. He sounded more shocked than upset.

"No," she said, her throat felt dry. "The pharmacist plays dominoes at our house almost every weekend. He'd tell my mother."

She tugged at her shirt, tried to smooth out its wrinkles with the palm of her hand, tried to smooth back her hair, which must be a mess. He simply stared at her, looking surprised.

"I could buy condoms," he proposed.

"Then he'll wonder who you are using them with. You don't socialize with anyone in town. And I... I live here. They'll think...

and they'll talk… and my mother, she'd kill me—"

"Christ, it's practically Victorian."

What did he expect in a place like this? In the capital, she was sure everyone did as they pleased. The women fucked men every other day and no one raised the alarm. Although maybe, even there, the elusive middle class morality held sway. And when you ventured off the anointed path and walked into the woods, you ended up like Viridiana's mother: married before her twenty-first birthday, sour-faced, a crease between her brows.

Men could leave. Her father had left. But a woman couldn't leave. Especially if she had a kid. A woman was chained.

He stared at her in silence. *Sharks do not blink, and it seemed to her Gregory had that unblinking quality, that he could stare at her for the entire evening, and if he opened his mouth he'd have rows of razor-sharp teeth.*

"Fine," he raised both of his palms up in surrender. "We said kisses, let's leave it at that. Maybe next time we can try something different."

"I told you, I can't—"

"I don't know what kind of chats about the birds and the bees you had at home, but you don't always need to put a penis in a vagina."

She did not reply.

They had no chats about birds and bees in her house, it was all oblique and allusions. The first time she'd menstruated, staining her jeans red, her mother had diligently taken the clothes away and handed her a sanitary napkin. She had said it would happen each month, she had said Viridiana must know all of this already, poking around as she did in books. Viridiana did know, she did have books, but somehow, she'd expected more than her mother's silence.

Viridiana thought, sometimes, that this had been the moment of her death. That she was now only half-alive, a living ghost, and they were counting the days left until they entombed her by way of marriage. To Manuel.

There had only ever been Manuel.

"Hey," Gregory said, grabbing her right hand. "Hey, you think I'm joking about Paris, don't you?"

"You can't be serious," she said. Her left hand rested on a pillow, which she clutched firmly as she spoke.

"Look, I'm tired of being Daisy's little errand boy. That's all I am to her. I've spent years following Daisy around, doing as she says, bumping with her from city to city. I'm tired of all that. I want to make it on my own, you know? Why not make it in Paris? Or somewhere equally far away."

"Yes, but I… you barely know me and I don't know you," she muttered, her grip on the pillow relaxing.

"I know you enough. Listen, I'm twenty-nine. You know what that means?"

"No."

"That's almost thirty," he said very seriously.

"I don't understand."

"It means I'm not getting any younger. Or any more charming, or anything at all. It means I need to think about the future. My future. Not somebody else's future. Come on, by the end of the summer I can do as I please. I can buy two tickets to Paris."

He rested a hand on her stomach, a finger sliding on the button of her jeans. He did not undo it, nor did he try to undo the zipper, he simply rubbed a finger there. She would have preferred if he tried to touch her some other way. This gesture, it made her shiver.

"Maybe," he said, "I fell in love with you at first sight, what do you think about that?"

"Since the first moment you saw me, even before you saw me," she said, paraphrasing Montgomery Clift when he spoke to Elizabeth Taylor. The only place she'd heard people speak like that was in the films.

"That's right."

He smiled and kissed her again. Lightly. Sweetly.

"Since you're a good girl, I'll be a good boy," he promised.

He stood up, gathered his glasses and his bottle of rum and went to the door. She followed him, a little confused, a little breathless, and she watched him walk down the hallway and away from her.

Chapter 8

For three days Gregory had ignored her. Viridiana did not expect him to make a big show of affection in front of the others, but he didn't make a show of anything at all. It was as if the conversation in her room had not happened, like she'd imagined the whole thing.

Three days Gregory and Daisy had gone down to the beach without her. She didn't think they would invite her to tag along every time they headed for a swim, but there was something about Daisy's attitude which made her feel she was entirely unwelcome. Perhaps Gregory had talked to Daisy about Viridiana and Daisy decided it wasn't right to socialize with her anymore.

Was it that? Was Daisy mad because Gregory was not paying enough attention to her? What did they say about her when she wasn't around? Did they make jokes about the help? Maybe the whole thing had been a joke.

"Come with me to Paris, I've fallen in love with you," certainly sounded like a joke. Like in *Now, Voyager*, one of those black and white movies they showed late at night, where Bette Davis has a sudden glamourous makeover. It was a favorite of her grandmother.

Viridiana applied herself with vigor to her work, trying not to think about Gregory and Daisy at the beach, taking notes. Ambrose droned on, and the office was warm. She focused her attention on the notepad between her hands. Then Ambrose would say it was enough for the day and Viridiana would look at the clock on the wall and felt deflated because it was too early. There were many hours left to kill and she did not want to kill them worrying about Gregory.

"I need you to take this letter to the post office. It's ridiculous that there's no mail delivery at this house," Ambrose said. "No mail! Who's heard of that?"

Viridiana did not tell him he was lucky there was a post office at all. Several small communities still depended on the whims of random truck drivers and fayuqueros to get their mail. Their little post office and telegraph station was a blessing, but, of course, Don Julio wasn't going to drive here for Ambrose. If Ambrose had wanted access to the post office or the telephone he could have stayed at the hotel, but she supposed he hadn't thought the whole trip through, or he merely wanted to play the part of the recluse.

Nevertheless, she was grateful. The errand would be a welcome distraction.

He handed her a letter. It said, "Mr. S.L. Landry" and had the address of a law firm in Mexico City. Ambrose wrote letters often—she supposed the lack of a telephone necessitated them — but the letters to his nephew he wrote on his own, by hand, instead of dictating them.

"Should I go right now?" Viridiana asked.

"Yes, go now." Ambrose said. "And I have something else, before I forget. This is for you, so you can deposit it in your bank account."

He handed her a second envelope, it was unsealed and contained a check. Viridiana wasn't expecting this, he had paid her in advance for her first few weeks working for them and no more money was due to her yet.

"I'll probably be heading back to Mexico City. I wanted to give you notice. The money, it's a bit of a bonus, I suppose. You've been a good kid, putting up with me and Daisy."

"You don't like it here?" she asked.

"I like it fine. My nephew, Stan, was supposed to be away until October, off in South America. But our lawyer wrote to say he's cutting his trip short and I'd rather spend my time with the boy. I have no children, only him."

Viridiana stared at the two envelopes between her hands.

"We might come back later, who knows," Ambrose said.

"Then it's decided."

"I have to see when Stan is back exactly. There's no sense in a move if he's not back from Peru. All these papers and things to ship away…"

"But wouldn't it be better the other way around," she said. "Maybe your nephew could come here?"

"He's a city boy, wouldn't know what to do with himself in this place. It's so quiet at night. You'd think you could listen to the stars. Kind of frightening. But of course, you must be used to it."

Stars, silence, who cared? She felt her heart, which had been ticking on merrily, stutter in pain as she pictured this house empty of its inhabitants. Empty of Gregory.

"Don't look so blue, girl. I'm sure you'll find another job," Ambrose said noticing her dejected expression.

"Yes, but I'll miss you, sir," she lied.

He laughed. "Not me. Maybe you'll miss Daisy, maybe Gregory. Not me."

Viridiana did not dare look at Ambrose, instead glancing sheepishly at the envelopes, opening the one with the check as if to make sure it was still there and had not evaporated. It did no good. Her expression had been too candid.

"Gregory, is it?" Ambrose said, smirking. "He's a parasite. You're best off cashing your check. I don't say that to be cruel, girl.

They're both parasites. God knows I've figured that out."

Ambrose opened a drawer and took out a packet of cigarettes, shaking it. It was empty and he crushed the cardboard box, shaking his head. On his desk there was a glass ashtray full to the brim with stubs.

"Anyway, off you go. I need that in the mail today. Get me more smokes, too, will you? You have petty cash to pay for everything?"

"Yes," she said, standing up.

"Good. You can take the car if you want."

"I'll ride my bicycle."

"Yes, you always do, don't you?" Ambrose mused. "It'd be faster to drive."

"I prefer the bicycle."

"Maybe you can buy yourself a new one with the money."

Viridiana did not reply. She grabbed her backpack, her hat, a pair of cheap plastic sunglasses with white frames, and rode to town. She dropped the check at the bank, where the bored teller was reading a copy of *Vanidades*, and then walked to the post office where Don Julio said no telegram or letters had come for Ambrose.

When Viridiana exited the post office she noticed that Cheng's truck was parked by the church. He was a fayuquero, selling odds and ends from town to town. The first fayuqueros had dragged their merchandise on mules, slicing across the sierra, but now they rolled around in trucks. Fayuqueros were better than a map for giving you directions, could help out if your car lay stalled on the side of the road, and brought in varied types of merchandise. In another place these peddlers might have been of little importance, but in tiny towns they took on mythical proportions.

Everyone knew Cheng, and Cheng knew everybody. If you wanted something he could get it. Information, goods, you name it. It didn't matter if you needed American goods or Mexican goods, he was the man for you. More reliable than the telegraph, too, he could send messages to a cousin in San Diego where letters would go astray.

Viridiana crossed the street and approached the truck, which on its side was emblazoned with the name Cheng'S ROYAL ROAD GOODS and pictures of cacti. Cheng had a tendency to the dramatic. Most fayuqueros didn't bother putting such signage on their trucks. Some of them merely tied packages and suitcases to the roofs of their cars with a rope.

"Viridiana," the man said when she approached him. He had taken out a stool from the back of his truck and was sitting on it, smoking a cigarette, before he unloaded the goods on the sidewalk so people could look at them.

"Hey, Cheng," she said. "Getting ready to work?"

"Getting there. The arthritis is mighty bad this month. Mighty bad," he said.

Cheng was missing two of his front teeth and two fingers on his right hand, so when he pressed the cigarette against his lips he didn't use the index and middle fingers, like most people did. He held the cigarette between his thumb and ring finger, nodding at her.

Viridiana didn't know how old Cheng was. He'd come to Mexico when the country was hungry for cheap Chinese workers and when the tide turned, and the government started expelling them because they didn't want them anymore, Cheng already had a truck and was rumbling around the peninsula. Let the fuckers catch him, he said. They never did.

"I got a box of books you can look at," Cheng said.

"Do you still have that radio you were carrying around last month?"

"It's there, rattling in the back. Help an old man take a few boxes out and I'll give you a discount."

"How much?"

"How many boxes you gonna help me take out?"

Viridiana smiled and opened the back of the truck. Cheng had bundles, boxes, suitcases. Most of them were labeled. Viridiana took out a folding table, set it next to Cheng, and then began piling boxes around it. She found the box labelled "electronics" and took out the radio. It was a bright yellow. The box with electronics also contained batteries and she slid two in, then turned it on, twisting the dial until disco music began playing.

"Sounds nice, no?" Cheng said.

"Sounds fine. Listen, are you carrying any makeup?"

"Sure. Check the little box on the passenger's seat."

"What about skirts?"

"Skirts? Try this suitcase," he said patting a brown suitcase by his feet.

Viridiana unzipped the suitcase and pulled out a short skirt. She changed inside the truck, shimming out of her jeans and putting on the skirt. Then she opened the box with the makeup. Inside she found an assortment of lipsticks, face powder, eyeshadow and mascara. Her mother sold such items, but Viridiana had never bothered using them, their abundance perhaps numbing her. She sat in the passenger's seat and pulled down the vanity mirror, applying eyeshadow and lipstick.

She looked at herself carefully, tilting her head.

She looked strange.

She went back to where Cheng was sitting. Alejandro Esparza and Paco Ibarra walked by. Alejandro was the other translator in town. His main talent was in cheating on his wife with whatever hotel guest he could get close to. Paco was his best buddy, owner of the only taxi in town which he used to drive tourists around, and man of all trades. Both lived a comfortable life because Alejandro was married to the hotel owner's only daughter. This assured them work during the tourist season. Off season, Alejandro borrowed money from his father-in-law, and Paco borrowed money from Alejandro.

Neither of them were friendly with Viridiana. She was Alejandro's competition. They thought her stiff, haughty. There had also been some small offense her father had committed against their parents, which they remembered. They steered themselves from her path on most occasions, in great part because she was Manuel's girlfriend. That was the measure of most women in town: who they were connected to.

But now Viridiana wasn't with Manuel.

They were lured to her side by the sight of a short skirt, which, like any good macho, they took to be an invitation. This coupled with the beers they had imbibed that afternoon emboldened them.

"Looking good, Dianita," Alejandro said. He was toying with a toothpick with one hand and grinned at her.

Viridiana raised her head and stared at him. She didn't like it when people called her that.

"Good afternoon," she said, her tone frosty.

"What you got there?" Alejandro asked, grabbing the radio which she had been about to stuff in her backpack. He turned it between his hands.

"Hey, you be careful with that."

"I ain't going to break it," he said, frowning, offended that she would speak to him like that. He flipped the radio upside down and handed it to Paco for him to inspect.

Viridiana crossed her arms, leaning against the folding table.

"That can't be cheap," Alejandro said. "It's American contraband."

Maybe it was. When it came to electronics not everyone wanted to pay sky-high tariffs, so yeah, maybe that little radio had been stuffed in someone's suitcase and taken across the border, but it was no big deal. It was ant trade, small-scale smuggling, like used clothes, boxes of powdered milk and other minutia which could be resold on the other side of the border.

"So?" Viridiana asked. "Are you a judicial now?"

"I'm making conversation. You're always jumpy, Dianita. Ain't she jumpy, Paco?"

"She's jumpy," Paco agreed.

"Can I have my radio back?" she demanded.

"You're working with those gringos on the cliff, ain't you?"

"You know I am," Viridiana said, clenching her jaw. She'd taken her hat and her sunglasses off and she wished she hadn't because she knew he was evaluating her lipstick and the blue eyeshadow she'd put on.

"Headed back there?"

"I've got stuff to do," Viridiana said, reaching forward and snatching the radio from Alejandro's hands. She stuffed it in her backpack. Both men chuckled.

"Want a ride back? We don't mind the detour. Gives us a chance to appreciate the scenery," Alejandro said, smirking like he'd told a dirty joke.

"No, thanks," she muttered, zipping the backpack closed.

"I was going to ask you if you wanted to help me with a group of Frenchies who are coming over this month, but I won't if you're going to be rude," he said.

"French?" Viridiana said, as if considering the offer.

"Yeah."

"They realize you don't even know what 'bonjour' means?"

"Fuck you."

Cheng, savvy to human behaviour like any peddler must be, recognized the beginning of a violent conflict. He rose from his stool and took his cigarette from his mouth, pointing at Alejandro with his free, whole hand.

"Hey, you going to buy something?" he asked.

"Shut up, old man."

"You going to buy something?" Cheng repeated, unperturbed by the young man's aggressive tone of voice.

"Yu go tu bye someting?" Alejandro said, in a high-pitched, mock voice that was probably supposed to approximate Cheng's slight accent.

"Exactly," Cheng replied.

Alejandro gave Cheng one look, Viridiana another, then motioned for Paco to follow him. They walked off, laughing, as if they had witnessed a very funny performance. Cheng took another drag from his cigarette and shook his head.

"Assholes," he muttered.

"Sorry about that."

"Not your fault, sweetheart."

Viridiana handed Cheng the money for the merchandise and he carefully placed it in a pouch which he carried at his waist. He had another pouch for coins and a small notebook in his back pocket for the people buying on credit.

"Ah, I almost forgot," Viridiana said. "Cigarettes."

"Smoking?"

"They're not for me."

Cheng nodded and handed her a package. When Viridiana attempted to take out her wallet, he shook his head.

"It's on the house."

"Thanks," she said.

When she got to The End she went upstairs to see if Gregory

was around, but he had not returned from the beach. She slid a note under his door telling him she had something to show him. Then she went to her room. He did not stop by to see her until late. She had reapplied the lipstick and eyeshadow, but lost all hope that he might come down, by the time he knocked on her door.

He was suddenly there, smiling at her like a matinee idol ready for his close-up, and as she looked up at him she forgot the cheeky greeting she had rehearsed. A witty line, to assure him she was not a small town nobody. As if the lipstick and the skirt could prove her sophistication.

"I've brought an offering. It's half a bottle of rum," he said, bottle in one hand, glasses in another.

"Thanks."

She wondered how many doorsteps he'd graced with similar gifts in hand. Flowers, chocolates, wine. Manuel had no need of such courtship, and high school dalliances were different, anyway. They used to hang out together so quite naturally, one day, he turned to her and simply said, "I'm like your boyfriend now, right?" and Viridiana figured sure, he was like her boyfriend, so they took it from there. He gave her small presents, but she thought them banal and unromantic. One time he'd won a goldfish for her. She'd heard that goldfish grow as big as their tank. Her goldfish, though, had a tiny bowl, but she sometimes wished to toss it in the sea so it could grow as big as a whale. Then the fish might swallow her whole.

"What's this thing you wanted to show me?" Gregory asked.

"It's right here. It's a radio."

He walked towards the desk were she'd placed the radio and set his bottle and glasses down.

"Will you look at that," Gregory said. "Does it work?"

"Sure. Give it a try."

He turned the radio on and switched through stations until Olivia Newton-John started singing. Then he opened the bottle of rum and filled their glasses.

"Where'd you get the radio?"

"A guy I know sold it to me."

"A guy? Are you fooling around with someone else?" he asked with a mock shocked face.

Viridiana chuckled. "He's a million years old."

"Who knows what kind of wild perversions you may have."

She sat on the bed, he sat by her side. They drank. She felt cozy and comfortable, as though she'd known him for a long time. Maybe it was the alcohol that made it seem so.

"Ambrose said you're headed back to Mexico City," she told him.

"When did he tell you that?"

"Today. He says he wants to go back there to be with his nephew."

Gregory grimaced and shook his head.

"I know. It's a horrifying idea. One of the only good things about puking my guts out while I was there is we didn't socialize with Ambrose's nephew except for a single breakfast we had together. Which was more than enough."

"What's wrong with him?"

"He's a pompous asshole. And he doesn't like Daisy and me."

"Why not?"

"Ambrose, he's old money. Not on his father's side, but on the mother's. The nephew, he's from that branch of the family, and boy does he know it. Daisy and I, we are definitely not old *anything*."

Parasites, Ambrose had said. Was that true? Gregory had alluded to business investments involving him and Daisy, so they must have their own money. Perhaps it was not enough money or the investments had gone badly, or Ambrose simply disapproved of Gregory's lack of a profession and his photography hobby. Did Ambrose's nephew work in Mexico City? The letter she'd posted had been addressed as in care of a law firm, but she did not think him a lawyer since she recognized the address from other correspondence. It was the firm that handled all of Ambrose's matters and where, presumably, all his mail was delivered and then rerouted as appropriate.

Ambrose, she knew, was in real estate. Daisy had once mockingly said he turned orange groves into condos. She had no idea about the nephew. He could be a trust fund boy, blissfully traveling South America aboard a yacht.

"Perhaps he might change his mind once you spend more time together," Viridiana said.

"That would be a neat trick. Anyway, we might not go. Daisy is trying to convince the old goat that we ought to stay."

"Really?" she said turning her head and looking at him hopefully.

"He's a stubborn asshole, but who knows. Hey, I definitely don't want to have to go anywhere far from you."

In her imagination, the one on the yacht was now Gregory, sunning on distant beaches, accompanied by a bevy of young women. Viridiana knew she was a little coarse, unvarnished, try as she might you could see her ragged edges and there would be other, worldlier women who could catch Gregory's attention. She didn't want to voice these thoughts, to express her doubts, but she found herself speaking too fast, too earnestly.

"You mean that? There's probably lots of girls in Mexico City and there's—"

"If there's a million girls, who cares?"

"I thought perhaps you didn't … I've hardly seen you this

week."

"That's Daisy's doing. She's got me carrying her parasol and sun tan lotion," he said rolling his eyes. "What else am I good for, right? But it doesn't mean I've forgotten you. I came downstairs with my offering, right? There's only one girl for me now."

He touched her chin, playful.

She looked at him but did not speak and he let out a sigh. "You don't believe me, do you?"

"People come, they come through town and then they leave," she said, looking at her glass. "You'll leave too."

"Don't say that. Wait, wait right here."

He got up and rushed out of the room. Viridiana waited, sitting in the center of the bed, afraid that she had scared him off, but he came back soon, a Polaroid camera in his hands. He gave it to her.

"Here, I can't get a bouquet right now so this will have to do. It's yours."

"You can't, it must—"

"Yes, I can. It's my camera. Now it's yours. Have you ever shot one of these?"

"Point and click."

"That's right."

Viridiana held the camera tentatively, looked through the view finder aiming it at him and pressed the proper button. The camera spit out a photo and she held it up, watching it develop before her eyes.

"Who's that handsome chap?" he asked sitting next to her.

"Are you terribly conceited?"

"Of course," he said and then he lay back and pulled her down so that she was also laying down next to him, side by side, both looking at each other.

Viridiana set the camera down and held the picture up, tracing its white border with a nail. Her nails were not pretty like Daisy's, but the woman had promised they could paint them together one evening.

"Why did you decide to take pictures?"

"That's a funny question. Most people ask me 'how' I started taking pictures."

"How did you and why?" she asked.

"Daisy and I met these people in New York. Artsy types. Models and film directors, Daisy likes that crowd. They shot experimental films in Esperanto in warehouses around Red Hook. Things like that. One of them took pictures and I became interested in them. Got a camera and started snapping pictures myself."

"What do you like to photograph? Aside from the sharks."

"The sharks are a novelty. I shoot a lot of people, a lot of cityscapes. Cars caught in traffic, women waiting in line to get into a club."

"There's none of that here."

"That's fine. Maybe I'm supposed to be a nature photographer. I know it my bones, you see, that I have to do something with photos. There's nothing else for me."

The pictured had dried and finished developing but the scent of its chemicals still lingered in the room.

"I have this tape recorder my father gave me and I like talking into it," Viridiana said. "And I like learning other languages. So sometimes I think I'd like to be some sort of radio correspondent. But whatever I'm supposed to be, I know it my bones, I won't find it here."

He took the photograph from her and flipped it around to look at it, grinning, and then set it aside on the night table where their glasses waited for them. But he did not grab a glass and resume drinking. Instead, he kissed her.

She twined her arms around his neck.

Everything was nice, everything was perfect, the radio playing love songs for them.

"Well, now," he said, "ever give a blow job?"

Viridiana frowned because that didn't sound terribly romantic. It sounded like the kind of thing the village boys might ask, and the answer was to say "no" every time, lest they think you easy, like poor Paloma Pineda, who no one ever invited to parties anymore.

Then, again, Viridiana thought, no one invited her anywhere anymore, either. Another idea popped into her head.

"Is that why you gave me the camera?" she asked, sitting up.

"No, no," he said. "I didn't mean it like that."

"But you'll get mad if I don't…"

"I won't get mad, but it's not like I'm a school kid. Neither are you. Come on, it'll be fun."

She thought of the women in town who took up with the occasional tourists. Poor women, women who drank with the outsiders and danced with them, and sometimes slept with them.

Nobody thought much of these women. They were a few notches above the mistresses of the fishermen and the two prostitutes of Desengaño. Easy virtue, easy living, her mother had always said. It didn't look that easy to Viridiana and she wondered what separated her from someone like that. Perhaps it was a matter of the size of the transaction.

"You said no condoms and no pills, what am I supposed to do?" he asked with an exasperated sigh.

Manuel had asked that, once, when they were hanging out at the beach. But then they almost got caught and they were too chicken after that. Besides, Viridiana didn't want to do anything serious with Manuel because then he got that look in his eye, and she could tell he was figuring out what was the best date for their wedding and the price of a honeymoon suite somewhere in Acapulco.

No sense in giving fuel to that fire.

But Gregory was another story and she had no idea what to do. She remembered how he'd said it was almost Victorian. He was referring to the town, but soon enough, he'd think the same of her. That she was nothing but a mochita—or worse, a cheap tease. Neither description had much to do with reality because the only reason why she made it to church each week was her family and she was not in the habit of flirting with boys, but rather of shutting them down.

She wanted to be... she wanted to be bold, she wanted to be *interesting*, she wanted to be the kind of girl who doesn't get left behind when the guy packs his bags and heads out of town.

"All right," she said, smiling a quick smile and she remembered this thing Manuel had said before they'd broken up. "You're all bluster." But she wasn't. Just because she thought things over, just because she let them rest and form and rise, that didn't mean she didn't *dare*.

That's probably what did their relationship in, the defining piece. That he had never understood the boldness she had deep in the marrow of her bones.

"All right," he repeated.

Gregory unzipped his jeans quickly, perhaps assuming she'd rethink it. But she didn't. Not that she found the activity terribly interesting, what with him digging his fingers into her hair a little too hard and the numerous instructions he provided, as if he was one of those filmmakers he'd known in New York directing a movie.

But the films she'd watched on the small TV set didn't have a woman bending over a man to swallow his cock. Liz Taylor and

Montgomery Cliff didn't go behind the bushes so she could swirl her tongue around his penis, and he didn't grunt at her and then come in her mouth, even though she had said she didn't like that idea, and he tasted horrible.

It's one thing to picture love and another entirely to be faced with the stark reality that love might mean the guy zips up his pants and gives you a pat on the head.

At least he didn't shake her hand. Rethinking it, or perhaps noticing her dismayed expression, he did plant a kiss on her cheek before rising from the bed. This was a sweet gesture, but it did nothing to resolve the knot in her stomach, nor the fact that she was trembling a little, and her cheeks were very warm, and she knew she was never going to be able to go to sleep.

"Gregory," she muttered.

"Yeah?"

"It wasn't too fun."

"I'm sure you'll improve," Gregory he said, because apparently that was that.

When he had left she collected the dirty glasses and the bottle he'd left behind and took them to the bathroom. One of the glasses still had an inch of rum in it and she held it up to the stark bathroom light, observing its deep, brown color. She took a sip, let it swish in her mouth, and spit it out.

Viridiana set the glasses by the sink and went to get the camera. She stood in front of the mirror and shot a picture of her reflection, slowly fanning herself with the Polaroid.

Then she stared at herself in the mirror, at the smudged makeup and the faint traces of crimson on her lips.

Chapter 9

The day dawned scorching hot and she ought to have known something would happen because she felt that familiar prickle down her spine. A day for omens, Grandmother used to say. The old woman also told her you could summon a storm by tying or untying knots. Viridiana still had blue and white bracelets against the evil eye, although she had brought none of them to the Americans' house. She had also left behind her medallion of Saint Benedict, which was used to chase away the devil. It lies in the crooks of rocks, in the brush, this devil. Grandmother said so.

The air outside could bake bread. It was the right month for sharks in Baja. The time of the year when the fishermen around the peninsula would ready themselves for a bounty. On the beaches the men would toil, finning the animals, cutting off their skin, holding up the slabs of pale flesh to dry. Viridiana derived joy from these rituals.

She would have loved to go down to the beach, to watch the little boats pushing into the ocean. She might have taken the camera Gregory had given her or the recorder and her microphone, to fix on audio tape or instant film these moments because she would miss the beach, the sharks, the ritual, once she was far and away from the peninsula.

But she had no chance to venture out of the house that morning. Ambrose wanted to work on his manuscript. He dictated to Viridiana and Viridiana scribbled in her notepad. However, when it was close to noon, a respite arrived in the shape of Daisy and Gregory.

"Let's go out," Daisy said. She wore the crocheted bikini Viridiana had borrowed on their previous outing. "I need to work on my tan."

"I guess we could," Ambrose said. "It's so hot inside. A little dip in the water could cool us down. I'll get changed."

"I'm thinking later we can go for dinner at that hotel in town. It's the only place that looks worth it," Daisy said.

"There's a restaurant with some fun décor if you are willing to drive a bit down the coast," Viridiana said. "I'll be happy to take you there."

"I was thinking it would be the three of us," Daisy said, pointedly.

"We can't leave her to be bored here by herself," Gregory quickly replied. "Ambrose, take my side."

Daisy gave Gregory such a look of utter contempt that Viridiana thought her cause was lost, but Ambrose got up from behind his desk and spoke. "Let the girl come with us," he said. "She's earned a dip in the ocean."

Ambrose left the office. Daisy did not try to conceal her displeasure and she informed Viridiana that she didn't have a bathing suit she could borrow that day, so she'd have to come up with her own beach attire and she'd better do it quick because she wasn't willing to wait for her.

Viridiana felt it was very unfair, especially when she had done nothing to deserve such treatment, but she kept her mouth wisely shut and rushed into her room. She had packed no bathing suit but she did bring a pair of blue denim shorts she seldom wore and a black sleeveless t-shirt. She tied her hair in a ponytail and hurried to wait by the car.

Despite Daisy's pronouncement that they would leave in five

minutes, it took more than half an hour for the others to emerge from the house. Daisy shoved a bunch of towels in Viridiana's face and Viridiana placed them in the trunk, along with the sun tan lotion and other beach paraphernalia.

"Where are we headed?" Ambrose said, taking the wheel.

"There's a beach I found in the tourist guide. It sounds very nice," Daisy said.

"Tell me how to get there."

Viridiana and Gregory sat in the back of the car. He discreetly ran a hand up and down her bare leg, touched her arm, and flashed her such a smile that Viridiana paid little attention to the road. They could have been headed to the bottom of the ocean and she would not have cared because his knee was bumping her knee, a finger rested on her thigh for a few seconds, and then that finger carelessly pushed a stray lock of hair behind her ear.

In fact, it wasn't until Ambrose parked the car that Viridiana recognized where they were. Santa Caridad, with its treacherous waves.

"It's pretty," Ambrose declared. "Very pretty."

"This beach is not good for swimming," Viridiana said. "The undertow—"

"Viridiana, set down the towels and the blankets," Daisy said. "There's no need for you to be sputtering on."

Viridiana frowned, but Gregory helped her with the towels, and soon enough they had two beach umbrellas up shading them. Gregory had brought the portable radio and he turned it on. Ambrose was in a very good mood. When he was like this, it was difficult to remember how obnoxious he could be. He was telling stories and jokes. He had a good repertoire. After a while he dozed off.

Gregory, for his part, was smoking a cigarette and forming

perfect rings with the smoke. He showed off to Viridiana, who appreciated the performance with an open eagerness which earned her a roll of the eyes from Daisy. It was obvious, judging by Daisy's face, that she had watched Gregory acting like this before, and it was all very hokey to her.

Gregory's pleasure, however, was palpable, and when he leaned close to Viridiana and whispered in her ear a simple nothing of a compliment (hey, love) she felt her heart soar high.

Daisy stood up abruptly and nudged Ambrose with her right foot.

"Come on, let's go swimming," she said.

"Alright," Ambrose said, lifting himself slowly. He had not gone down to the beach often and unlike Daisy and Gregory, who were perfectly tanned, Ambrose's skin was still pale, like a fish's belly. He himself resembled a disgruntled sea lion, murmuring as he shed his shirt and remained only in his swim trunks.

"But you don't intend to really swim, do you?" Viridiana asked. Daisy did not reply and Viridiana ought to have left it at that, but she felt compelled to elaborate. "It isn't safe."

"The undertow, yes," Daisy said. "How bad can it be?"

"Very bad."

"It looks peaceful," Ambrose said, skeptically.

"It's treacherous. You don't want to be going in there. I thought you only wanted to tan."

"On top of speaking all those languages are you also an expert on ocean currents?" Daisy asked.

"Quiet," Ambrose commanded. "The girl lives here, she knows the area. I'm not swimming today."

Daisy placed her hands on her hips and shot Viridiana a murderous glance. Viridiana had started on the right foot with Daisy, but these days it seemed the woman had nothing but hostility for the girl. Viridiana did not know exactly what it was she had done wrong.

They remained at the beach for another half hour. At that point Daisy said she wanted to head back and they packed their things. As soon as they walked in Ambrose declared that he had to take a nap.

"It's too hot for anything else," he said. "Maybe tonight we can type more letters, alright Viridiana?"

"Sure," she muttered, watching the man head upstairs.

Gregory lingered at the foot of the staircase. Viridiana thought maybe they'd have a chance to talk a little more, but he told her he wanted to take a shower to cool down and Viridiana guessed that was it for them.

At least for this afternoon.

At night, who knew. Maybe he'd sneak into her room to see her. He would whisper sweet words into her ear. Things like "I love you, too. It scares me. But it is a wonderful feeling." Like the movies. Like Monty and Liz.

How she wished they could go into town together. There was the bar at the hotel, where they could have drinks and a nice dinner. But then everyone would know about them, and it would be hell to pay for her. One day, though. Somewhere else, far away, they could do as they pleased and go wherever they wanted, and Viridiana wouldn't have to worry about busybodies who liked to wag their tongues when she walked by.

Viridiana went to her room and turned on the fan, lay down on the bed. She dreamt she was walking in the desert and beneath her feet she could feel tarantulas slumbering in their burrows. And then she heard a voice call out to her. Like Grandmother said the devil would call, leading travelers astray until they tumbled down the side of a cliff and to their death.

The invisible voice beckoned Viridiana and she listened, even though she knew it was not a good idea to listen to voices in the desert.

And she recalled what some relative of hers had said once, that in Baja California there is only the devil or the nothing. But there was something there, there was someone, leaning over a clump of cacti. The cacti were engorged with water, their flowers blooming red. And when she moved closer—even though she didn't want to move closer, but the voice, the voices around her compelled her to step forward —she could see that the man (it was a man, she knew this) leaning over the cacti was dressed in a yellow habit. And when Viridiana stretched out a hand to touch his shoulder, he turned and looked at her and his mouth was filled with jagged shark teeth and blood was streaming from that mouth because he had bitten into the cacti, bitten into it, spines and all.

She awoke slowly. Despite the nightmare she was not startled. Instead her eyelids lifted gently and she heard the voices still around her. The fan had stopped working while she slept and Viridiana lay covered in a thin layer of sweat.

The voices from the dream continued speaking and she frowned.

But then she realized that the voices were not in her imagination, that this was not the lingering dream. Someone was arguing.

Viridiana stood up and went to the door of her room, opening it and standing in the hallway.

Ambrose was yelling, then Daisy.

They were shouting at each other.

She could not make out the precise words. They were too far off, but so loud the tenor of their conversation was still obvious.

Just as she thought of returning to her room and shutting the door, there came a single, piercing scream and a loud thud. Then a silence.

The silence was more piercing than the scream.

Viridiana stood immobile, and she recalled a passage that she had read in an old book about the history of the area. It leapt into her mind, as clear as if she held the book between her hands and paged through it: "They sinned by eating human meat and they sacrificed themselves to the Devil and they would not make the sign of the cross."

Neither the scream nor the silence which stretched on were any of her business, but she still walked forward, as she had walked forward in the dream. When she emerged in the living room she almost expected to find the man in yellow there, tearing a piece of prickly pear and stuffing it in his greedy mouth. Instead, she was greeted by a different, equally macabre sight.

Ambrose lay at the bottom of the stairs.

Gregory was kneeling next to him, his hand on Ambrose's neck. He did not look at Viridiana as she approached them. But Daisy was staring at her.

"He fell," Daisy said.

Viridiana looked down at Ambrose. There was a scratch on his cheek and his eyes were closed. She couldn't tell if he was breathing, when she tried to bend down to take a closer look at him, Daisy grabbed her arm, as if to pull her away.

"We need a doctor," Gregory muttered.

"I think he's dead," Daisy said.

"We need…"

"I heard you the first time!"

Viridiana had only seen one dead person before: her grandmother dressed in her favorite blue skirt, a photo of her in her youth placed by the coffin. She could not tell if Ambrose was dead or gravely injured, and there was no point in debating. Viridiana hurried to the door.

"Where are you going?" Daisy asked.

"He's right. We need a doctor," Viridiana said, and she grabbed the car keys in the Talavera dish.

"Hurry up."

The sun was setting as she drove into the town and the sky was like a purple bruise. She rang the bell on the side door of Doctor Navarro's house, where he had his attendance room. Navarro saw people from four in the afternoon until eight at night. He had no patient with him that night and the doctor opened the door quickly.

"Yes?" he said.

"One of the Americans, over at The End, he had an accident," she said. "You have to come and look."

"Is it bad? I have a card game in half an hour."

Viridiana had forgotten that on Fridays the man usually ignored the hours painted on his door and went to meet friends. She was lucky she'd grabbed him before he started downing beers.

"Yes. He might be dead."

"All right. You better get Cipriano," Doctor Navarro said. "If the man is really dead, he'll be needed anyway."

Navarro looked put off, probably on account of missing his card game. Viridiana nodded and jumped back into the car. Cipriano lived on the other side of town. He was the funeral home owner although to call this a "funeral home" was doing it a great favor. It was a white-washed house, very small. Most rooms of it were littered with coffins, boxes filled with candles and wooden planks. Cipriano was a carpenter by trade, the coffins were a side-business, like the fireworks he sold in December. He did know something about the dead, having lived in Guadalajara where he worked for a real funeral home.

Viridiana knocked on his door and told Cipriano about Ambrose and that Navarro had said they should head back to the house. Cipriano called his son, a surly boy of about fourteen, and they got into their pickup truck with the blue tarp. This was what passed for a hearse in her town.

When they arrived at the house, Navarro was sitting on a couch and Ambrose's body was still sprawled on the floor. Someone had tossed a blanket on top of it. Daisy sat on another couch, across from the doctor, while Gregory stood behind his sister.

"Good, you're here," Navarro said. "He is very much dead. I have to ask them some questions so you'll have to translate."

"Sure," Viridiana said, and she sat down slowly, next to the doctor. "The doctor wants to ask you a few questions."

Daisy was lighting a cigarette Gregory had handed her. She nodded, her manicured fingers pressing the cigarette against her lips. Daisy and Viridiana had never done their nails together, even though Daisy had promised. She got the feeling Daisy was full of empty promises.

Viridiana looked at those hands and noticed the broken nail. A single red, broken nail, standing out starkly against the others.

There had been a scratch on Ambrose's face.

"What happened to him?" the doctor asked.

Viridiana quickly repeated the question in English.

"He fell," Daisy said. Daisy's hand was shaking a little, her golden bangles clashing for a second, but the answer was short and simple. Viridiana licked her lips and said it in Spanish.

"How did he fall?"

"He was coming down the stairs, and he fell."

"Just like that?"

"He tripped."

Navarro was frowning. He had a stern face and a deep frown, it used to terrify Viridiana whenever she visited him for a checkup as a little girl. He'd shine a light in her ears, ask her to stick out her tongue, all while frowning. Viridiana always feared she was coming down with a horrid disease by the way he frowned and seemed displeased, though inevitably it turned out to be a minor issue.

Daisy stared at the doctor and Gregory placed a hand on his sister's shoulder squeezing it lightly.

"He'd been drinking," Gregory said quickly, the words so quick he almost sounded breathless.

Daisy tapped her cigarette against an ashtray. Viridiana stared at the broken nail. Daisy was looking down, she looked terribly upset and her hand trembled again. The bracelets clinked gently together. Four gold bracelets, one of them with jade embellishments. Daisy had casually mentioned Ambrose had bought them for her before they took the ferry to Baja.

Navarro sighed. "This is going to be more annoying than that hippie who stabbed his friend," he said.

That incident had taken place a few years before. A group of friends who had been camping by the beach, drinking, doing drugs, and God knew what else. They had gotten into a scuffle which turned violent when one of them took out a knife—so much for love and peace, although she wasn't sure those folks had been hippies it's just that any outsider was liable to be called a hippie— and stabbed another hippie in the arm. It wasn't fatal or anything like it, but the Americans had flapped their hands and said charges needed to be laid against the man while everyone else rolled their eyes.

It was the kind of event which precipitated needless paperwork. For Navarro, it meant he'd likely have to waste his Friday night examining the body and writing a death certificate. The doctor took out a handkerchief and pressed it against his forehead. The ceiling fan was on but it could not cool the room properly. Air conditioned was needed. A pity the previous owner had never bothered installing it.

Navarro stood up and went to take another look at the body. He shook his head.

"Tell them we have to take the body," the doctor said, finally.

"Why would they take the body? Aren't the cops supposed to come?" Daisy asked.

Viridian translated Daisy's question. Navarro shook his head. "Cops! She thinks there are, plural, 'cops.' But he's an American. They'll expect a proper examination and I can't examine him here."

"What?"

"They should talk to Maximiliano and Homero in the morning," the doctor said, sounding slightly annoyed as he turned to Cipriano. "Put him in your truck, all right?"

"What's happening?"

"He'll examine the body, issue a medical certificate and give it to Maximiliano. That's the civil registry clerk, and then the civil registry clerk will, if necessary, get the district attorney involved. Only there's no district attorney here. There is one cop, Homero, so he'll be called tomorrow," Viridiana said, trying to explain. At least, this was what she thought would happen. It's more or less what had happened with the hippies. Now that she recalled, Navarro had called them "beatnicks," as he complained about that episode while playing dominoes at Viridiana's house. Navarro was older. To him hippies and beatnicks were the same thing.

"Tomorrow? And they'd call a district attorney?"

"If the civil registry clerk deems it necessary," Viridiana said. "If he suspects a violent death."

"He fell."

"Maximiliano and Homero will talk about that tomorrow. Maximiliano Parra is the clerk, Homero Flores is the cop."

"Yes, who cares about their names. Then there's no statements? There's what, whatever they *feel* like believing? Whatever he feels like writing down on that certificate?" Daisy asked. She sounded agitated.

"Daisy, why don't you go upstairs?" Gregory said. "They're moving the body, anyway."

Cipriano and his son had grabbed hold of Ambrose, one lifting him by the shoulders, the other taking the legs, and they were walking out. He'd be dumped onto the pick-up truck and tossed in the doctor's office for him to examine.

Daisy crossed her arms but she didn't go upstairs.

Navarro bid them goodnight and told Viridiana they should speak to Maximiliano at eleven the next morning. He'd have his certificate done by then. Suddenly they were alone.

"Should we… should we call the consulate?" Viridiana asked.

"You forgot there's no phone here," Daisy said.

They could drive into town, use the phone cabins in the hotel.

"Anyway, I don't care about the consulate. Not now. There's no need for it, we'll explain everything, tell them how it was. He was drunk and he fell."

"Only he wouldn't have been drunk," Viridiana said, because she had translated that, but she had not believed it. She couldn't. Ambrose had been adhering to his vow of sobriety. Besides, the house was dry. Except for Gregory's stash.

"And you'd know this because you were in the room?"

"I wasn't, but he was very clear, that it was—"

"That it was *what*, little girl?" Daisy said, standing up straight, her hands closed into fists. "What exactly are you going to tell these people?"

"Take a sleeping pill and try to rest," Gregory said brusquely.

Daisy turned her head, giving her brother an outraged look. "Take a pill, huh? And you? Don't you need your beauty sleep?"

"I'll sleep soon enough. Go up."

Daisy glared at Gregory, but she clamped her mouth shut and stood up, excusing herself.

Viridiana looked at the stairs, following Daisy as she walked up. Then her gaze swept from the top of the stairs to the bottom, and she stared at the floor at the foot of them. There was blood there. A dark smear on the white tiles.

"Why did you say he was drunk?" she asked.

Gregory did not reply.

"He didn't drink anymore," Viridiana insisted.

"I was nervous. Look, I need a glass of water. Come to the kitchen," Gregory said, glancing up the stairs and waiting for a couple of minutes, making sure Daisy was out of sight.

They went into the kitchen and Gregory took a pitcher of lemonade out of the refrigerator. He placed it on the counter. Gregory had not bothered turning on the light when they walked into the kitchen. They stood in the semi-darkness, the light filtering through the rectangle of a door providing the only illumination.

"He wasn't drinking, I was," Gregory admitted. "He found the booze in my room and he got mad. Really mad. He said it was forbidden, that he was going to pour it down the drain. Daisy heard him and came over. And then he told her he was going to have me tossed out.

"They were yelling at each other. And then he said he'd have *her* tossed out. It wasn't the first time he'd said that. He'd done it before, for show, or to humiliate her, God knows. He went after her. I tried to intervene. Bastard hit me in the groin. He grabbed her by the arm and pulled her down the hallway and he was dragging her down the stairs."

Viridiana had seen Ambrose being mean to Daisy more than once. There had been that slap on her leg. It was mostly words, though. Cruel words or gestures when Ambrose lost his temper. Back and forth they went on at least two occasions.

She could believe the scene Gregory was describing.

"Daisy was mad. She slapped him, tried to kick him… and then, I don't know how it happened. Daisy, she moved or elbowed him or something and he fell down the stairs. He fucking rolled down the stairs."

Gregory poured himself a full glass of lemonade and drank it in a few gulps. Sweat beaded his hairline and his eyes were unfocused, he was not looking at her, at anything, as he spoke.

"But you didn't tell that to the doctor," Viridiana said.

Gregory turned his head.

He tiredly ran a hand through his hair.

"I've heard about Mexican jails. I thought if we told them that part they'd cart us off to jail and then we'd have to pay through the nose to get out. If we could. And that damn doctor kept staring at us."

Gregory pressed the cold glass against his forehead. He closed his eyes.

"There's a story I heard, once, that William S. Burroughs killed his wife during a game of William Tell. They were in Mexico City at the time. And I remember they called him a 'pernicious foreigner' and he had to flee, or they'd had him rotting in jail. I mean, his own lawyer skipped town after *he* killed a guy. What kind of country is this, where your lawyer murders someone?"

"His lawyer also got Burroughs out on bail in record time," Viridiana said. "Thirteen days once he paid a bond of more than

$2,000."

"You know the story."

"I read it in one Reynier's books."

"We don't have thousands of dollars. And he spent those thirteen days in a hellhole called the 'Black Palace,' right?"

"That would be Lecumberri."

Gregory put the glass down on the counter, he moved closer to Viridiana and spoke in a whisper.

"Look, there was something in California... something that happened there. The reason why Ambrose decided to go clean."

"His doctor said he needed to, didn't he?"

"No... the doctor said so, but the doctor had said so for years and years. Ambrose didn't take it seriously."

"Then?"

"Daisy got pregnant. She was happy. I've never cared about kids, and Ambrose didn't look too thrilled either, but she was glad to have a baby. I thought, I guess it's time to be an uncle. Then she lost the kid. Told me it happened one night, she'd been sleeping and woke up feeling pain in her abdomen and it was gone.

"Tonight, after you went to get the doctor, Daisy told me something I didn't know. She told me Ambrose had caused the miscarriage. He'd given her a shove and she'd fallen."

"So, she shoved him back," Viridiana whispered.

"Maybe. I didn't see it. I said he was drunk because it sounded better. Yes, it sounded better that way. Because otherwise they might ask her... and then... she told me she hoped he was dead. God, you can't tell them what I said, alright? You can't tell Daisy I told you, either."

Gregory took hold of Viridiana's wrists, holding them tight. Then he put his arms around her and embraced her. He was trembling.

Viridiana did not know what to do. She held him too, awkwardly, her left hand reaching up and gently touching his hair.

It made sense, the whole thing.

The yelling,

Ambrose's scratch on his face,

Daisy's broken nail.

He was an annoying, horrid man. Daisy could turn cruel. She switched moods like a cat. But then who could blame her? Married to that prickly bastard.

Who could blame her if she had indeed shoved the old man down the stairs.

"Promise you won't tell them," Gregory said, raising his head, looking down at her. The light trickling into the kitchen bounced on his hair, it made it golden.

Viridiana held her breath for a moment. "I...they should know."

"No, no, it will be bad if they think she did it. Daisy can't be going to jail. God, I have no money. How would I pay for a lawyer?"

"Daisy has money."

"Daisy doesn't have anything. It's all his. Ambrose's. If Ambrose's nephew hears she could be responsible for his death, she won't see a penny of anything, ever. He'll make sure of that. Daisy in jail. God, *me* in jail."

"Why you?"

"I don't know. Because I didn't stop her. She had a look on her face when she confronted him. This awful look. I should have slugged him, then, and maybe this wouldn't have happened."

Gregory muttered something Viridiana did not understand. His voice was thick with distress.

"It'll be fine," she said, touching his cheek.

"How can it be fine?"

"They're lazy. Maximiliano and Homero, they won't want to bother with any extra paperwork, with any trouble."

"That sounds crazy."

"Maybe."

"You'll help us, right?" Gregory said. It wasn't truly a question, and he firmly wrapped an arm around her waist.

Viridiana knew that they shouldn't be having this conversation at all.

That a man had died, he'd been pushed down the stairs and they had lied, saying he'd been drunk.

That it was best to come clean and tell the doctor, tell *someone*, the truth. But when did the truth do anyone any good? Her aunt's husband beat her. No one cared. When the beatings got too bad, she moved in with them until the husband circled around to collect her.

And so it went.

The answer, when a man beat you, was to be nicer to him. Everyone said so. Viridiana did not believe that. At least her father had never done a thing like that to her mother. He might have been a loser, but he kept his hands to himself.

She pictured Daisy shoving Ambrose down the stairs. Pictured her face flushed with anger, her beautiful, manicured hands resting against the man's back and pushing hard. Pictured Daisy's blonde hair in her face, her eyes narrow and angry and wild.

She found she didn't care how it had happened. She liked Daisy, she liked Gregory. She hadn't liked Ambrose much. She didn't want to see them in trouble.

She cared about them. That meant there was no sense in caring about Ambrose.

There was too, behind everything, that fuzzy dream of Paris. Of running away with this handsome man. Only there couldn't be any running if his sister was in a jail cell, or worse, if he was in the cell with her. They wouldn't even be in the local jail, but transported to a larger city. They could end up as far as Tijuana.

She refused that fate.

"I'll help you," she muttered.

He took her face between his hands. He smiled at her, brushed her hair behind her ear, traced the outline of her jaw with his fingertips.

"Good girl," he whispered.

People die every day, people die everywhere, and that was that. He fell.

They death certificate would state he fell and a week from now this would all be forgotten. If she willed it, then it would be. Her grandmother had said this.

That was how you summoned winds.

She placed a hand on his chest, over the space where his heart lay and then she recalled that her grandmother also said the devil awaits in the rocks and crevices, in the brush, in the desert.

Chapter 10

When Viridiana came into the living room the next morning, she was surprised to see that the tiles at the bottom of the stairs were sparkling clean. Not that she had expected the blood to remain there eternally, but Daisy or Gregory must have gotten up early and wiped the mess away.

She asked him about that.

"I couldn't leave it there," Gregory said. "I grabbed a brush and soap, and washed it. Doesn't make a difference, does it?"

At this point, Viridiana supposed it didn't. She couldn't discuss it with him because Daisy came down the stairs, wearing sunglasses and a black hat, and told them she was ready.

The civil registry office also served as the office of the mayor of Desengaño, but the mayor was never around. He owned the gas station, several plots of land and buildings, and a fat bank account. He was a hypochondriac who was always suffering from a new disease and flying to Mexico City to meet with specialists. When he was in Baja, he tended to spend his days in La Paz, which he considered more hospitable. This pleased Maximiliano because the office was small. The police station, located around the corner, was equally minuscule. It had a jail cell which could contain at most three people and which was scarcely used.

When they walked into the civil registry office Maximiliano was sitting behind his desk, typing, a cigarette between his teeth.

"Doctor Navarro and Homero should be here soon," Maximiliano said without bothering to look at them, and kept on typing.

Daisy, Gregory and Viridiana sat down on a bench set against the wall and across from Maximiliano. After fifteen minutes Daisy angrily turned toward Viridiana. She had not taken off her sunglasses and Viridiana saw herself reflected in the lenses.

"Will he ever speak to us?"

"It's not odd to be late for meetings, here," Viridiana said.

"What do you mean it's not odd? It's rude as hell."

"Navarro might have had an urgent patient. Who knows."

Daisy did not seem convinced by her explanation. She sat clutching her purse, blue eyes blazing. Gregory was more relaxed than his sister, although by the tapping of his left foot Viridiana could tell he wasn't calm.

Viridiana tried to think of something, anything, to keep herself in check. If they thought she was nervous they'd pry. They'd ask what was up and it was so hot in there, it would be easy to slip and admit to a dozen crimes.

She thought about her father and the time he'd shown her the bezoar. The little stone cool against her hand and she focused her thoughts on that single stone.

The bezoar, cut from the belly of a beast.

Gregory tapped his foot and it was steaming hot in this office, you'd think they were going to boil lobsters. But no, think of something else.

The bezoar. The serpent stone. Things hidden. Things that are not what they seem.

At half past eleven, in walked Doctor Navarro and Homero. Homero was only a few years older than Viridiana, and she remembered him as a terrible bully in high school. He'd never bothered with her, but she'd seen him fuck around with others. His father had been the police officer in town and when he retired he passed down the torch to Homero, as though this was a nobility title.

"It seems we're all here," Maximiliano said, setting down his half-smoked cigarette and shaking everyone's hands. "Please pull up chairs."

There weren't enough, so Viridiana let Daisy and Gregory sit while she remained standing. Homero also remained on his feet.

"You've looked at the body?" Maximiliano asked.

"I have. I need to fill some gaps, of course. Age, full name, all the standard details," Navarro said, taking out a notepad. "You have his passport?"

Viridiana told Daisy to hand over Ambrose's passport. Navarro looked at it, asked a couple of basic questions and jotted down the answers. Then he scribbled a few more things.

Daisy asked what was happening, and Viridiana told her to wait. There was a rhythm to these things. If they seemed desperate or eager, they would notice something was amiss—surely even Homero could sniff out a criminal if the criminal began to twist like a worm on a hook. They must not notice.

"Wait," Viridiana whispered.

Maximiliano hummed to himself, pausing to pick up his cigarette again.

"So he smashed his head against the floor, huh?" Maximiliano asked.

"He had a laceration on the back of his head," Navarro said. "There was quite a bit of blood. There were bruises on the rest of the body."

"How did that happen?" Homero asked, looking at Daisy. Viridiana translated.

"He'd been drinking," Viridiana said in Spanish. "He was heading downstairs and lost his footing."

"Was he a big drinker?"

"He was. He drank too much," Viridiana said. A bead of sweat was sliding down her temple. She tried to maintain a serene tone of voice.

"How did you find him?"

"They heard a noise and saw he'd fallen. He wasn't moving, he wasn't talking." Just hold still, she thought. Hold perfectly still, play it natural. It's an old dead guy. Homero asked more questions and Viridiana stuck to the plain answers and even though there was a point at which she could have sworn there was a bezoar in her stomach, she didn't flinch. Quick, simple.

Homero leaned backwards, looked at Daisy, then at Viridiana. He seemed to think the whole thing through, nodding and frowning. "Then that's it," Homero said slowly. "It was an accident."

It sounded almost as if he were asking a question. A question directed at Maximiliano and Navarro, but Maximiliano shrugged helplessly. He was used to signing and stamping documents, not questioning them. The doctor, however, did not look convinced.

"What I find interesting is the laceration," Navarro said, taking out a handkerchief and dabbing his forehead with it, which was an elegant way to say, "I don't believe this."

"Really? He fell," Homero replied, glancing at Daisy. He had apparently chosen what line he'd follow. When it came to policing, Homero didn't do much of it and she guessed he was simply trying to keep it all manageable.

"Maybe," Navarro said. "I'd recommend an autopsy, but I realize..."

He trailed off. It was obvious Navarro wasn't absolutely sold on this story of a drunkard falling down the steps, but it was also obvious it was a fuzzy situation. It wasn't that Navarro was a bad doctor, it's just that he knew the way things go and that you needed to be able to say "let's leave it like that" or you'd be asking for trouble.

"Now that would be a major hassle," Homero said, shaking his head. "A hassle we don't want. But if it's needed, can't oppose it. Doctor Navarro, it's up to you. What should we do?"

"Viridiana, there's nothing else you want to tell us?" Navarro asked.

Doctor Navarro stared at Viridiana. Why has he looking at her? What was he expecting to see? She stared back at him blankly.

She thought of nothing. If he was searching for clues, he wouldn't find them in her eyes.

"No," she said.

"An autopsy would be a problem and I'm not sure it's necessary," Navarro said finally. "Accidents do happen."

Homero nodded. Maximiliano smiled and laced his fingers together, leaning forward, making a few papers rustle. "They do," Maximiliano agreed.

The doctor was still looking at her, but he shrugged and turned to the men. "In that case, this should be enough to issue the death certificate. My medical certificate states it's an accidental death," Navarro said, signing and tearing off the page from his notepad and giving it to Maximiliano.

"Damn hot day to have to type it up," Maximiliano said, shaking his head. "Damn hot, and it would be nice to buy ourselves a few drinks before getting to work."

Viridiana realized two things right then.

One, that nobody in that room cared about what had happened to Ambrose, not even a bit. She had been nervous for no reason. The doctor, the clerk and the cop were all trying to avoid paperwork and questions. They didn't get paid enough to launch tedious inquiries and on top of that they probably thought if Viridiana wasn't willing to levy accusations against the Americans, they weren't willing to go there either. Which led to number two: they wanted a bribe. The old, "Hey, buddy, how about money for our sodas?"

Viridiana informed Daisy and Gregory of the turn of events.

"What are we supposed to do, write them a check right here?" Daisy asked, taking off her sunglasses.

"Cash," Viridiana said. "They'll want cash."

Daisy looked inside her purse and took out several bills. She set them on the desk and stared at the clerk.

"Mrs. Allerton realizes that the issuing of documentation requires a fee, she wants to be able to bury her husband."

"Why, of course," Maxmiliano said. "It's very hot, so we wouldn't want to hold anything up. Why don't you folks get the funeral arrangements going right away? I'll fix this paperwork."

That much made sense. The body was going to rot and would stink quickly. Maximiliano said they should pick a good suit for the deceased, go to Cipriano's place and pay for a coffin, then stop by the church to see about a burial. Ambrose's body was locked in Navarro's receiving room, but Cipriano would go pick it up once the arrangements were in place.

Normally, they would have taken the body back to their home, where a wake would be held. The coffin would be set in a room, a crucifix hanging from the coffin, and friends would be allowed to pay the widow their respects. But the Americans had no friends. They simply wanted Ambrose to be dressed properly, in the navy suit Daisy picked for him, and buried. Cipriano, however, informed them that they would not be able to bury the body right that instant: the gravedigger lived in a nearby town and they'd have to fetch him.

Besides, a wake was the decent thing to do.

Cipriano rented out one of the rooms in his house to the poor fishermen and their families who could not hold a wake in their house because it was too small. This was deemed the solution to their problem. Cipriano asked if they would like to drape a purple sheet over the coffin, and whether flowers would be necessary. Daisy and Gregory agreed to this, but when they headed to the church to speak to the priest they were less tractable.

The priest salivated at the idea of a grand mass. He would be paid to say the name of the deceased and ask for special blessings for him. No doubt he thought he could price-gauge them for this, but Daisy balked.

"He was not Catholic. And I don't want to sit in a church and listen to a mass," Daisy said, once Viridiana explained what the process was like.

The priest looked peeved. He made a comment about how, in that case, burying a Protestant in their cemetery might not be the most palatable idea, but Viridiana soothed him.

"Mrs. Allerton wants to donate to the fund for the restoration of the Virgin's altar," Viridiana said, figuring that was the best course of action.

Again, out came the money and the priest informed them they could bury Ambrose the next afternoon.

Once that transaction was concluded it was time to go around the doctor's house again, to pay him his fee, and let him know Cipriano was picking up the body, although there was no need for that because when they arrived Navarro told them the man had already come by.

"That was quick," Viridiana said. The swiftness of it all seemed close to sacrilege.

"Why waste time?" the doctor said. "And the sooner they get the corpse in there, the sooner they can head out to the bar. It's the weekend, after all."

It was indeed. When Viridiana's grandmother died they all huddled around her coffin for the wake, praying the rosary. Grandmother was not left alone during the night, but neither Daisy nor Gregory were going to sit next to the coffin. This worried her, and she wondered if she should pray for him that night, even if it was from the comfort of her room.

"Yes, I suppose it is," Viridiana whispered. She felt kind of bad now. Relieved, but bad, and she rubbed a hand against her eyes.

They were feeling dangerously moist.

The doctor must have thought she was grieving because he gave her a pat on the shoulder. "Go see your mother. She'll be wondering what happened."

He was right. She needed to speak to her mother. If she didn't, the woman would no doubt show up at their doorstep demanding to know what was going on. By now the whole town must be aware one of the Americans had died and they'd be gossiping about it.

"I have to take care of some things," Viridiana told Gregory. They were waiting in the car, outside the post office while Daisy made a phone call to Ambrose's lawyer in Mexico City. "My family, they'll be wanting to speak to me."

"About what happened?"

"Yes. They'll be curious. Everyone will be curious about you. Small town, big hell," she said, but she said the last part in Spanish and had to translate it into English. The literal translation did not make much sense, so she told Gregory it meant small town, big fuss.

"I guess," Gregory said, frowning. "You think people will talk about us, then?"

"Yes," she said.

"At least we don't live in the town. Pretty hard to hear gossip up on that cliff. Tell them what you must to calm them down."

"I will, and I'll catch up with you later."

"Catch up, how? You don't have your bicycle," Gregory pointed out.

"I can get a ride or walk it if it comes to it."

"You sure?"

"Yeah."

"Hurry back, then, and be careful."

Gregory squeezed her hand for one quick moment and she got

out of the car.

Viridiana hurried to her mother's shop. It was small, its modest collection of dresses, shirts and jeans were hardly the latest in fashion. There was a corner with makeup products. Lipstick, tweezers, blush. When she walked in, two teenage girls were looking at lipstick and her mother was watching the girls like a hawk.

Nobody stole from Marta.

She had to wait to speak to her, but once the girls exited, her mother motioned for Viridiana to head behind the counter. She obeyed.

"What's happening?" Marta asked, immediately extending a hand to smooth back Viridiana's hair. It always looked a little wild and her mother disliked this, trying to press it into place with lemon juice and hair spray. "I heard from your godfather that one of the gringos died."

"Ambrose, he had a bad fall. They're burying him tomorrow."

"What a thing, I heard he was drunk. You didn't say he drank."

Viridiana didn't want to lie, so she chose her words carefully. Her mother smelled untruths easily. "It was not my business and I didn't drink with him, so how should I know what he did?"

"And the burial, *here*? I would have thought they'd take the body back to their country."

"He liked it here." That's what Daisy had said. Also, that if Ambrose's nephew wanted to have the corpse hauled to the American cemetery in Mexico City, he could arrange for that himself. Viridiana suspected Daisy didn't much care where her deceased husband's body ended up.

"When are you bringing your things back home? Is your last day tomorrow or the day after?"

"I'm still working for them."

Marta stopped fussing with Viridiana's hair and stared at her daughter.

"How?"

"I'll be doing the same stuff I was already doing. Typing letters, translating stuff. They have to talk with lawyers and all that. They can't up and leave today, especially when they don't speak Spanish," she said.

"But a man died in that house. You can't stay there. It's bad luck."

Viridiana looked down at the floor and nudged aside one of many cardboard boxes hidden under the counter. "Grandmother died in ours."

"Of old age," her mother said.

"Death is not contagious."

Her mother leaned down to open a box under the counter and took out a few blouses, placing them on the counter and folding them, her face tense.

"I could use some help around here, at home."

"I have no interest in the shop."

"You have no interest in anything except in flipping through dictionaries and smiling at tourists."

"It's work, Mother."

"Ha! Work. Seven hours behind a counter is work, a couple of hours showing people the beach and pointing out the church or the lighthouse is not real work."

Viridiana grabbed one of the blouses and began folding it but her mother shook her head and took the piece of clothing out of her hands, folding it herself.

"You always do it wrong," she chided.

"Then why do you want me around?"

"Because of that. Because you have to learn the business."

"We both know the business is not going to go to me," Viridiana said.

Marta had a bunch of children from her second marriage. Her siblings would be the ones to reap the benefits of the shop. Viridiana was a mistake, the other kids were the do-over.

"Maybe you'll have your own shop one day," Marta said.

Viridiana leaned back against the counter, resting her elbows on it and chuckled. "I know the shop you imagine for me. The stationery store."

"He has no brothers or sisters."

He. Manuel, Manuel, always Manuel. The more her family tried to shove him in her face, the more Viridiana recoiled. She wanted Gregory. Devilish sparkle in his eyes and the twist of the head as he smiled at her. Gregory looked like a matinee idol, but reconfigured for the modern age. Skin tanned to perfection and dirty blond hair that was growing lighter under the Baja Californian sun and the playful waves.

"I don't want to talk about him, I came to say a quick hi and I'll head back out," Viridiana said airily, the way Daisy might do it.

"You better stop by tomorrow for mass and stay for supper."

"There's the funeral."

"You can attend both things," Marta said. "It's not like the funeral will take all day."

"Fine."

"And you better stay for a while. Don't think I don't notice how you dash out after an hour."

"It's boring," Viridiana said. "Playing dominoes every week with the same people."

"You could open your mouth and have a conversation once in a while."

"About what?"

"You'll stay until nighttime tomorrow," her mother said as she carefully folded another shirt.

"I shouldn't ride my bicycle back in the dark."

"Someone can drive you back."

Someone.

Manuel and his pickup truck. Viridiana moved away from the counter and stood in front of a calendar where each day was carefully crossed out with a marker. As if Monday made any difference from Thursday in this place.

"I don't have anything black, can I grab a shirt?" Viridiana asked, because she might as well get something out of the bargain.

"Of course."

She grabbed a plastic bag and tossed in a simple black shirt with white cuffs and a pair of stockings, which she normally didn't wear. Then she headed out of the shop, adjusting her hat. It would be a bit of a walk back to the house but the other option was asking someone in town for a ride. She would have enough of her family the next day and decided it was preferable to make her way on her own.

How prosaic this whole business of life and death was, she thought, as the plastic bag dangled from her wrist. One moment here and then gone.

Liar.

The word, it rattled in her head and it made her stop on the side of the dusty road, catching her breath because for a moment she thought someone had whispered the word in her ear, that it had not been her mind conjuring it.

And she thought of the devil but when she turned her head there was only the desert around her, quiet and still. She saw a snake stirring in the crepuscule, not far from her. It had eyes a black as onyx and a dark strip running down its back. Although it might thrash wildly if you tried to pick it up, it was not dangerous. Nevertheless, she recoiled in fear. Not of the snake, but of something else.

And that something followed her home, as keen as her shadow.

Chapter 11

The funeral was a quiet affair. Aside from the priest and the gravedigger, Viridiana was the only local. She wore the black shirt from her mother's store, which looked cheap next to Daisy's simple, elegant black ensemble. Gregory must not have had any mourning clothes because he had on a tan jacket and a white shirt. When the priest finished reciting his brief words he shook hands with Daisy and Gregory.

Viridiana went home after that. Her mother had made pastel de tres leches in a quiet bid to please her. But it didn't improve Viridiana's evening. She watched the men play dominoes and shared a few words with the people around her.

She did not feel like socializing. The funeral had left a bitter taste in her mouth. She hadn't liked Ambrose, yet she kept worrying about the fact that no one was going to say a rosary for him. She knew it didn't really matter, but that nagged at her more than the fact that she had lied to the authorities.

She hadn't lied out of malice. She didn't want Daisy and Gregory to get in trouble. It was for them.

This is a bad situation but these are not bad people, she told herself.

Anyway, she couldn't say anything *now*. It wasn't like the truth was going to bring Ambrose back to life, was it?

Viridiana stayed longer than usual that evening, hoping to pacify her mother, and she let her ex-boyfriend take her back to the house, which had to count for something.

Manuel placed her bicycle in the back of his pickup truck and drove slowly. The radio played sugary-sweet ballads. She turned down the volume with a quick flick of her wrist. Their taste in music, like other matters, had always been at odds.

He parked outside the house and spoke before she could thank him for the ride and haul her bike off the truck.

"We're gonna go to the movies next weekend," he said. "All of us. Maybe you'd like to come."

She had not been invited to any outings since their breakup. Not that she had attempted to socialize. She could have talked to Patricia or Trinidad, reconstructed her circle of friends or built a new one. It seemed too difficult. Too pointless. She wished only to get up late and read a bit from her books, and then watch black and white movies on the TV set. The arrival of Daisy and Gregory had changed her routine, got her interested in something after wanting nothing of this stinking town.

"I don't know. Won't they be irritated?" she asked.

"Because you're there? Viridiana, they're not mad at you."

"That's not true. They are. And so are you."

She unlocked the door and got out. He got out too, and helped her with the bicycle, setting it down next to her and resting a hand on it.

"It can be the way it was before," he said.

Viridiana stared at him. He thought "before" was a good thing. As if she was not desperately running away from "before". She had felt sick talking about a wedding, physically nauseous. She couldn't swallow a bite of food. A weight had been lifted off her shoulders when they'd broken up. And while it was true that afterwards she had found herself in a state of confusion and depression, she had no desire to return to the way it was "before".

No, she was looking ahead, looking to something entirely different.

"I'd like to go out with all of you," she said, "but perhaps another day."

She meant it, too. Now...now was not the time to start mending friendships. If she moved away with Gregory, if Paris was indeed their destination, *then* she would write copious letters to her mother, to her friends, to Manuel.

"Things are a little bit chaotic around here," she said, crossing her arms and glancing at the house. "You understand, right? Thanks, though. Thanks for asking."

It wasn't the answer Manuel had expected. He didn't look pleased, but he also didn't ask her again. He nodded and got into his truck. Viridiana waved goodbye.

When he was gone she looked up at the moon, which was round and shining bright. The Kiliwa said Coyote, who came from the place in the south where everything was yellow, made the earth and with the skin of his testicles he made the sky and when he perished he became the moon. The moon was male. *Nyiew halah.* Black moon, the number zero and death. She didn't speak Kiliwa, but then, who did? The missionaries came to teach everyone the proper language and the proper religion, and then the missions crumbled and now there wasn't even that.

Viridiana spoke English and French and Spanish, but these tongues, too, would fade someday. For the here and now, those were the only tools she required. Those were the artifacts that allowed her to be employed each summer, speaking words for people who had never bothered to read a sentence in another language.

She felt empty some nights and that night she was emptier, and sad.

Perhaps that is why she thought of Ambrose, or how Ambrose

bought forth the sadness and the loneliness. Back in her room, she prayed a rosary without any beads to aid her, marking each prayer with dots on a piece of paper.

When she was done, she took out the tape recorder and spoke to it. This had been, for a long time now, not only her diary but a method of confession. She felt it more secure than the blessing of the priest, sacrilegious as that might be. It was clean and holy in its own way.

She had not made a full confession to the recorder since she'd arrived in the house, although she had whispered to the tapes her attraction to Gregory. The blow job, his hands in her hair—that she hadn't dared to speak out loud. Now those were minuscule compared to this sin.

"I've lied," she told the tape. "It's not as if I wanted to lie, but I don't have a choice. The cops couldn't know the truth, because if they had then it would have been a mess so it was for the best. He's dead and the world is for the living. Isn't it? Does anyone suspect me?"

She stopped the recording and lay back on her bed. Outside her window, the moon watched her, but it did not judge her. The moon was pure. And she thought of Coyote, who dreamt beautiful yellow dreams and thus created the world. But when she slept she dreamt of a shark with massive jaws, jaws taller than her. The shark's belly glowed and she ventured inside of it, looking for the source of light, which was the moon, plucked from the sky.

* * *

The week after Ambrose's funeral the mood at the house was odd. Not sad, just odd. Delfina cooked for them on the days when she cleaned the house. She left meals in the refrigerator. Ambrose had also cooked a meal or two a week, because he liked it. Now that he wasn't around, neither Gregory nor Daisy picked up the slack. Instead, Daisy told Viridiana to whip them dinner.

Viridiana had been very clear since the beginning that she wasn't there to play maid or cook, but Daisy seemed to have forgotten.

She cooked the meal, anyway, and afterward Daisy was extra nice. Daisy did her toenails and let Viridiana use her nail polish. Daisy painted them a bright red, and they chatted like they were fast friends.

You would have believed Daisy a young girl by the way she smiled and was so excited. It reminded Viridiana of her first day in the house. Maybe things would go back to being nice between them. As Daisy applied the polish to her toenails, Viridiana remembered her broken nail. Daisy had cut them and filed them down to the same length, there was nothing which might differentiate them. But Viridiana still thought about the broken nail. You could lacquer it a dozen times, she'd still be able to identify it.

But who cared about that?

It had been the ring finger.

After their nails were dry, they went down to the beach together. Daisy laid herself out on a towel, sunbathing, while Gregory asked Viridiana more about the sharks. She told him that in Santa Rosalía they still hunted sharks with varillas.

They harpooned it, first the neck and then the back, and then they dragged it onto the boat.

No hooks with bait, no nets, but brute force. The fishermen beat the shark with a baseball bat— nail affixed to it.

Then he asked her about the peninsula, its people, the geography. She told him that the east is calm and full of life, but the west is naked rocks. It is harsh. It is cruel.

She told him about all the creatures you can find in the sea, not only the sharks, but the great sea turtles, the lobsters, and the industries that had vanished many years before. Like the cannery down south which closed down, and the famous pearl divers who dived no more because the pearl beds had sickened and died.

But she did not tell him the stories about the moon and the coyote. She wanted to keep certain things to herself. There are only so many stories you can tell about yourself, about your land, before you grow empty.

"Hear that? We ought to head to Santa Rosalía," Gregory said to Daisy. "I could take pictures there. Or what was that other place you said?"

"Isla de Cedros," Viridiana answered. That had been a mining town. They mined for gold. Then, that also ceased. This seemed to be the fate of everything in Baja California: a stillness, which overcame any attempt at movement.

"What's there?"

"Sea lions," Viridiana said. "Sardines, shrimp, lobster and snails. People dive for snails."

"What a bore," Daisy said, examining her nails.

"She's not much of a fishing enthusiast," Gregory said.

"Neither are you. Why can't you take pictures of the fishermen and their boats and their sharks *here*?"

"I have pictures from here, and now I want pictures from other places around Baja. I might as well do it since we're in Mexico."

"You're right, we are," Daisy said, taking off her sun glasses and frowning.

Then they went home and that night Viridiana prayed another rosary for Ambrose while the electric generator hummed outside her window. She even recorded herself saying a Hail Mary. When she played it back she thought her voice sounded odd. Like it wasn't her.

As if, like the coyote, she had removed her skin. This made

her think of sharks and the fishermen making their quick, efficient cuts, tugging at the shark's hide. A slit down the back, then they scraped all flesh from the skin until it was as neat as a glove.

Brigida used to say she was an odd girl, skeptical about her son's choice for a girlfriend, although ultimately, she figured Viridiana could be tamed. She could be cut and made into someone new, like the hide of the shark would cease to encase a monstrous fish and become a pair of shoes.

Reconfiguration, transmutation, it was possible. What Viridiana needed, they all agreed in town, was to settle down and stop dreaming. Stop with her books of foreign phrases and her reckless choices.

Viridiana didn't know, some nights, if she was right in fighting. At the center of her being there was a blank space.

Friday afternoon they went to the post office so Daisy could make a phone call and check her mail. When the woman returned to the car she was furious. She got in and banged the door shut, immediately demanding a cigarette. Gregory handed it to her.

"Light it, for fuck's sake," Daisy said, raising her voice and her hands in the air.

Gregory obeyed her. Daisy took a drag.

"Let's go," she said.

"What happened?"

"I'll tell you when we're back home," she replied and glanced at Viridiana through the rear-view mirror.

"Tell me now," Gregory said.

"*She's* here."

"Yes," Gregory replied blankly.

"Why can't you—"

"Tell me now. I don't want to wait."

"Fine. Start driving."

Gregory frowned, but he started the car. Daisy adjusted the rear-view mirror, her lips pursed, still looking at Viridiana. Viridiana crossed her arms and glanced down.

"He made a new will," Daisy said.

"When?" Gregory asked. He was gripping the wheel tight with both hands.

"I don't know. I spoke to his lawyer and he said there was a new will, that changes had been made."

"What kind of changes?"

"He wouldn't tell me. He said someone from the law firm is headed here, to talk about that...and to look at the death certificate."

"All right."

"And they froze the bank account," Daisy said.

"They can't do that."

"They did."

Daisy let out a little laugh as she rolled down the window and tossed out her cigarette. She had hardly taken more than two puffs.

"We should leave," Gregory said, his voice grave.

"Run away? The only thing you're good at," Daisy said, chuckling and she shook a finger in the air. "No, we are not leaving. Not now."

"Then what?"

"We wait until that stupid man from the law firm gets here and then we see what's what."

"Don't you thi—"

"Shut up," Daisy said and she flipped on the radio, cranking the volume.

They didn't speak after that, not until they got home and began climbing the stairs, arguing. Gregory was saying something about money, about savings, and Daisy was furiously rebuffing him.

Viridiana stood, at the bottom of the stairs, her arms still crossed against her chest.

She went to the office and looked at some of the notes she had typed, neatly piled on a desk. Ambrose's sad attempt at a book, this was what was left of it.

There was nothing for her to do, now. She rested the palm of her hand against the desk. After an hour she ventured upstairs and knocked softly on Gregory's door.

"Yeah?" he said.

"It's me," she replied.

"Come in."

She'd never been in his room. When she walked in, he sat up. The room was bigger than her own and it had a full-size bed. There was also a walk-in closet, the door half open, and a door leading to what she assumed was a bathroom.

He'd been napping, his hair was tousled and the covers were wrapped around his legs. He'd taken his shirt off to sleep.

Viridiana stood at the foot of the bed, sliding her hands into her jeans' pockets.

"I wanted to see how you're doing," she said.

"Not that great. You heard. Ambrose's asshole of a nephew has frozen the bank account," Gregory said with a sigh.

"Do you know why?"

"Because he doesn't want us to get our fair share. Daisy earned that money by not vomiting every time Ambrose went near her, for Christ's sake. And now? Now he's trying to take away our money."

"Daisy must receive something, as his widow."

"Something! God knows what scraps that lawyer is going to try and toss to us. It's worse than New York."

"What happened in New York?"

"Nothing," Gregory said.

"Daisy said something about running away."

He stood up and reached for her, pulling Viridiana towards the bed. There was a wooden ceiling fan, which whirred rather lazily above them.

"Let me show you a magic trick," he said as he laid her back against the bright yellow bedspread.

"I think I know your tricks already," she replied. She was naïve, but not entirely stupid. He was trying to distract her. New York must be important.

He smiled, a slightly crooked smile. Endearing. Not really Montgomery Clift because Clift had been too honest-looking for such an expression, but some other film star. Errol Flynn or Pedro Infante dyed blond. All swagger.

"Bet you don't know this one. I am a professional magician."

"Rabbits out of hats," she said. "Guessing the right card. But it's sleight of hand and not real magic."

"Sleight of hand, ha! Says who, Viri-diana?" He drew out the syllables as he popped open the button of her jeans. "Quite the name, that."

She shared a name with a film. Movies, cinema, melodrama and illusions. Her father had liked Buñuel's surrealism and her grandmother had liked any flick that Televisa transmitted.

"What are you doing?" she asked, because he was tugging at her jeans. "I told you—"

"Don't worry."

Which is what every boy said, along with "only the tip," but it turned out he was telling the truth because he didn't take off his clothes, content with pulling the jeans down her legs and then kissing her stomach. This was all right, very all right. Then it got weird because he began to kiss her below, kiss her thigh, then between her thighs, then he licked her. It was the oddest sensation, it made her jerk her hips up, and it made him smile. She could feel his smile against her, a Cheshire Cat's grin.

Since he didn't use his fingers, maybe it wasn't sleight of hand. Not that it mattered much, because whatever it was that he'd done, it melted her sinews to jelly, made her hot and fervid, plastered her hair to her face. Until she was shaking and felt as if she was falling, although he had her firmly on the bed.

He laughed then, and she didn't appreciate that bit. Not that she disliked his laughter per se, but sometimes he laughed low, and it was entirely different to his nice laughter. Too much mockery.

She was overthinking it.

When her tremors subsided, he laid back next to her, casually, and began unzipping his own pants.

"Your turn," he said.

She didn't realize she had signed up for another blow job. Perhaps she should have assumed it was implicit in the bargain. Tit for tat. She frowned, but he stared at her. She didn't want to be a bad sport about it, she didn't want to ruin it. God knew she was always ruining something with people. If she hadn't broken up with Manuel, surely he would have called it quits soon.

It had almost been a pre-emptive move.

"Okay," Viridiana said.

She didn't like the taste of him, but that was a small matter. And afterwards, when he closed his eyes, content, she curled up next to him.

"I can see you. I can hold you next to me," she whispered, so low he wouldn't hear her. The words weren't for his sake, but for her pleasure. She parroted the lines from an old movie.

Montgomery Clift's lines, because she had decided she was the plucky boy from the wrong side of the tracks, and Gregory had to be the sophisticated socialite Liz Taylor had played. The movie, reversed.

There had been a murder in that movie, a drowning. Only it might have been an accident.

Suddenly, she didn't enjoy the analogy of the film and rose from the bed, going to the bathroom.

She looked for mouthwash. There was a tall shelf by the sink, crammed with things. All of that bathroom stuff couldn't possibly belong to Gregory, some of it must be from the previous tenant. Or had they shipped a full container of stuff from the States? She pushed a stick of deodorant aside and knocked over a plastic tray. Viridiana knelt down quickly to pick everything up.

She hoped she hadn't broken anything.

On the floor there was a black leather wallet. Two cards had slipped out from it.

Viridiana grabbed them, ready to tuck them back in place.

Until something made her pause.

Both of the cards were driver's licenses. Both had a picture of Gregory, smile on display.

But the names were different.

One belonged to James Haskins of Nevada and the other to Jerry Nichols of New York.

The date was wrong, too. Gregory had said he was twenty-nine. But James Haskins was twenty-eight and Jerry Nichols was thirty-one.

Viridiana sat on the toilet seat, staring.

She *knew* Gregory and Daisy. They had talked, had gone to the beach, had meals together. But when she considered it, when she thought carefully about it, Viridiana actually knew little about them. The details of their lives were vague. Ambrose had been very specific. Part of that had been because she'd been taking notes for him and he'd told her about his childhood, his brother who died when he was a teenager and his only sister who died of cancer years ago, his real-estate business...

So, did she really know *anything* about Gregory? Did Daisy have similar IDs in her room? Viridiana thought about whether she might find out the answer, but she couldn't right away. If Daisy saw her riffling through her things, she'd be mad as hell.

Of course, she could ask Gregory what the driver licenses were about, but she wasn't so silly that she thought this could be explained as a harmless misunderstanding.

She opened the wallet again and found more than a hundred dollars in cash, and a card for the Off Road Club, NY. On the back of it he'd scribbled two phone numbers and the name Lucas. She memorized the numbers.

Viridiana promptly placed everything back in the wallet, put all the items in the plastic tray, and set them on the shelf. When she poked her head in Gregory's room, he looked fast asleep, and she hurried back to her room. She scribbled down the numbers and the name, mostly to make sure she wouldn't forget them, but also to remind herself that she had seen them. It had not been a dream.

Viridiana prayed no more rosaries and she did not record another message.

Chapter 12

There was nobody to confide in. She couldn't talk to Manuel because he was her ex and they weren't exactly on good terms, she had been shunned by her friends and shunned them in turn, and speaking to her mother would only invite disaster. She could attempt to phone her father, but he might, in turn, phone her mother. That left Reynier.

Viridiana's relationship with Reynier was warm, but rested on a bedrock of chess and other board games, books, and foreign languages. Offhandedly, she had mentioned some difficulties she had at home, but was vague. This would be a very specific problem.

Although, she didn't even know if it was a problem. It was odd. Worrisome. But maybe it wasn't *her* problem. If people were walking around using false IDs, that was their business, and she could remove herself from their presence quickly. It wouldn't take long to pack.

But every time Viridiana looked around her room, she realized leaving Gregory and Daisy meant heading back to her home. No Paris.

She rode the bicycle to town and stopped in the town square, propping her bicycle next to the coin-operated horse which had an "out of order" sign. A bus had stopped on the other side of the street, and she spotted people with cameras around their necks—a small flock of tourists—and some locals who had gone to another town and now returned. Her period had started that morning, and she bought a box of sanitary napkins, gum, and more cigarettes for Daisy and Gregory at the pharmacy.

When she went outside again, she stuffed her purchases in her backpack. A young man with a suitcase, Panama hat on his head, was standing on the sidewalk, resting a hand on the head of the coin-operated horse. He was talking in English to Alejandro Esparza and Paco Ibarra.

"1050 Aristoteles?" the foreigner asked. He sounded American. "You know the street?"

"Sure, we drop you off there after the tour is done," Alejandro said, pointing to a car. Paco was holding the door open. The car looked like any other, but Paco had affixed a "Licensed Tours and Taxi" sign to the side of it. It didn't mean anything, because there wasn't any office that licensed tours and taxis in town.

"No, I don't think you understand," the American said, a book under his arm. "I'm looking for 1050 Aristoteles, not a tour."

"We'll drop you off. The tour is eight dollars."

"You're going to Reynier's house?" Viridiana asked.

The American turned around. He wore sunglasses, which he took off and tucked in the back pocket of his trousers. He was neatly dressed, but that was all she could say about him. A neat man, in his twenties, but not a backpacker or a stray party boy, which is what younger people who came here tended to be. The older visitors were a mix of fly fishermen and families.

"Yes. You know him?" the man asked.

"I'm headed there," Viridiana said. "We can walk together, if you want. It's five blocks."

Viridiana walked her bike while the guy grabbed his luggage. Alejandro Esparza and Paco Ibarra looked at them with ill-concealed irritation.

"Thanks. They wouldn't let off and kept insisting on a tour," the man said.

"They were trying to fleece you. Eight dollars is way too much for a spin around town."

If Alejandro Esparza and Paco Ibarra hadn't been such monumental assholes to her the last time they met, maybe she wouldn't have said anything. But they had been, and they were being real cheeky trying to get eight dollars out of the guy when all he needed was a simple set of directions.

"I'm so tired and sweaty I might have paid them twenty to leave me alone."

"I can walk you back to them," Viridiana said with a shrug.

"Of course not," he replied, seriously.

She didn't want him to feel like she truly meant it, so she tried to make her tone sound friendlier. Could be he might need a tour guide later on, after all. A fair one, not one who tried to scam him out of his cash.

As they walked, he paused to take off his suit jacket. His shirt clung to his skin, drenched with sweat, but it was buttoned up to his chin, like he was a clerk or government functionary who couldn't quite shed his formal wear. The color of the jacket and the shirt did him no favors, either. Brown jacket and beige shirt. Slacks and shirts were supposed to have a little color, these days.

"You must have taken the public bus, now that's bravery," she said, while he looked at her, perplexed. "There's no air conditioning in it."

"You tell me," he said, grabbing his book and fanning himself with it, and now he tried to sound friendly, although his eyes still seemed serious.

"You ought to have taken the tour bus. It's more comfortable."

"But it only runs once a week."

It was also more expensive. He didn't look like a backpacker but he also might not be flush with money. If he was headed to see Reynier, he could be the son of a friend, trying to find a spare room to sleep in. A boy on a budget. If that was the case, he'd try to save face and might use the schedule as an excuse.

"It's right there," Viridiana said, pointing at the yellow house on the other side of the street.

The man set down his suitcase, as if to ring the bell.

"The bell does not work. It's open, anyway."

"Open?" the man said. "I'd never leave my front door open."

"You're from a big city," she replied, giving the door a shove.

"I'm from Boston."

"You don't have the accent."

She set her bicycle by the door and held the door open for him. He nodded and walked in, looking around the foyer which was small and dark. The whole house was poorly lit. A marvel in a town with such a sun. Yet Reynier lived like a delicate plant which requires its shade.

"Did you paak the caa in Haavaad yard?" he drawled.

"In the beginning there was the word," she intoned. "That accent is non-rhotic. They have it in Wales, too. You know, the really posh accent of Hollywood movies does not exist?"

She headed towards the office because that was where she always headed when she visited Reynier. When he was home they could play chess and when he wasn't she might wait for him and read a book.

"What kinds of movies?"

"Black and white. Bette Davis and Cary Grant films. If you heard it, you'd know what I'm talking about. It's called a Mid-Atlantic accent. They invented it so it would be the 'correct' sort of English, but any linguist will tell you there is no 'correct' way to use a language. They're living things."

The American TV shows were dubbed, but they'd show the old films with subtitles, which was the best way to view them. You could get the right cadence of the English language listening to the actors declaim their dramatic lines. Joan Crawford, Katharine Hepburn, she'd picked up many things from the TV set.

"I had no idea."

The office was empty, the shades drawn. But the fan was gone, this meant Reynier was about. She pulled a cord, by the couch, which rang a bell upstairs.

"He'll know we're here and come down," she said.

"He doesn't have a doorbell but he has a bell *inside*?"

"A quirk."

The man had been carrying his luggage with him the entire time, but now he finally set it down by the window and put his book on a side table. It was a travel guide of Baja California. She recognized the red cover, it was a popular line for maps and travel guides found at every tourist shop. *Guía de Lugares de Interés Turístico: Baja California.*

An old tabby cat lazily walked into the room and rubbed itself against her legs. She picked it up, scratching its head. It was a stray. It came and went as it pleased.

She came and went, too.

"God, I forgot. I'm Lawrence. But everyone calls me Law," the man said, sticking his hand out for her to shake.

Viridiana put the cat down and shook it.

"I'm Viridiana. Don't call me Diana," she said.

He had been smiling, and the smile did not quite die away, but it suddenly acquired a certain crispness which had not been there.

"You knew my uncle," he said.

She did not reply, merely sliding her hand away and bent down to pet the cat again, and her fingers trembled a little against the animal's fur.

"I'm Stanley Lawrence Landry."

"S.L. Landry. I put his letters in the mail for you," she said and looked up at him.

His nephew. And she'd thought he was a boy on a budget. And she'd chatted mindlessly with him, but that was what she did often with tourists. Tried to seem friendly and approachable because that is how you get good tips.

She attempted to find something in his face which resembled Ambrose, but there was little of his uncle in him. He was plain-faced, bordering on the sour (in this perhaps he *did* resemble Ambrose), although his eyebrows had an elegant curve to them. The eyebrows had been stolen from another face, from an old portrait in a fine Boston house with equally fine linens and teacups.

"Yes," he said.

She looked down, again pretending to be interested in the cat. Thankfully, she heard Reynier's hallmark stride.

"Viridiana," the older man said. "You've brought a friend."

Not a friend. God knows what this man was. But she nodded and stood up.

"Sir, we spoke on the phone. I'm Lawrence," the young man said.

"Mr. Landry," Reynier said. "I hope you had a good trip. Are you thirsty?"

"A glass of water would be nice."

"I'll fetch it," Viridiana offered, needing to get out of the room.

She filled a pitcher with water and took out an ice tray from the freezer. Struggling with the tray, she dislodged a handful of ice cubs, but dropped half on the floor. Cursing, she picked them up and tossed them in the sink.

She managed to find a tray and a placed couple of glasses and the pitcher on it. When she walked back into the office, Lawrence was sitting in the chair she normally used.

"… by bus," Lawrence was saying. "I don't like driving, if I can help it."

"The town is small enough that you won't need it. You could borrow my car if it's necessary. I don't drive much either, these days."

She set the tray down on a table. "Thank you," Reynier said. "Aren't you having a glass of water?"

"I only came by to return a book," Viridiana said, taking out her copy of *Bel Ami* and also setting it on the circular table, next to the guidebook. "It was nice meeting you," she told Lawrence.

He stood up to bid her goodbye. "Thank you for showing me the way. I'll stop by to see Daisy and Gregory tomorrow."

Viridiana clutched one of her backpack's straps, nodding. She did not hurry out of the room, but once she was outside, she quickly grabbed her bicycle and pedaled furiously. She saw none of the scenery, like she normally would. The giant cardons, which she found so pleasant as they stood against a blue sky like painted enamel, were of no importance today.

When she arrived in the house she was drenched in sweat. She took off her hat as she walked into the living room. Daisy and Gregory were sitting there, smoking. They had a bottle of rum and a couple glasses, plus a plate with cold cuts. A deck of cards sat by the plate.

"Ambrose's nephew is in town," she said.

Gregory lifted his head to look at her. Daisy held her cigarette against her lips, frowning.

"Are you sure?" Daisy asked.

"I spoke to him!"

"Are you kidding me?" Gregory said. "They said they were

sending a lawyer. What's *he* doing here?"

"I don't know. He was at Reynier's house."

Gregory stood up, running a hand through his hair. He looked outraged and very, very worried. Viridiana was worried, too.

"Fuck," Gregory said. "Fuck that asshole. What are we going to do? Should we get packing?"

"For the last time, have a bit of a spine," Daisy said tartly. She held her cigarette in her right hand and looked at Viridiana instead of speaking to Gregory. As if he was not worthy of her attention.

"A spine?"

"A spine, yes. Or a drink. Pour yourself a fucking drink."

Gregory frowned, but he obeyed.

"You too," Daisy said to Viridiana.

"I don't know—"

"Relax," Daisy said, smiling at her. "It doesn't mean anything that he's here. It's only an obnoxious relative who is not going to spoil our fun. Because we were having fun, weren't we? Gregory, get the girl a clean glass."

Viridiana bit her lip, which Daisy must have taken as a sign of acceptance, because she smiled even more, and when Gregory returned with the glass, she filled it to the rim. Viridiana pressed the glass against the hollow of her throat. It felt cold.

"How about a little music?" Daisy asked.

She switched on the stereo, tuning to a radio station which was playing disco music. Viridiana had been suffering for the whole day, racked with doubt. She had thought very bad things about Gregory and Daisy. She wondered about the kind of people they might be. But now that she was back there, with them all that didn't seem serious. Daisy was so self-assured and calm, the worries melted away.

She knew she should not be standing there, drinking with

them, but she was. And the rum was quickly putting her in a good mood, and the beat of the music was pleasant, and Gregory had sat down, and she was sitting next to him.

"How's your poker?" Daisy asked.

"I don't play cards."

"No cards?"

"I'm good at chess," she ventured. "And dominoes."

"No smoking or makeup either."

Viridiana blushed, recalling that night when she had put on lipstick and mascara for Gregory. It was the first time she'd given him a blow job.

"Bit of a saint, aren't you? We'll teach you," Daisy offered.

She'd seen them playing cards before, the three of them. When there had been three. Viridiana had not been invited to partake in those games and it was a good thing, since Ambrose bet real money.

Ambrose.

"Gregory, would you deal?" Daisy said.

Daisy had a great voice. Or, no, not a great *voice*, but it was the way she said the words and how the words matched her gestures. Like now, how she shook her head, making her earrings sparkle. Viridiana touched her own earlobe, which was bare.

Viridiana told them she'd play one hand of cards, but she ended playing five or six. She didn't know how many glasses of rum she had. Where did the booze come from? Gregory must have gone to town and bought half the liquor store.

What a difference. Ambrose would not have allowed a drop of beer near him. It had only been a few days since he died, and already the house felt entirely scrubbed of his presence. Daisy had not even worn mourning clothes, not beyond the day of the funeral. She was draped in a fluid, vibrant blue dress which felt

Grecian in its cut.

When Viridiana tried to excuse herself, Daisy said it was time to do Viridiana's makeup. She thought the woman was joking, but Daisy urged Viridiana upstairs, glasses in hand, to her room. Viridiana sat in front of Daisy's vanity, which was littered with eyebrow pencils and lipsticks and eyeshadows.

"You don't wear makeup at all, ever?" Daisy said, as she opened a shiny compact.

"My mother is strict," Viridiana replied, looking down at her hands and blushed again.

She felt a child with these people, sometimes. A naughty child who was playing doctor with Gregory and now dress up with Daisy.

Daisy tipped Viridiana's chin up and looked at her carefully. "Gregory thinks you're pretty. He's right, but pretty doesn't really mean much at all. The important part is improvising. I wonder if you can improvise?"

Viridiana had no idea what she meant. It was no doubt something very clever. Daisy seemed the very clever type. Clever and sophisticated, her blonde hair out of a glossy magazine ad. Viridiana always jumped to the back pages of those magazines, which was where you found the romance stories and the serialized novels. Sometimes the stories were illustrated, and the drawings featured women like Daisy.

"I guess we'll find out," Daisy said and she handed Viridiana the cigarette she had been smoking. Viridiana took a puff and coughed. Daisy laughed at her.

Chapter 13

Viridiana woke up late, with a massive hangover. She didn't remember how much she'd had to drink, although she did remember vomiting her guts out in the bathroom and then rolling into her bed. Daisy and Gregory had been amused by her lack of tolerance. They could probably drink the night away.

Viridiana showered, and when she came out, she found Delfina and her daughter cleaning the living room. It was Wednesday already? The visits from Delfina were the only thing that helped her to keep track of the calendar.

"Thank God you're awake," Daisy said, walking down the stairs, leaning against the banister and sighing dramatically. "Could you tell them not to cook the fish in that horrid tomato sauce, like last time? Keep it simple. And nothing that stinks, all right?"

Daisy walked back upstairs. Viridiana explained what Daisy wanted.

"We brought cazón," Delfina said. "How else would you cook if not with jitomate?"

What a pity. This was a nice bit of shark, and would taste best with a bit of chile habanero and tomatoes.

"Don't you have anything else?" Viridiana asked.

"Shrimp."

"Good. I think a cocktail would suit her fine. You must have brought some other fish. Maybe you can bake it with garlic and lemon."

Delfina didn't seem pleased with the idea, and the way she was eyeing the living room, with the overflowing ashtray and the dirty glasses. Viridiana knew she was wondering if whatever carousing had taken place the night before had involved three people. Rather than giving her a chance to question her, Viridiana escaped back to her room.

When she came out again, Delfina and her daughter had departed. Gregory and Daisy were sitting outside, on the patio with the white chairs and the large umbrella. They'd eaten their shrimp cocktails already and were languidly resting, doing nothing, like lizards sunning themselves.

Daisy was wearing a fabulous green dress, with a pattern of palm trees, and a matching green hat. Her sandals were white, the ones she normally wore when they went to the beach. Gregory was in his bright orange Hawaiian shirt. What might have been too gaudy on other men was perfect for him.

The bell rang. Neither Gregory nor Daisy moved a muscle. Viridiana knew this meant she ought to open the door.

As expected, it was Lawrence. He looked up sharply at her, and for a few seconds Viridiana did not know what to say.

"Hello," she muttered. "They're in the back."

Simple, really. She was not required to say anything else, even if she felt the impulse to assure him she had prayed the rosary for Ambrose.

When they walked onto the patio Daisy and Gregory finally shifted their limbs and stood up. There were polite greetings.

"They said a lawyer would be visiting us," Daisy told him, "but we didn't realize they meant you. If you had sent a telegram ahead of time—"

"I didn't think I could come until the last minute," Lawrence said. He pulled a chair and sat down under the table with the umbrella. Gregory and Daisy joined him. Viridiana, not knowing if she should even be there, hovered by the big glass door which led back into the house.

Lawrence was again neatly dressed, hair parted and perfectly combed. His neatness contrasted with Gregory's tousled hair, which was growing lighter from the salt and sun, and Daisy's elegant face. There really wasn't much elegance in Lawrence, merely a spotlessness that made her think of a Boy Scout. He wore jeans, yes, but also a pressed shirt and a suede jacket. She might almost swear that the jeans were an odd concession. An attempt to acclimatize himself. Or else, to seem more relaxed. But this man, she could tell, was not relaxed. Ever. He did not drink a couple of bottles of rum and smoke half a pack of cigarettes in one night, rolling out of bed around noon, like Gregory and Daisy did these days when they didn't have to maintain pretenses.

These days, with Ambrose dead and buried.

By looking at him, she could tell Lawrence was lying about "last minute." Perhaps he had been pressed for time, but he had always fully intended to come, himself. She could not be certain, but she was. Sixth sense, omens. Her grandmother said you can tell your future by looking at the path a snake leaves in the sand.

"I'm sorry you had to be dragged all the way here over what I'm sure is a trivial mistake," Daisy said. "When I spoke to Ambrose's lawyers, they mentioned there had been a change to his will, but I'm sure that's wrong."

"He had a new will made."

"He never mentioned it. Do you have a copy?" Daisy asked. Her voice was calm.

"Not here. I can tell you the gist of it. You are to get a million dollars."

"Then there is no change."

146

Silvia Moreno-Garcia

"No, there *is* a change. I control Ambrose's estate and the disbursement of any funds, including this amount. It will be at my discretion, whether I choose to provide you with the bequest, or whether nothing is provided at all."

"What do you mean, nothing?" Daisy asked, but she said this leisurely, as though it hardly mattered.

"Exactly that. Ambrose was contemplating a divorce, wasn't he?"

Daisy stretched her hand and reached for a dish filled with green grapes. Carelessly she grabbed one and popped it into her mouth.

"Your uncle and I had our fights, but there was no talk of divorce."

"He mentioned it when he was in Mexico City," Lawrence replied.

"With all due respect, you must be mistaken," Gregory said. "Ambrose never spoke a word of divorce."

"Were you his confidant?"

Gregory shook his head. "No. But when you share a house you get to know the people in it."

"I don't expect he'd talk about problems with his wife with his brother-in-law."

"Are you here to tell us then, that we should vacate the premises? That I should pack my bags and head back to the States, a widow without a single cent?" Daisy asked. "Will you dare such a thing?"

She stared at Lawrence, her hard, lacquered stare. Gregory could never hold his gaze like that. Daisy did. Viridiana had seen her use that stare on her brother. On the occasions when she had looked at Viridiana with those determined eyes, Viridiana had hated the woman because those were the eyes of someone who

147

knows she is the master.

But Lawrence was not cowed. He either did not see it or did not mind.

"I've come to investigate my uncle's death," he said simply.

"What is there to investigate?" Gregory asked. "He had an accident."

"I'll determine that."

"The police have investigated already."

Rather than reply to Gregory, Lawrence looked at Daisy when he spoke. "I've hired a translator to help me speak with the local authorities, and I've booked my stay at the only hotel in town. I'll remain here for a few days, and then we'll see."

"Will we?" Daisy said.

"I don't intend to cheat you out of money. If I find nothing, then it'll be yours."

Daisy stood up and gave her back to them.

"If you find nothing. That implies you expect to find *something*. What exactly are you accusing me of?"

Then she turned around, precisely, slowly, and blasted Lawrence again with her hard stare. This time he did seem affected by it and blinked.

"I don't very much care what you are up to. Go around town, ask your questions and when you are done being silly, please do come back with a copy of the will and we will chat amicably," Daisy said with finality. "I'd invite you to stay with us, but you're probably safer at the hotel. After all, I'm a murderess."

"I—"

"Shut up."

The woman walked back into the house with quick steps and Viridiana moved aside, pressing her back against the wall, so that she could go past.

Lawrence looked uncomfortable, but the fight seemed to have perked up Gregory, who stood and smiled.

"Look, I'm sorry about that," he said, "but this has been very stressful for her, and you really shouldn't be… ah, forget it, I'll go calm her down. You should come back some other time."

With that he was gone and it was only Lawrence and Viridiana standing outside.

"I'll walk you out," Viridiana said, because she didn't think there was anything else to say, and because he was making her nervous.

He followed her in silence. When she opened the front door she saw the old car parked outside.

"You have Reynier's car," she said, noticing for the first time.

"Yes," Lawrence said. "He's lent it to me. For the duration of my stay."

"You really are staying in town?"

"That's what I said," he told her, sounding a little irritated.

Of course. He had not flown all the way to Baja California merely to jump on a bus again after five minutes. It had been an idiotic thing to ask, but she'd hoped he would take one look at the town and walk right out. Viridiana scratched her arm and glanced down at her feet.

"Sorry. I'll see you around, all right?" he said, softening his tone.

She nodded. When she walked back into the living room, Daisy was coming leisurely down the stairs. Her anger evaporated. Had she even been upset or was it merely a performance?

"Is he gone?" Daisy asked.

"Yes."

"Good. Get me a mineral water."

Viridiana recalled how Ambrose had Daisy fetch him

everything and she frowned, but she went to the kitchen, filled a glass with ice cubes and set it on a tray. When she returned to the living room, Daisy was sitting on the yellow egg-shaped chair, her head thrown back.

Sometimes she liked Daisy and other times she hated her. Like right now. And Daisy knew it. Viridiana suspected she delighted in causing this flipping of emotions.

"What translator would he hire? I don't get the impression there are many."

"There's only Alejandro Esparza," Viridiana said, setting the tray down on the side table.

"Is he any good?"

"Not really."

"Can't compare to your brilliance? Miss I-Speak-Four-Languages," Daisy said and she showed her teeth when she smiled at her this time. "Gregory thinks you're a genius."

"It doesn't take a genius to speak several languages. You have to pay attention. And improvise."

Daisy laughed at that, and leaned forward, the glass dangling between her fingers, blue eyes zeroing on Viridiana.

Who the hell are you? Viridiana thought. *Who are both of you?*

Chapter 14

Two days passed. Daisy and Gregory went down to the beach. Viridiana stayed behind. She had formed a plan to search inside Daisy and Gregory's rooms for more clues about their identity. She took a quick look around Gregory's room, but aside from the IDs she had already found, she did not notice anything else. It was hard to find anything at all due to the chaos Gregory maintained all around him. Rather than waste her time there, she went to Daisy's bedroom.

She opened the closet and looked at the clothes on the hangers, unzipped a suitcase resting in a corner, and opened the drawers of the nightstand. No passports or driver licenses. Daisy was more careful with her documents than her brother, more careful with everything, as all of Daisy's things seemed to be in order. She did not leave half empty glasses with cigarette stubs by the bed, nor did she abandon her clothes in a pile for the cleaning lady to pick up.

The nightstand yielded an address book and Viridiana flipped through it. Several names were crossed out. But there was nothing truly significant about it except that there was an entry labeled "Off Road Club," and the name "Gehry" next to it was circled with a red pen. The card she'd found in Gregory's room was from that club. And since that card had two phone numbers on the back, she decided to try her luck with those.

It's not like she had anything else.

She rode her bicycle into town and mulled her options on the way there. She could place a call from the post office, but everyone would hear what she said since the telephone was a heavy, green thing which rested on a side of the counter. If she wanted more privacy, the answer was obvious: the hotel.

She went directly into one of the two solid mahogany booths in the lobby. They were worn and scratched, but proved La Sirena had once possessed great aspirations.

Like Viridiana.

She closed the door and asked the operator to connect her to the first of the two numbers. It was disconnected. The second one was a phone answering service. A woman promptly asked for her name.

"I'm getting my boss's messages," Viridiana said.

"What's your boss's name, then?"

Viridiana almost said Gregory, but she decided to go with James Haskins. She could always phone again and try the other two names if that one didn't pan out. Or maybe she'd chicken out and forget about this. She wasn't entirely sure what she was doing.

"What is his password?"

"Password," Viridiana said.

"Yes. His password."

Viridiana frowned. "Lucas," she said, since that was the only other thing that had been written on the back of the card.

"Thank you. Let's see. There's only one message, from Mr. McDaniels, saying to call him urgently. Do you have pen and paper?"

"Yes," Viridiana said, scrawling the name and number on a notepad.

She hung up and immediately tried Mr. McDaniels, before she lost her nerve. The phone rang six times before someone picked up.

"Who's this?" asked a man.

Viridiana did not reply, the receiver pressed against her ear. All she had to do was gently set the receiver back in its cradle and walk out of the booth. She didn't need to have this conversation. She could pretend she had never seen those two driver's licenses.

Smart people did that. Smart people looked the other way.

"Hello?"

"Yes," Viridiana said.

"Who's this?" the man repeated.

"You left a message for James Haskins—"

"You're not Lillian."

"No," Viridiana said.

"Where's Lillian?"

"I wouldn't know."

"Fuck and damn it. Has he got a new girlfriend? Are *you* his new girlfriend?"

She held her breath. *New girlfriend?* Viridiana decided that the best thing to do was to provide as few details as possible and allow the man to do the talking.

"Uh-huh," she said.

"Where the hell is James? It's been weeks since I've heard one damn word from him. Frank Gehry is furious."

Viridiana scribbled down the name in her notepad and circled it.

"Hello? Are you listening to me?"

"Yes, you said Gehry is furious."

"Damn right he is. He's been looking for him, asking everyone who knows James about his whereabouts. He's hounding me, and if James has a fraction of a brain in that big head of his… what the fuck is James up to?"

"Why is Gehry mad?" she countered.

"Hasn't he told you? That would be like him, wouldn't it. And he's rid himself of Lillian," the man muttered.

Lillian. She wrote down that name down too and bit her lip, trying to figure what to say next.

"Gehry wants his money back. Look, please, tell me. Where the hell is he? Where are you phoning from?"

"How much money does he owe him?" she asked instead.

"Your accent… Mexico. Is he there with that old bastard in Mexico? Did he really do it?"

Viridiana pushed back her hair from her face.

The fucking accent. If she hadn't been so nervous she would have gone for a more neutral English, though even then she might not have managed it. Her father had learned British English at school, and that's the way Reynier spoke too. She tried to pick up things from movies but under pressure who knew how the hell she sounded. Mid-Atlantic accent. Far from it right now.

"Do you have a message for James?" she asked.

"A message. Yes. The message is that Gehry is mad as hell and I'm getting out of this fucking city. And James should put as much distance as he can between him and Gehry, if he knows what's good for him. The bastard is probably going to send Henry looking for him. God help James if he does."

"Henry?"

"Don't phone again."

He hung up. She placed the receiver back in its cradle and rested a hand against the rotary dial, her fingers brushing over the painted numbers. She thought about phoning the man back but could not think what to say. She shouldn't have called in the first place.

Viridiana pushed the booth door open and stepped out back into the lobby. She felt odd. She was being deceived by Daisy and

Gregory, but now *she* was doing the deceiving. Snooping in their rooms, phoning this man behind their backs.

I'm not to blame, she told herself, but her hands were shaking a bit.

Girlfriend, money, and trouble. None of those things were good.

She needed to sit down. Maybe have a coffee. She hadn't had breakfast that morning. They'd gone over to the beach early, Daisy and Gregory, and instead of frying herself an egg, Viridiana had been busy quickly rummaging through drawers.

What she needed was a coffee, yes.

She marched into the restaurant of the hotel and almost as quickly she wished to march out. The place was almost empty. Three German tourists were sitting at a table, drinking orange juice and eating toast with butter and jam. Lawrence was the only other person there, and he saw her and waved to her.

Viridiana could not run out without looking suspicious. She did not relish this encounter.

"Hello," she said, approaching his table and stuffing her notebook in her backpack.

"Hi," he said. "Having brunch?"

"No. I wanted a quick coffee."

"You should sit down."

"I don't want to be a bother."

"It wouldn't be a bother. You'd keep me company and help me order," he said, putting away the book he had been reading. "Please."

Viridiana knew the menu, but she pretended to be interested in it. When Lawrence asked her opinion on the bread, she said it was fine and fresh. Lawrence ordered eggs, coffee and the pan dulce basket. She did not alter her plan: a cup of coffee.

She unfolded a napkin and placed it on her lap.

"You're getting along with Reynier's car?" she asked. She had to ask something and figured that pushing the conversation away from Ambrose's death was the best course.

"Yes. I'd rather walk any day, but it's a fine car."

"It can be a bit temperamental. It doesn't always start. But it was quite the sight when he first moved into town, I'm told. He paid a pretty penny to have it brought here."

"How long has he lived here?"

"Forever, it seems."

"Then you must know him well."

"All my life. He was my father's friend," Viridiana said. "And then, after my father was gone, he watched over me."

Lawrence looked at her carefully. "Your father, he's dead?"

"No," Viridiana said, chuckling. "Divorced. He lives in Mexico City."

She felt stupid for referring to her father in the past tense, for making Lawrence think about death when her aim was to keep herself entirely off the subject. Luckily, the waiter returned then with their coffee, the eggs and the bread basket, which he showed to Lawrence, inviting him to choose. Lawrence pointed to a pink-colored concha, which the waiter set on a plate with a pair of silver tongs.

Viridiana shook her head, refusing.

"I think the greatest culinary achievement of the Mexican people is this bread," Lawrence said, tearing off a chunk of concha.

"It's definitely prettier than a donut," she said, looking at the spiral sugar surface mimicking the ridges of a seashell.

"And it's cheap. You can buy a whole bag at La Vasconia for nothing."

"I wouldn't know."

"It's a large bakery in downtown Mexico City. The office of my uncle's lawyers is not far from there."

"Never been to Mexico City," she said.

Never been anywhere, although she had plans. Big plans. Paris was involved. Only… who knew since Gregory wasn't Gregory, and it was probably idiotic to get any more attached to that idea than she already was.

Okay, even if she didn't go to Paris— forget Paris—she could cobble enough money to make it to Mexico City. She should, and leave Gregory and Daisy to do whatever they wanted.

"You must travel a lot, since you were in Mexico City and Peru."

"I travel a bit," he said. "The family has a penthouse in Polanco so it seemed easy enough to fly in to Mexico City and then catch a plane to other places."

"But you live in Boston? Or are you an expat?"

"I've spent a total of one month in Mexico and three weeks in Peru. We have business interests throughout Latin America, but frankly most of the Landrys stick to Massachusetts. This is supposed to be my grand tour of the region."

She had, through her father, enough of an understanding of where the expats gathered in the city, since he had done a bit of translation work for Brits and Americans before making his way to Baja California. Enough of an understanding that she might picture Lawrence's apartment, large and lavish, with a view of the park.

"Then you're adventurous."

"Hardly. You know, I was terrified that if I did have to rent a car here the roads would be terrible and I'd end up with a flat tire and no way to change it. I'm useless when it comes to any excitement. But I don't think the roads are that bad. Are they?"

"More or less. It's not the roads you should fear, but the air conditioning in the car failing."

He actually looked concerned when she said that, as if she could will it to happen.

Viridiana traced the rim of her cup with her index finger, readying herself to say goodbye to Mr. Landry. Surely this had been enough of a conversation. It would not be rude.

"You can't be named after the Buñuel movie, can you? You'd be too young," he said, curious.

She looked up at him, equally intrigued. He'd gotten the movie reference right. "Eighteen. It came out the year I was born."

Her father subscribed to *Cahiers du cinéma*. Her father read every news story he could about Buñuel and watched all his films as a student. Her father did not trust "mediocre people," which is why he'd given her a glorious, distinctive name. Viridiana. Never to be shortened as the tacky "Viri" or the lazy "Diana."

"Eighteen. Have you even finished high school?"

"Yes. A year early, to boot."

Not that it had done her any good. Finishing school meant her mother wanted her behind the counter, full-time, and married off. She believed Viridiana would rot as quickly as a banana, her appeal gone by the time she hit twenty.

"You must be a smart kid," he said, and she supposed it could be interpreted as a compliment but she absolutely hated the way it sounded. *Kid.* As if he was standing at the upper rung of a ladder, which he absolutely was since he was a man on a grand tour.

"You don't look too much older than me. You look like a kid too, I could take you for a high schooler," she said, meaning it as a jab. And it was no lie. She bet he still had a crop of pimples popping out now and then.

One boy is the same as another, she thought, remembering

Manuel, *but a man is a different story.*

Gregory was a man.

"I'm twenty-four, so, a bit older."

"You must have come to Mexico right after university. Looking for an exotic adventure, no doubt. Like they all do. Backpackers, surfers, people on tour buses. Doesn't matter if you can or can't change a tire, I'm sure someone can do it for you for a pittance."

He frowned.

She pushed her coffee cup aside, ready to bid him a goodbye, but he must have sensed that was her next move.

"I've got a favor to ask you," he said.

"Me?" she replied, actually surprised by that.

"I'm supposed to meet with your town's police officer today. I'd like you to translate for me."

"Didn't you hire a translator?"

"Alejandro Esparza."

"It didn't work out?" Viridiana asked, confused.

"I don't think he's a very good translator. Let's say I want a second opinion."

"I really can't. Alejandro doesn't like me, he'll be pissed off if I'm standing there with you."

"He's getting paid. He'll do as I say."

He reminded her of Ambrose then, the way his mouth seemed to almost set into a sneer, but not quite. He looked fully his age when he did that, the boy vanishing.

"I don't trust him," Lawrence said, crossing his arms. "He tried to cheat me when I got into town."

"It doesn't mean he can't translate."

"I'd pay you. It wouldn't be for free."

Money. Good money, no doubt, and wasn't that what she needed? Cold hard cash. Gregory was an illusion, a dream. There was no Paris, was there? And who'd go to Paris with a stranger, a liar.

I might, she thought. *In the end, I might.*

She was curious, too. Curious about where all this was headed and what Lawrence intended. It made sense to keep an eye on him if she could, to keep informed.

"Would it take long?"

"I don't think so," Lawrence said, checking his watch. "I could pay you in cash, right now, beforehand, if you don't—"

He opened his wallet.

"No," she said, stretching a hand out and setting it atop his. "Later is fine."

She had not finished her coffee, so she did that.

* * *

Alejandro did not even try to pretend cordiality.

"What the fuck are you doing with this guy?" he asked in Spanish, glancing from her to Lawrence, and then back at her.

"Helping him out with some stuff," she said coolly.

"Sucking cock, I bet."

Viridiana did not waste her words on him, turning her head away. When Lawrence explained in English that Viridiana was his friend, Alejandro's face was pure disbelief, but he did not contest her appearance at the police station. Lawrence held the door open for her and she walked in.

The police station was small and on certain days it smelled of whatever fritanga Homero was eating, but he had refrained that day. Likely because he knew he'd have company.

Homero was as courteous as he could be, which is to say he offered the three of them a cold soda from the mini refrigerator. That he did not offer them a beer, however, indicated he was not *too* pleased to see them. He drank liberally with his friends and used the station more for sweet talking women than actual work. On his desk there were several stacks of raunchy comic books— cowboy stories, all of them —along with old copies of *Alarma!*

Behind the desk hung a massive map of Baja California and a corkboard. In a corner, there was a neglected typewriter.

Homero made much show of moving a stack of papers and folders away before he began addressing them, as if he'd been hard at work.

Lawrence had a bunch of questions, which Alejandro translated. Back and forth they went. For most of the conversation, Homero fiddled with a paper clip, before breaking it, frowning, and grabbing another one.

His courtesy eroded after a few minutes. He was fed up, and turning to Alejandro, said, "What the hell is wrong with this guy? Can't he be done now? I'm hungry, and can't be chit-chatting all day long. Who does this guy think he is? Does he fancy himself a private investigator?"

It went on like that until Homero finally declared he had nothing else to say and ushered them out the door. Lawrence paid Alejandro and Alejandro took care to give Viridiana a bitter, long stare before departing.

"Let's find a place to talk," Lawrence said.

"This way," she said, and guided him towards a narrow side street that was actually pretty, because there wasn't very much that was pretty in Desengaño. The sea was beautiful and so was the desert, but those were not part of the town proper.

On the west side of the street ran a wall made of red bricks, and next to it grew a succession of bugambilias, which, with their explosive purple colors, contrasted with the palo blanco trees that shone, slender, smooth and pale, under the sun. This was the vast garden of the widow Allende, who had come from Guadalajara thirty years before and tried to make herself comfortable in this peninsula of salt and sand by tending to her plants.

Viridiana sat on a section of the wall which had tumbled down and therefore offered a low perch. Lawrence sat next to her.

"I don't think I've seen this tree before," he said, looking at the palo blanco.

"The Cochimi called it gokio," she said. "They used it to treat sores. And that one, over there, that's the tree where jumping beans come from."

She pointed at clump of tall shrubs with serrated leafs.

"Really?"

"It's very dangerous. If you sleep under it you'll go blind."

"You're a liar, since you are smiling," he said, sounding amused.

"Believe what you want."

"A shrub can't really blind you, can it?"

"Maybe the blinding, that's a tall-tale. But it was used to poison arrows. And if you threw it in the water it would poison the fish."

Viridiana kicked her heels back and looked up at the foliage. She had done this same thing many times, following the red wall, with a stick between her hands, and resting there, hidden from everyone since the only thing across the street was an empty lot with weeds. She liked it better here than at the lighthouse, although both offered convenient pools of solitude.

"I could speak more about the flora of the region, but I suspect it doesn't interest you. What is it that you needed from me?" she asked.

"Exactly what I asked for. A translation. You heard what Alejandro said, do you think he spoke well?"

"Well enough, I guess."

"You guess?"

"He omitted things."

"Can you elaborate?"

"Mostly Homero's slurs," she said. "Homero was being rude at points. And there were some bits... I don't know, he told you that the doctor examined the body the night of the accident, but that's not what Homero said. Homero said he thought perhaps the doctor looked at the body during the night, perhaps the morning, he couldn't know."

"What else?"

Viridiana tried to recall the conversation as best she could and pointed out half a dozen mistakes Alejandro had made. When she finished talking Lawrence was frowning.

"You're telling me that he's worthless, then."

"I didn't say that," Viridiana replied. "He spoke the gist of it."

"The gist wouldn't do at an inquest."

"This is not an inquest."

Lawrence stood up and placed his hands in his pockets, looking at her with his sober, plain face made even more sober at this very moment.

"I'm meeting the physician who examined my uncle's body the day after tomorrow. I want you translating for me."

"I already did you a favor today," she said.

"Then do me a favor again."

Viridiana did not reply, lifting her hand which had been resting against the bricks and looking at her palm, as if she'd found something of interest there. Her aunt read books about zodiac signs and palmistry, and had promised her a long life full of luxuries.

"You hired Alejandro already, and he doesn't like me."

"It doesn't matter what he likes. It was clearly a mistake."

"I'm busy," she said and stood up, ready to walk back to the town square where she'd left her bicycle around the corner from the police station.

He raised both of his hands and pressed them together in front of his face. "Please," he said, with an unexpected vehemence which made Viridiana sit down again.

A line of ants was running by the wall, diligently going in one direction. She observed them, knowing she could easily stomp her foot down and kill a dozen or so. She thought about Ambrose, in his wooden coffin, and the feast the insects and maggots must be enjoying there.

She felt sick, pressed a hand against her mouth, turning her head.

I did nothing wrong, she thought. *I prayed him the rosary, I owe you nothing.*

"What time are you meeting him?" she asked, nevertheless.

"Seven o'clock, at his house."

"I'll drop by."

"Thank you."

Viridiana nodded. He sat down next to her. One of the ants was carrying a large crust of bread. She watched it march away with its bounty. Viridiana took off her hat and set it on her lap.

"Is that really a jumping bean tree?" Lawrence asked.

"Yes. But they wouldn't be jumping this time of year. The shrubs, and its pods, are the home of the larva of a gray moth. They consume the pod from within and then burst out. The larva wriggling inside is what makes the bean move. But right now, the moth hasn't laid its eggs yet."

"I think I had some of those beans when I was a kid. When I cupped them in my hand they moved."

"It's the warmth of your hand making the larva twitch. Did you have sea monkeys, too?"

"Yes," he said, smiling. "And I do know those are not monkeys, despite what the back of my comic books claimed."

"Brine shrimp. It's all illusions and make-believe, Mr. Landry."

"Law," he said. "You can call me Law."

"Hmm," Viridiana said.

"You're going to call me Mr. Landry, aren't you?"

"Probably."

"I hate being Mr. Landry. It makes it sound like I'm my uncle now. It's strange. And you were right in what you said before, I suppose I do look young and it is ridiculous to have anyone say 'Mister' to me. Although it's all 'Señor' this and that at the hotel."

"If it helps, you can be Lawrence to me. Laurentum. You are a tree. Not as pretty as our bugambilia."

She'd have no problem calling Gregory "Greg" at some point, but that was different.

Of course, Gregory was not really Gregory. He was three men and who knew which one was the true him. James. Jerry. Gregory. His nickname could be anything.

Lawrence gave her a searching look. Solemn and searching, like he was doing a crossword. Like he was trying to figure her out. She couldn't figure herself out, God knew what he was going to find.

"I ought to head back," she said, putting on her hat again and tucking away a stray lock of hair.

"I'll walk with you."

Chapter 15

That night she lay on the bed with the tape recorder at her side, not uttering any words, telling herself she would press the button any minute now. Then Gregory came by, sat on her bed, flashed a grin at her. Viridiana put the tape recorder under the bed.

He made a couple of jokes, laughed, told her she ought to have gone down to the beach with them. She regarded him dubiously. But when he touched her breasts and laid her back on the bed, she allowed it. She wanted to be touched, that much she was sure of, and she didn't mind caressing him back.

It soured quickly when he tried to get her undressed, pulling the hem of her shirt up. Viridiana pulled it down.

"I want to fuck you," he said, breathed it against her ear. Perhaps he thought it was sexy to put it like that, to be blunt and raw. It only served to make her recoil.

"I told you, no," she said, scooting back from him.

He had been full of good humor when he arrived, but that was evaporating. He stared at her.

"Look, I'm not an idiot boy. I can pull out if you're worried about that."

She laughed at him because he didn't get it. He couldn't. Machos and Madonnas, and how you had to be a good girl or you were trash. Plus that idiocy about pulling out. Even in her inexperience she wouldn't have fallen for that line.

"There's a place near Monterrey where girls go to have their virginity fixed again, do you understand? People talk, in a place like this they talk and they expect certain things from you and… it's the only thing I have."

"It's a shit town if that's the case," he said.

"Yes, but it's *my* shit town. It's the place where I live. No other place for me."

He sighed and shook his head. She knew exactly what he was thinking: idiot and prude. It maddened her to be considered inferior, faulty.

"Not forever. There's Paris," he said.

"There's Paris," she said, and fixed her gaze on him. She could not hold her tongue any longer, she could not accept this bullshit. "What's your real name?"

"What do you mean?" he asked, frowning.

"I saw the driver's licenses in your bathroom."

"Damn," he said it without inflection.

"Yeah, damn. James-Jerry-Gregory. There is no Paris," she said, getting up from the bed. Her voice was high-pitched, girlish. Silly.

He stood up, caught Viridiana by the arm and tugged at her, pulling her towards him. Her back rested against his chest.

"Bartholomew," he said. "My name is Bartholomew."

Bartholomew. She savored each syllable.

"You aren't lying?"

"Why would I lie about a name like that? Give me some credit."

He had released her arm, but ran his fingers upon and down her sides, from her shoulders to her wrists, casually. Barely brushing her skin and she felt his chin coming to rest upon the top of her head.

"What else do you want to know?" he asked.

"Why do you go by different names?"

She couldn't see him, but she knew he was frowning, and she

felt the way he took a deep breath.

"Daisy must not know I've told you, all right? She'll be pissed if she knows I've told you."

"I won't speak to her."

"Remember how I said Daisy and I had business investments? It's not what you might call a traditional business."

"Go on."

"It's… people are greedy. And that old saying, there's one born every minute? Damn right. You tell someone you'll double, triple their money, they listen. Even if it's a bit too outrageous and it doesn't make that much sense when you add it all up."

"You're a thief?"

"Let's say…some of our business ventures worked and others not so much, and when they didn't it was time to move on."

"A grifter."

He spun her around and settled his hands on her waist, casually, and smiled and shrugged—she figured he used that little shrug and that sly smile often. Because it worked.

"Look, if I told you I could sell you the Mona Lisa for $20,000 you wouldn't believe me would you?"

"That was your game, then? Selling art?"

"No. It's an example."

She looked at him in silence. Gregory didn't like silences, she'd figured as much hanging out with him these past few weeks and sure enough he started talking after an uncomfortable pause.

"Daisy has an uncanny ability to spot people with money. Give her two minutes, she'll wind up at the right of the richest guy in the room, chatting with him like they're old friends. And a fool and his money will soon part ways. There were other things we did, too. Insurance claims. Daisy's property has an uncanny knack for going up in flames, literally."

"Do you douse the houses in gasoline or does Daisy do that?"

He chuckled and gave her another shrug.

"Truth is Daisy is the brains. I'm backup and yes, I get to drag the stupid cans of gasoline."

"What about Ambrose? Did you kill him?"

"God, point blank, eh?" he replied, although he didn't look too startled by her words. It was a pretty big elephant in the damn room.

"No," he said, sullenly. "I thought Ambrose was going to keep us fed for a while. He was generous to his ex-wives. He had five of them. I thought we were headed to lucky number six and he'd ditch us somewhere in Mexico, where we could have cocktails by the pool."

"Did he push Daisy down the stairs? Did he cause her to lose her baby?"

"No. He couldn't have kids. That's why the nephew was such a big deal to him."

So that was the truth. She was standing next to a run-of-the-mill con-artist, no better than the men at the cheap bar where the fishermen gathered, men who tried to wheedle fools and encourage them to bet their cash on the weekends. Gregory dressed better, but he was no better.

She sighed.

"Hey," he said, grasping her chin, tilting it up, "hey, you asked. It's the truth."

"Are you really twenty-nine?"

"Yes. A Libra. My birthday is not far on the horizon," he said and rubbed his cheek, thoughtful. "We've all got shelf-lives, Viridiana. Daisy and I can't keep this up forever. And I, for one, am serious about calling it quits."

"Sure," she said looking down at the floor.

"I'm from a shit town in Kansas. That's why I know what you are feeling. Goldfish will grow as big as their bowl, and bowls like this don't allow you to grow an inch. Am I wrong?"

She wanted to grow, yes. She wanted to float to sea and turn into a shark. A huge beast, fierce, with rows of teeth and sleek skin. Nobody thought her capable of anything. Her mother considered her a failure and Viridiana suspected half the town thought her stupid for wanting to leave, and everyone was betting she would end her days unmarried, behind her mother's counter, slowly opening and closing the cash register.

Her father, after all, had accomplished very little, and when they spoke on the phone it was all about how busy he was, how he never made quite enough money, and a complaint or two regarding his new wife.

"I get it. I do," Gregory said.

He looked sincere as he spoke. Kansas was real, she thought. He pressed a palm against her cheek and she could feel beneath his skin the truth of it. Shitty little town with shitty little people. She could picture Daisy, firstborn, bolder than Gregory, making her way out of there fast. And then Gregory reuniting with her, in a big city. By then she'd learnt a few tricks, she was the brains, and convinced Gregory that it was easier conning people when you do it in twos.

She could picture the whole bit, like the first reel of a movie. The film spooled before her eyes.

"You won't take me with you," she said. "There's some other girl for you, a girl stashed back in the States."

Lillian, she thought. Although she couldn't say that, but the name burned on her tongue. She swallowed.

"I had a girl. But that's been over for a while. There's no one waiting back for me there, and nothing at all back in that country.

No friends, no lovers, no pets. I'm here now."

He sat down on the bed and sat her down on his lap.

"We'll have money, all right? A little bit of patience and we'll have a wad of cash. Ask me for something. Ask me for anything. A string of pearls, a diamond ring, I'll deliver."

"Please," she muttered.

"We're going to run away together. You're going to run away with a highwayman, with a brigand. With the man with the blackest of hearts, and his heart is for you. Isn't that exciting? Like the movies you tell me about."

He was in high spirits and it was hard to remain morose when that happened. But she glanced down at her hands, at her nails.

"What was it? How did it go? 'I've loved you since the first moment I saw you. I guess maybe I've even loved you before I saw you,'" he quipped.

She looked at him.

He didn't sound *exactly* like Montgomery Clift, but close enough, and the way he was tilting his head and the way the light reflected on his hair, you would have thought he was being professionally photographed. He really looked wonderful, even if he was worth as much as a tattered romance novel, but then that had its appeal. Like he'd said. Brigand. Blackguard. Rogue.

Not Clift, who seemed a tad too sweet, but an alluring wickedness all his own.

"Yes," Viridiana whispered.

"I love you. We'll have money. We'll go away," he promised and he didn't smile at that, he didn't joke.

He lay on the bed, but this time there was no sex play. He held her tight, his head on her chest, quietly. Viridiana ran a hand through his hair and she bit her lower lip and she thought about moving him away, but she didn't.

She wanted to lie like that with him for a very long time. She tried to picture them alone, in the middle of the desert, under the starry skies. In the places where time ceases to run as it should. Or in the ocean, deep beneath the waves. Nothing would matter there, whoever he'd been before. It could all be washed away. Who said it hadn't been washed away already? He wanted to begin anew, after all.

"Let's go down to the beach, you and me, tomorrow," he said. "I'll take photos. You can bring the Polaroid, too. What do you think?"

He looked up at her and Viridiana nodded.

"We can pretend the world has ended and it's the two of us down there, collecting sea shells," she said, softly. She'd fallen half-asleep in his embrace and her thoughts were fantastical, bloated by dreams.

"The apocalypse?"

"The world wouldn't end, not really. It's always a cycle."

"Says who?"

"The Mayans. The Aztecs. This is the fifth sun, but there were four suns before them."

"Were they any fun?"

"Jaguars ate everyone during one of the suns. And during another fire rained from the sky and turned the world to ashes. And now during the fifth sun we must offer blood and sacrifices, or the sun will go black and the world will end."

"That's morbid," he said, but she could feel him grinning. "You're a morbid girl, Viridiana."

"Probably."

"I don't mind, if you don't mind my faults."

"I don't even know what to call you," she said as he shifted his position, depositing a kiss on her neck.

"Don't call me Bartholomew. I do hate that fucking name. I suppose you like your name. Viri-diana. There must be a saint with that name, no? Everyone is named after a saint here and your names are so terribly long."

"Yes, there is a Saint Viridiana."

"Did she do anything interesting, Saint Viridiana?"

"She was a hermit and spent more than thirty years alone in a small cell. Two snakes came into that cell one day."

"Did they bite her?"

"No, she lived with them."

He kissed her again and pulled her closer and it was her turn to rest her head against his chest. Under her fingers she felt his heart, heard him breathe gently.

I can hold you next to me, she thought. Life couldn't be a movie, she knew that. Yet it seemed close now, the possibility of the glitz and the glamour and the excitement and him. Him most of all.

Chapter 16

The water lapped at her feet, the stench of the dead sharks was pungent enough to make her eyes water. She raised her hands, rubbing her eyes. Viridiana thought about bezoars again. She had been thinking about them since she was a little kid, those little lumps of flesh that looked like stones. They made her wonder, what is the true nature of a thing?

This question assailed her constantly. It was, perhaps, the query from which all her issues stemmed. Had she not wondered so much about her true nature, she might have accepted life as it was. She might have smiled like the other kids her age smiled, done as her family wanted, lived and died happily in Desengaño. But she thought a lot about hidden things, she spent too many days peering at the mounds of shark flesh on the beach. Watching the men strip the carcasses of their glossy skin and revealed the pale meat beneath, pale as ivory under the blazing sun.

So that day there she was again at the beach, thinking of bezoars, secrets written in the flesh.

She was restless and the sea seemed to mimic her emotions, the wind tossing her hair against her face. She had been fine that morning, but that changed, dread steadily building in her belly. Once the sun began to dip and she approached the doctor's house, she bit her lip and thought of turning back.

She did not want to speak to Lawrence. But she had ridden there, and he'd be waiting for her. Wouldn't it look worse if she didn't show up? What exactly did he want? What if the doctor said something that incriminated Viridiana? What, what, what.

Lawrence was by the doctor's house already when she arrived and she needed to stop fretting because he'd notice and then it would be worse. She attempted a smile. It came out wrong, too timid.

"Thanks for coming," he said.

"Sure."

"Let's go in, then."

"Shouldn't we wait for Alejandro?" she asked.

"I fired him," he said simply.

"You did? Why?"

"You said he was a bad translator."

"I didn't say that," Viridiana corrected quickly.

"But you *are* the better choice, aren't you?"

She did not reply and rang the bell instead.

Doctor Navarro let them into his attendance room. He had the charts and posters she imagined all physicians owned, framed diploma behind his desk, jars filled with Q-tips and wooden tongue depressors, and in a corner, dusty and forgotten, a stuffed armadillo that he had bought from an ambulant seller of taxidermied animals when he first moved to Baja California, for Navarro had been a capitalino, sophisticated and aloof like Viridiana's father, before he too had ambled onto the distant peninsula. But unlike Viridiana's father they didn't think him an uppity, fucking chilango. Her father had an annoying face, he spoke out of turn, and despite his natural charm he eventually rubbed everyone the wrong way.

That's what happens with certain people, they're too much, too bright, like the sun which burns incessant in the true-blue Baja California sky, and one day you find you are sick of them. That's probably what happened to her mother, to the whole town. One day they woke up and they discovered that the chilango Marta had brought over really didn't amount to much despite speaking all his languages and his witty lines.

One day, they were all going to figure out Viridiana wasn't worth a damn either. Maybe they already knew.

There's a bezoar in my chest, she thought and then, *cut it out, calm down.*

"I can't spend more than half an hour speaking to you, I have an appointment," Navarro told them, after they'd taken a seat. "So, let's do this. What do you need?"

Lawrence took out a notebook and a pen, and started rattling off questions. He wanted to know what the doctor had seen when he arrived at the house, the state of the body, his conclusions. Navarro was brisk and to the point. Not rude, like Homero had been, but also not terribly warm. Lawrence was an annoyance, and although Navarro wasn't going to point that out, he also wasn't going to waste too much time with him. After all, Ambrose *was* already buried, which he did literally say as he stared at Lawrence.

"An autopsy might have been performed," Lawrence countered. She glanced at his notebook, his compact handwriting. He had written several words in Spanish, several sentences.

He was taking notes in Spanish.

Viridiana realized he could understand what the doctor was saying without any assistance. She felt a little sick, like the bezoar in her belly was expanding, but she focused on the words being said and translated mechanically. She should have known when she saw the travel guide. She had agreed to do this and if she tried to fudge the truth – if somehow Navarro gave an indication that she'd helped cover up a crime, Lawrence Landry would be able to point his finger at her.

Lawrence Landry could have her jailed.

"An autopsy? Not here," Navarro replied and she hoped to God he stuck to those sort of answers, brief and calm. For her part, she spoke mechanically, betraying no emotion.

"But somewhere else."

"What would be the point of that?"

"You said there was a wound, on the back of his head."

"It might have been a number of things."

"Hence an autopsy, you could have done an autopsy."

"Mr. Landry," Navarro said, shaking his head, "we can wonder about the things we might have done, but it was not performed. I'm sorry."

"Could we do one now?"

"Would that be truly necessary?" Navarro asked with a sigh.

By then, their time was up and it was a good thing because Lawrence was very upset. He closed his notebook, tucked away his pen. Outside, Viridiana walked her bicycle and glanced at him.

"I can't believe this bullshit," Lawrence complained. "How long did that guy speak to us? Barely twenty minutes?"

"You're lucky. It's Friday."

"So?"

"Fridays he is itching to play dominoes and have a few beers. He was being nice to you by seeing you tonight."

"Nice to me?" Lawrence repeated.

"Of course."

Lawrence shook his head skeptically. The explanation, if anything, had made him more irritable. Viridiana did not know what he was expecting. He was no cop, no consular authority, he was a rich young man who had stumbled into town playing detective. No one was going to take him seriously.

"My uncle could have been stabbed twenty times and everyone would have shrugged it away," he muttered.

"He was not stabbed."

"I know he wasn't! No, 'he fell down the stairs', drunk. As if I'd believe it. He wouldn't drink. He had promised he wouldn't anymore, he'd stopped all of that."

Lawrence stood in the middle of the street and crossed his arms. Viridiana stopped the bicycle next to him.

"He might have—," she began, but he wouldn't even let her complete the sentence. He raised his irate eyes at her.

"He might have what? He might have picked up the bottle again? Like Daisy claims? Bullshit. My uncle gave all his ex-wives very generous settlements, but do you know why he altered his will? Because he didn't trust Daisy. He told me so. And he was right."

Lawrence began walking again, faster, his hands in his pockets.

"He was good to her, he was good to her and she repaid him by either getting him drunk and shoving him down the stairs, or shoving him down when he was stone-cold sober. He was alright, he never did a single thing to deserve this, never treated her wrong and that bitch—"

"He yelled at her. He was mean."

Viridiana didn't want to blurt that out. Hell, Daisy wasn't always nice to Viridiana but she wasn't all bad either. And she'd seen Ambrose angry. She'd seen the ruckus he could make.

"What are you saying?" Lawrence asked.

"That he wasn't a saint and maybe...maybe he wasn't in his right mind that night."

"How? You said he yelled at her that night?"

"Not just that one time. I saw him slap her leg once, too."

It was not polite to speak ill of the dead. More than that, Lawrence looked a bit heartbroken, he shook his head. She wondered what she'd do if someone said bad things about her father.

The ache in her belly which had flared at the doctor's house increased as Lawrence stared at her.

"What did you see that night? How did he die?" he asked.

"I didn't see anything. I was in my room and I heard people arguing, and when I walked into the living room he was at the foot of the stairs. I went to get the doctor, but he was already dead."

"You're lying."

"I'm not! But you are," she shot back.

"What?"

He looked at her blankly, but it was not the blankness of innocence, he simply did not know what to say. She tightened her fingers around the handles of the bicycle.

"You don't need a translator. You could probably write an essay in Spanish. I saw you back there, you... you and your stupid notebook. You were testing me," she said.

He blushed a vivid crimson, like a boy caught scarfing down a cake. Deception did not suit him. Viridiana wondered if it suited her? She'd never been much of a liar, but these days she was learning dissimulation. That was not quite like lying. Not yet. But it might be. People like Gregory and Daisy must have started somewhere. Did they pile little tricks together and build up to outright fraudulence? Or had they known insincerity from the start?

Maybe it was a simple case of metamorphosis and, like a caterpillar, once you stuff yourself with enough falsehood, you'll naturally transform into a butterfly. No one can chide the caterpillar for doing this. It was, after all, a butterfly all along even if it didn't know it.

"All right, I was. I don't know who to trust in this town." Lawrence said. "It's obvious the authorities don't care about anything that happens here, and they might not be honest with me, but they might with a local. I couldn't be sure you, or any of them, weren't going to fudge facts."

"I didn't."

"I know. And I know now that you aren't bullshitting me, unlike everyone else."

"That's great. But you've caused me a lot of trouble."

"What are you talking about?"

"Forget it," she said, shaking her head. "It's Friday. Go have a beer or find something to do."

Viridiana got on her bicycle and rode toward the pharmacy. She needed to purchase an Alka-Seltzer or she'd never make it back to the house. The pharmacist, however, was busy conversing with Patricia and took his time counting the change and bidding her goodbye. When Viridiana stepped out, she found four men lounging next to the entrance, right where she had left her bicycle.

Alejandro, Paco and their friends.

They'd been drinking. They still carried with them a bottle which they were passing around. Perhaps they were getting ready to hit the cantina, or to pile into a car and drive to the next town, where they had a pool hall. They might have passed through the town square without pausing, but Viridiana was sure Alejandro had spotted her bicycle.

He'd spotted it and rested his back against the wall of the pharmacy and waited for her.

Why did it have to be Friday? If it hadn't been Friday, things would have been much better, she was sure of it. But Friday was party night for the young people in town. Or as close as they could get to a party. Cheap beer, for sure, and perhaps music if someone had a place and a record player. Friday and these assholes were looking for sport, for a game, and she was the amusement that would open their evening.

She could walk back into the pharmacy and wait until they were gone. She could also ask the pharmacist to fetch her mother, like a child who must be held by the hand and escorted home. That would not go well.

She could brave it. Alejandro might be drunk and irritable, but the night was early. He could be almost sober and less likely to lash out at her.

There was no use in cowering. Viridiana put her purchase in her backpack, walked forward and looked straight at Alejandro, who was casually resting one hand on the bike.

"Do you mind? I need to go," she said.

"This is yours?" he replied, but he didn't move his hand.

"You know it's mine."

"You're probably right. Since so many things in town are yours. My money, for example."

Alejandro stretched out a hand and Paco handed him the bottle. He drank, wiped his mouth with the back of his hand, returned the bottle to Paco, all while staring at her and blocking her way.

"Your gringo friend fired me, Dianita. He said he didn't need me to translate for him anymore."

"He's not my friend," she replied. Her stomach still hurt, she hadn't even had the chance to sit down to drink the damn Alka-Seltzer, and now her mouth tasted sour, too. What a fucking day.

"He said you were. And you sure were friendly to him, costing Paco and me a fare that day he arrived in town. And now, costing me more work. You owe me."

"I didn't say anything bad about you."

"I don't believe that," Alejandro said. "You're always saying shit about me. So, yeah. You owe me. Why don't you go down with me to the beach, to talk the terms of your debt."

"The day I get a lobotomy, sure," she said. There was no sense in being nice to Alejandro if he was already in one of his moods.

"How'd you get him to fire me and hire you? Did you spread your legs wide?"

"Fuck you. You're a pig."

"What a bitch you've always been," he said, shaking his head. "You don't even realize I'm joking."

"Move away," she ordered. "Pig. Asshole."

She tried to shove him aside and he did not move, arms crossed, standing firmly in front of the bicycle.

His friends laughed.

"Hey, do you want it?" he asked. "Okay, okay, you can have it."

Alejandro grabbed the bicycle and tossed it on the ground, then he began stomping on it. Viridiana tried to pull him aside, to make him stop, but he laughed and tried to pin her against the wall, at which point she slapped him.

"What the hell is going on?"

Alejandro turned around and his friends, who had been hooting and clapping, stopped as everyone looked at Lawrence. A couple of elderly ladies, carrying bags filled with bread, halted their steps, as did two men who were headed to the tiendita, and the butcher who had closed up for the day and was going home. It wasn't that odd to see young men harassing a woman, but when the woman in question was a girl like Viridiana, and when an out-of-towner American was about to get involved in the confrontation, it caused heads to spin.

"Nothing's going on," Alejandro said. "And if anything is going on, it's not your business."

"Maybe it's the business of the police," Lawrence replied.

"Really? You want to get Homero involved?" Alejandro turned

to his friends and spoke in Spanish, chuckling. "This pendejo thinks he can sic Homero on us."

"Ah, you don't want no problems with that asshole," Paco said. "He thinks he's Erik Estrada these days, it'll cost you."

The men agreed that it was best to head wherever they had been headed in the first place. Viridiana knew they did not do this out of courtesy, but self-preservation. Homero played cards often, and often lost, so he took bribes liberally and he would no doubt ask each and every one of the men to pony up money. Which is why nobody but an idiot would call the cop to the site of a brawl in the first place, but Lawrence, being American probably didn't know this rule.

"Bye, Dianita," Alejandro said, blowing her a kiss. "No hard feelings, alright?"

Viridiana crossed her arms and watched as the men walked away. The two elderly ladies shook their heads. Viridiana knew they'd tell her mother about this.

"Hey, everything okay?" Lawrence asked.

"Lovely," she said.

He grabbed the bicycle, righting it, and she practically snatched it from his hands, checking to make sure it looked to be in decent shape. In the scuffle she'd misplaced her hat, and Lawrence bent down to pick that up too. He held it out to her.

"I could get the car," he said. "Drive you back. It's dark."

"I noticed," she said, looking up at the lamppost, a couple of moths circling around it. She got on the bike.

A boy, no older than ten, climbed onto the coin-operated horse outside the pharmacy, ignoring the "out of order" sign and making a bucking motion. He was accompanied by two other boys who urged him on, even though they knew that the pharmacist hated it in when they did that.

Alejandro and his cronies had once been like those boys, engaging in small pranks and devilries which turned slowly more unpleasant. They had emerged from their cocoons to become something dangerous.

She guessed that was the other reason why she'd dumped her boyfriend: she couldn't tell what he'd turn into. Nice guy, but what if he shed his skin one day and revealed a new beast? At least with Gregory she knew she was standing next to a chameleon, a proven liar, and that somewhat simplified things.

She looked at Lawrence, Boy Scout and cowboy, wishing to brandish a tin sheriff's star like the one they'd played with when they were kids, and she wondered what animal existed under his hide.

Then she shoved all those dark thoughts, shoved the bezoar back into the pit of her belly, tried to tell herself Paris was around the corner and Gregory looked like a matinee idol, and that's what mattered. Love, adventure, passion.

She wanted to be in a romance movie. Wanted to be Audrey Hepburn with her fabulous dresses and her breakfast at Tiffany's.

Though, as she pedaled, she wondered if she hadn't wandered into the dark streets of a noir.

Chapter 17

Daisy was in a mood. Not exactly angry. She paced around the living room. Round and round she went, until Viridiana, not knowing what to do with herself, went to her bedroom to listen to the radio. When she came out for lunch, Daisy had vanished and since Delfina had already left for the day, Viridiana felt like she could finally relax.

But not long after she sat down, the doorbell rang, and she found herself staring at Lawrence. He'd driven there again in Reynier's car. The top of the convertible was off, and in the backseat there was a bicycle.

"Hey," he said, smiling at her, speaking quickly. "I brought this for you."

Viridiana looked at him, then at the car. She felt as though she had been out too much in the sun, even if she'd spent the whole day inside. Like she was looking at a mirage. "What? The bicycle?"

"Yes. It's brand new."

"I can't take that," she said.

"Why not? Look, I saw what those guys did to your bike the other day."

"It's not broken."

"No, but you could use a new bicycle, couldn't you?"

He turned his head to look at her old bicycle, which was propped by the front of the house. It really did look like shit. The seat ripped and taped back in place, the frame scratched and the paint chipped, the handles wrapped in electrical tape. "Maybe, but why would you get me one? I don't understand."

"Because I feel bad. You were right. I caused you a lot of trouble."

She pushed a strand of hair behind her ear and placed her hands in the pockets of her jeans, giving him a shrug. "It's okay."

"Then you'll keep it?"

"God, I don't know," she said.

"Mind if I park it here then? And you can decide later? I'm hoping Daisy is around, I want to ask her something."

"Come in."

He took the new bicycle out and set it next to her old one. There was no comparison. His bicycle even glinted.

Viridiana went to get Daisy, who headed downstairs quickly, smiled at Lawrence coolly, and shook his hand.

"I'm sorry about our last meeting, I upset you," Lawrence said.

"It was upsetting, but I understand," Daisy said. "You cared about Ambrose."

She said this with a certain queenliness, as if she were a mother accepting the apologies of an unruly child. Viridiana had seen her act like this before. She disliked it very much. It reminded her of her incipient youth. Age had granted Daisy gravitas.

"I did."

Daisy picked up a pack of cigarettes and a lighter which had been carelessly left on the living room's coffee table. "How can I help you today?" she asked.

"I was hoping to have a look at my uncle's papers. The stuff he would have had in his office."

"Why?" she replied carefully running a manicured nail against the edge of her cigarette case, her eyes on Lawrence, her smile was turned on bright, like a light switch. Ninety watts right there, and with the oh-so-crimson lips the effect was hypnotic, but he didn't seem much affected.

"For one, I must ensure all his affairs are in order. For another, it may help me make a determination on the matter of his will."

Daisy seemed to think it through, then nodded, lighting her cigarette and making a lazy movement with her right hand, as if indicating the direction of the office.

"I'm sure we both want everything dealt with as quickly as possible. Viridiana can show you. She knows where he kept everything, I paid little attention to his papers."

"Thank you."

"Perhaps later you can join us for dinner?"

"I'd like that."

With that, they walked away. Since that one day, Viridiana had not bothered to spend time in Ambrose's office. She had avoided it out of a superstitious fear. Ghosts clung to the living, her grandmother said. They could follow you onto the street, and even into a new home, if you let them. Ambrose was buried in the cemetery and she had prayed for him, but there was still too much of him in this room.

All around them were the books which had belonged to the previous owner—another dead man—and the volumes Ambrose had shipped here himself. Most of all there were papers. Ambrose carried with him many things, both important and meaningless. She had ordered it all as best she could.

Lawrence looked at a pile of pages stacked by the typewriter.

"Was he really making progress on his book?" he asked.

"Bit by bit. He was too undisciplined at times," she said, mindful of her choice of words.

The young man lifted the top page from the pile, scanning its contents, then looked at the ones beneath, carefully lifting a few more and returning them to their place on the stack.

"What about the rest? His correspondence? Notes?"

"Some of it is in this drawer," she said opening a cabinet. "Some of it here," she indicated the shelf on which the letters he had received were stacked, as well as the carbon copies of the ones he'd mailed. Lawrence unfolded a couple of them and peered at the envelopes.

"What are you hoping to find?" she asked.

"He liked writing things down. I don't know, I'm looking for clues. For something."

He opened a box, but it only contained carbon paper.

"You're sure Daisy killed him."

He placed the top back on the box and set it back in its place. Then he leaned against the open door of the cabinet, frowning. A tired scout who had hiked through the wilderness.

"I'm not sure she killed him. I'm not sure of anything, that's the problem. All I know is he was heading back to Mexico City, and I don't think it was for the fresh air," he said.

"Did your uncle mention something?"

"Not enough for me to get a clear picture of what was happening. But he was fed up with Daisy."

"You said he gave his wives generous settlements. If he was fed up with her, wouldn't Daisy still have collected her check?"

"Not if he was really upset. Or concerned."

It would have to be a really big concern, wouldn't it? Viridiana remembered the IDs she'd found in the bathroom. Maybe Ambrose had found similar identity documents amongst Daisy's things. That could have set him off.

Lawrence turned his head, to look at her, and she wondered if she looked terribly guilty because his eyes narrowed, turning hard. "He never mentioned anything to you? Maybe he said why he was cutting his trip here short."

"He wouldn't have had to explain anything, and he didn't. He gave me a check for the remaining weeks I was supposed to work here and he…"

If she hadn't looked guilty before, she sure as hell looked guilty now. She thought of Gregory, which made her blush, as she recalled the day Ambrose handed her that check. Or rather, the night. Gregory had come to her room. She'd shown him the radio she'd bought, and he'd asked her to give him a blow job.

"What?" Lawrence asked, when she trailed off.

"He said Daisy and Gregory were parasites."

"They are. Gregory doesn't have a job. He lives off his sister, apparently. And she lived off my uncle."

"Was that so bad? Daisy is beautiful, young, smart."

"And Ambrose wasn't. Is that what you are saying?"

"You think she's a gold-digger. What's so wrong about that? He wanted a younger wife, she was there. They worked out an arrangement."

"Except maybe the arrangement wasn't enough."

"Or he was reneging on it," she countered back, thinking of all the times she'd seen Ambrose be rude to Daisy. He was a clown, a bore, even cruel.

Lawrence ran a hand across the desk, the tip of his index finger resting on a silver letter opener. He looked at her.

"You didn't like him at all, did you? And you like her."

He seemed surprised, and that almost made Viridiana chuckle because he must know his uncle was a prickly man. Sure, at his best Ambrose had been jolly, even generous—that check he'd given her could attest to it—but he wasn't a *likeable* person. Then again, she supposed people are always different in front of a special audience, they changed their flesh masks. Ambrose might have been a saint to his nephew. Now that she thought about it, everyone in this house—Ambrose, Gregory, Daisy—existed under the cover of a different identity.

Same for her.

Viridiana was not who she thought she had been. The summer heat was stripping layers off herself, like peeling bark from a tree. She was, at present, not quite an accomplice, not quite an innocent, but certainly not quite the original Viridiana.

"I didn't like him, and I do like her. Maybe you're right and she did kill him. But she probably didn't leave a note in here, for you to find," Viridiana said.

"I can't figure if you are trying to help me or hinder me," he said. "I trust you either way. Stupidly, perhaps."

"Now that you've tested me."

"I *am* sorry about that, and the business with those men in town. You should keep the bicycle."

She picked up the letter opener he had been toying with and held it up. A ray of light bounced off it and she angled it, like she'd done when she was little and she had a cat. It had chased the light across the room. But it had been her father's cat, and he'd taken it to Mexico City with him.

"I'm not helping *or* hindering you," Viridiana said.

His eyes bored straight into hers.

She'd once thought Gregory looked a bit like San Judas Tadeo and a bit like a movie star, and to her, right then, Lawrence resembled Claudio Brook playing the ascetic in Buñuel's film. The look of a man who has spent a long time in the desert and is thirsty.

Daisy appeared at the door. "Dinner is ready. Delfina made some wonderful fish, and I've assembled a perfect salad. Won't you come with me?" she asked.

Daisy's bad mood had evaporated, like turning the dial and

switching to a different frequency. It surprised Viridiana because she figured the woman would be irritable with Lawrence around them, but she was terribly pleasant.

Viridiana didn't enjoy the meal. She still felt a pain in her belly, that imaginary bezoar which was growing in size, and when she looked at the fish on her plate she had grim thoughts of pale sharks caught in nets. When she raised her head, invariably Lawrence seemed to be looking at her and although he lifted his eyes and turned to Daisy or Gregory, she could not help but feel unnerved.

"You've seen nothing of the area," Daisy said.

"Nothing except the view from my window," Lawrence replied.

"That's a shame. Viridiana took my brother to see sharks."

"Is that so?"

"Apparently they fish them here. And wasn't there that other thing? A lighthouse?"

"It's abandoned," Viridian said.

"Still. You should ask Viridiana to take you on a tour. She knows all the coves and beaches in this area," Daisy said. "Don't you think, Greg?"

She didn't like them offering her up like that, like she was a trained monkey who would do tricks for the visitor. But Gregory was smiling.

"She does. Maybe she can get you a discount on one of those big shark jaws we saw," Gregory said. "You can hang it in your office."

"A souvenir," Daisy concluded.

The conversation went on. Viridiana was amazed at how easy it was for Daisy to talk about nothing of importance and yet never give the impression of boredom. The weather, the sea, the pottery that could be found around the house, they were all spoken about in an easy, light way. Yet Lawrence's regard still felt heavy on

Viridiana and when she walked him to the door, only then did the stone in her belly melt away.

"Tell me, then," Lawrence said pointing at the new bicycle. "Will you keep it?"

The sun was setting and as the dark loomed close she could almost feel the desert coming alive around them. But it would not do it slowly. The desert was yawning and it would wait, and then all of a sudden, when stars dotted the sky, it would tremble and palpitate, wood rats emerging from their burrows, the moon cutting the sky like a scythe. Coyote's moon, ravenous and masculine.

"Yes," she said, because she wanted him gone. The evening had worn her down. She closed the door, her hand resting on the wall. She could feel the night outside taking shape. Viridiana walked back into the living room where Daisy and Gregory sat in perfect comfort.

"Come, sit down," Daisy said, as she filled three little glasses with rum. "Let's chat."

"I should head to bed," Viridiana said. "I haven't been feeling right."

"That's a pity. But it won't take long. Anyway, alcohol always fortifies the body," Daisy declared. "At least, it makes everything taste better."

Viridiana sat down, grabbed a glass and held it between her hands. Daisy, pleased with her cooperation, tossed her a friendly smile.

"We were talking, earlier, about how we should best tackle the question of dear Stanley Lawrence Landry. I think at this point it's obvious it should be *you* who convinces him," Daisy said, glancing at her brother and back at Viridiana.

"I'm not following you," Viridiana said.

"The problem is obvious. We are entirely dependent on this man's good will. He's a nosy little junior detective, prying everywhere. We need him to acknowledge that no foul play took place here and give us the money that is due to us."

It was Viridiana's turn to glance at Gregory. He looked at her, serious. Daisy still spun her smile for Viridiana but Gregory had no glee left.

"So, my idea is that you should simply convince him to stop the prying and hand us the money," Daisy concluded.

"Simply," Viridiana said. "Me? I don't have special mind powers."

"But he trusts you. That's what he said and I'm inclined to believe him."

"You were listening to us?"

Viridiana set her glass down on the coffee table.

"Of course," Daisy said, unencumbered by guilt.

Viridiana crossed her arms, tensing. "That's great," she muttered.

"It is what it is."

"Just because someone says something, it doesn't mean they are honest," Viridiana replied, sarcastic. "You ought to know that."

"Of course I know. I also know how to read people. Every gesture, the way they talk, how they move. What it means when they cross their arms in a protective way, like you do."

Viridiana opened her mouth a little and closed it quickly. She pressed her hands against her lap. Her sarcasm had not served her at all, the little dig had been turned against her.

"Lawrence Landry likes you. Don't ask me why, the appeal of dark-haired Madonnas escapes me," Daisy said, "but he is not immune to your... charms. Which is great news to us, since we could use a bit of that little-girl prettiness to our advantage."

"I've helped you quite a bit already, and I'm not—"

"You want to go to Paris?" Daisy asked setting her glass down, right next to Viridiana's own.

Viridiana stared again at Gregory. He looked at her, helplessly, a fish on a hook, startled and upset. Then he looked down at the coffee table, as if inspecting it for scuff marks and stains.

"Don't deny it. I've heard the whole thing already from Gregory. You are both looking forward to a new life in France. But you need money. The three of us need money. I am not going to dispute it, I'm happy to give Gregory his share and enable you two to sail off into the sunset," Daisy made a dismissive hand motion. "That means the *three* of us have to make sure that rat bastard unfreezes the accounts and gives me my cut. We all profit."

"You're saying I should do exactly what?" Viridiana asked stiffly.

"I don't know. Try the same things you've been doing with my brother, see if that smooths things out between all of us."

There. Exactly what she had been wondering. Gregory had spoken candidly, he had revealed everything. Viridiana felt her cheeks flaming. The embarrassment was almost enough to render her mute.

"He wants you, plain and simple," Daisy said. "He has it bad for you."

"I'm not trying anything with Lawrence Landry," Viridiana said, standing up.

"Sit down," Daisy said, her voice rising a little, but only a little. She wasn't willing to scream.

Viridiana did not, in fact, sit down. But she did not move, either. Which seemed enough for Daisy, who stood up, too. She was taller than Viridiana, but finer-boned. Skin like delicate china. For a split second, Viridiana wondered what would happen if she gave her a shove, if she struck that skin with her knuckles. She was not one for scuffles, but that could change. She was changing.

"You're going to do as I say, for one, because as I explained, we need the money. No money, you don't get Gregory and macaroons and whatever the hell you are picturing in France. Second of all, if you don't help us, I'm going to have to tell Lawrence Landry and the authorities about how you killed Ambrose."

"*I* killed Ambrose?" Viridiana said, she scoffed. "You're nuts."

"No. I have the proof. There's a recording where you go on and on about guilt and the dead guy—"

"You were in my room? What the fuck?"

"Cut it out. You were in *my* room, too."

Viridiana curled her fingers into a closed fist.

"Yes, don't think I didn't notice. Unlike my brother, I keep my things out of sight and all in order. I know someone was riffling through my drawers. It's only fair I listened to your tapes."

"There's nothing incriminating on that tape," Viridiana muttered, but she was desperately trying to recall exactly what she had said. It had all been nonsense. She always talked nonsense to the recorder, it didn't mean anything. She labelled the cassettes so neatly too, with the date on them. Daisy would have found it easy to pop the right one in and find her thoughts after the funeral.

"No? Then why are you trembling?"

She was, fear made physical. The tape had enough words which strung together would look very bad.

Hit her, she thought. *Hit her.*

Yet there was no way to strike Daisy, a black eye would fix nothing, and she didn't even know how to throw a punch in the first place. It would be like trying to fight a shark in the water, hands slapping against the great white body, fists meeting teeth.

"Here's how I see it. Of course, a single tape is not going to shift all the blame on to you, and if you start talking, you'll get us in trouble quickly. But, I'll make sure we all go down together for this."

"Bitch," Viridiana whispered.

Daisy chuckled. "Look, call me whatever you want, I'm making things clear. You want to play that game, we can. Or we can be nice and civil to each other, divvy up the money. Then we go our separate ways."

Viridiana drew in her breath. She did not speak a word, the bezoar seemed to have moved to her chest, she could feel it protruding there.

"Viridiana," Gregory said, filling the silence, like a coin tumbling into a well.

She stood up and rushed to her bedroom. He followed her. She tried to close the door on him, but he forced it open, wedged his way inside and Viridian stepped back, her back bumping against her desk.

"God, will you get out?" she said, her voice high-pitched, like a girl's.

She *was* a girl. A stupid one.

"Give me five minutes and I will," he told her.

"I don't want to talk to you for five seconds. You're blackmailing me!"

"I'm not. Daisy is."

"Yeah, *Daisy*. You told her everything about us, about our plans."

"She guessed most of it, and I had to tell her, alright? You think Daisy has stuff on *you*? She has *real* stuff on me."

Of course, there had to be stuff. Gregory had hinted at plenty and she ought to have guessed the rest already. Theft, identity forgery, embezzlement. Murder, maybe? Ambrose was dead and Lawrence was right, these two had killed him. Or they hadn't saved him. Who knew what they had done while Viridiana had driven to town for the doctor?

If they could rack one murder they could rack two, three…

Viridiana shook her head. "I don't care. You could have lied, you could—"

"She has a fucking bullshit radar, besides, she needed to know about us at some point. Better now."

She pressed a hand against her chest, against the pointy end of the bezoar which she was sure was protruding between her breasts. Viridiana grabbed hold of the chair by the desk and sat down. Her right foot grazed the waste basket. She remembered that Daisy had been in her room, she had taken at least one of her tapes and gone through her things.

It only helped to make her feel sicker. Seeing this, Gregory loomed closer. He set a hand on her shoulders before he knelt in front of her. He grabbed her hands, his thumbs on her wrists, gently massaging her skin.

"She has a point. We desperately need that cash and if you play your cards right Lawrence Landry will do as you say."

"Why would he?"

"Because I recognize the looks he's giving you."

"What damn looks?" she asked.

Viridiana stared down at him and he ran his hands slowly up her arms. "Don't play coy. You can get anything in life if you understand what people want," Gregory said.

What *she* wanted was pretty dumb, Viridiana thought. Love, life, city lights. Was it too much to ask, those three things? They seemed small in comparison to whatever they must be envisioning. No doubt Daisy pictured a distant island, white sands, an exotic cocktail in her hand, sunglasses, a red parasol to match her bathing suit. A boat in the distance with her name on it.

"I'm not saying fuck the guy. But he seems a bit stupid. Lead him on." Gregory told her

"Lead him on to what? Christ, you both… you both think—"

"We know people can be manipulated."

"I'm sure," Viridiana whispered.

"We've all got to survive somehow," he said, his words sour.

His hands, which had stopped at her elbows, now crept up.

"I'm not lying about you and me. I'm not. I need to make a clean exit and I can't without the money. Daisy doesn't get her share, she'll pin it on us. We don't get our share, we are going nowhere. I've got to get out of this mess."

"Yes, *you* get out, I—"

"I can't alone. More than ever, now. Not alone."

"You're going to drag me into it, then."

"You are already in it, Viridiana. From the very first day."

She thought he'd try to take her clothes off, that he'd convince her to play another sexual game, but instead Gregory settled his head against her lap, holding on to her waist with one arm. Viridiana was very still until at last she touched his hair, running her fingers through it.

She thought, ironically, she might look like the dark-haired Madonna Daisy had mentioned right now. Pietà. The sacrilege of the thought made her smirk and she turned her head away.

"You thought you loved me until now, didn't you?" he said. "Have you stopped?"

The room was curiously quiet. The hum of the generator, which troubled her most nights, had ceased. It was only the night outside, gnawing at the windows, but a night without any of the proper sounds which came with it.

"I love you," she said.

He lifted his head, she could see the movement of his throat as he swallowed. He nodded.

"Good," he said.

Chapter 18

It was early in the morning, too early for coherent thought. Since Ambrose's death, their days had been spent in a lazy haze. To be woken up that early, to have the curtain drawn, was a shock. This is partly why Viridiana squinted, looked straight at the face of the stranger in her room, and didn't immediately scream.

The other reason was because she'd been dreaming, and the dream confused her. It had involved the appearance of two yellow dogs in her room, which began biting her legs and tearing off chunks of flesh. This dream, this nightmare, had made her limbs so heavy that even when she opened her eyes her body felt like it was made of lead. She rose slowly from the embrace of the dream and stared at the man.

Gregory, who had been dozing off next to her, had also woken up, bumping his back against the bed's headboard.

"Hi," said the stranger. "It's been a while, Jimmy."

The stranger was short and strong, dressed in jeans and a t-shirt that said "La Paz" with a picture of a smiling sun on it. He had a red bandana around his head. Like an ordinary tourist. But she didn't think he was ordinary at all.

"Scott," Gregory said, running a hand through his hair. "Why, it's good to see you."

"I suspect it's not. Come on over to the living room. We need to have ourselves a chat."

They were both fully clothed, which made getting out of bed

a lot easier. The night before, Gregory had slept with her, but that had been all, it was nice when it didn't have to be all hand jobs and blow jobs and him groping her breasts.

They sat on the couch, side by side, and Daisy walked into the room with another stranger. This guy was tall and stick-thin, his hair cropped short, no jeans for him. He wore a velvet jacket and had a long, grave face. If he was playing the role of a tourist, it was the professor on a trip to study the flora of the region, not the frat boy.

The thin man sat down in front of them, Daisy by his side. The short man, Scott, remained standing, leaning a hand against the back of Gregory and Viridiana's couch.

"It's a nice place you have here," the thin man said.

"It's not ours," Gregory said. "It's a rental."

"Still," the man said. He took out a cigarette case from his jacket and it sprung open with one quick motion of his fingers. "Is the water okay for swimming?"

"It's fine."

"A pity you didn't ask us over for a swim, you know."

The thin man held the case open, for Daisy to have her pick. She did, and then he grabbed a cigarette too, snapped the case closed and put it away.

"I know we haven't been in touch much—"

"Where's the money?" the thin man asked. He didn't sound rude or forceful. He sounded quite casual, as if he had asked what time it was. Not that this made Viridiana relax in the least.

"Henry, look Henry. It's… it's complicated, if I—"

"There's no money," Daisy said, interrupting Gregory. "My husband passed away and he's left me squat."

"That's a pity," the thin man sad.

The thin man lit Daisy's cigarette. She held herself perfectly straight and did not fidget, she did not look nervous at all, whereas Viridiana thought she was going to throw up because these two men were Very Bad People and some Very Bad Things were about to happen. The nightmare had announced them, riding ahead of them, infiltrating her room and biting into her mind. It had been a portent of doom.

"Lily," the thin man said shaking his head and lighting his own cigarette, "Lily, Lily. What am I going to have to do to you?"

Lily. Two syllables.

Suddenly she did not feel like hurling, the surprise took care of that.

Lily.

Gregory's girlfriend Lily.

Viridiana looked at Daisy and then at Gregory. She had believed their story that they were brother and sister, but they didn't really look alike, did they? Their hair was blond, but a different sort of blond and their features did not match. Not that all siblings resembled each other, but the more she looked at them the more she knew this was yet another lie.

How many layers of deception are there? she wondered.

"Henry, cut it out. You know you don't have to threaten me," Daisy said, rolling her eyes and then she raised her head, her bracelets clanking as she raised a slender arm. "Scott, pour us a drink, will you, honey?"

Scott obeyed, grabbing a bottle and two glasses and setting them before Henry and Daisy. Viridiana admired the way Daisy spoke, how she seemed to act as if this was a visit by two beloved friends. Gregory, meanwhile, had a sick look on his face.

She's the one who does the talking, Viridiana thought. *He's the shill.*

What was it Daisy had said? Improvisation was the most

important art.

"I'm not implying we are going to shortchange you," Daisy said. "If you've come to collect right this second, there's not much we can manage. But we have money coming down the pipeline very shortly and we'll settle our debts."

"How soon is 'shortly'?"

"I can't say. It doesn't work that way."

"You better wind it up, Lily. I wouldn't be here if a certain someone was not feeling impatient and more than a little pissed off that you vanished on him."

"I told you we were heading out of town for a while," Gregory interjected.

"Out of town doesn't mean out of the country," Henry replied.

"It's Mexico, not Europe. It practically doesn't count as going anywhere. How did you find us, anyway?"

"The usual. Asked around. You should remember: I know everything."

Viridiana recalled the phone call she'd placed. Could they have been bugging the line? Or maybe they had forced Gregory's friend to spill the beans about their location. It could be their discovery had nothing to do with Viridiana. She suspected it did, but what was done was done. They had to deal with the now.

"About the money… enlighten me on your cash flow situation," Henry said, lighting his own cigarette.

"My husband passed away recently. I thought it would be pretty cut and dry to get my share as instructed in the will, but turns out his nephew holds the purse strings. He's here in town. You're sure you don't know this? Since you know everything."

"So, the kid's in town? And?"

"A couple of phone calls from him and I get a million dollars."

Henry nodded, carefully inspecting the cigarette between his fingers. He raised his eyes, staring at Viridiana.

"Who's the girl?"

"Our translator and protégé," Daisy said.

"Is that what you call them these days?"

Daisy smiled as an answer. Viridiana should have been busy feeling frightened but right then she felt angry.

The man leaned forward. He wore glasses, round-rimmed, and they made Viridiana wonder what type of goon he was. She couldn't picture people who went around collecting money like this with glasses; he ought to have looked more like the beefy, shorter man. Henry looked like an accountant. Perhaps that's what he was, in some fucked up way.

"Translator, you have a name?"

She was able to answer without stammering. "Viridiana," she said.

The man, he looked at her with a dispassionate, careful gaze. She sensed that what she said and how she said it was very important and that she must try to maintain her cool, like Daisy did.

"Viridiana, you know anything about this situation? Is this woman lying to me?"

"She's not," Viridiana said.

"What's the nephew's name?"

"Stanley Lawrence Landry."

"Where's he staying?"

"There's only one hotel in town. I wouldn't know the room number."

"What's the hold up? Why is this Landry making Lily wait?"

The man took off his glasses and held them between two fingers. There was nothing sinister about the gesture and yet she thought for a few seconds that she could not speak any more, that if she did her voice would be a pitiful squeak. Viridiana took a deep breath.

"He thinks she murdered her husband," she said.

"That would put a damper on any inheritance. Right?"

The man was still looking at Viridiana, his gaze did not waver. "Maybe this Landry man is a hopeless cause. What do you think, protégé?"

Viridiana blinked. She intended to answer, but was prevented by Daisy. "I can talk any man into anything," Daisy said.

The thin man turned his head to look at Daisy. There was no derision in his face or words, but something about his eyes felt like mockery to Viridiana. It was not easy to spot, this man kept his cards pressed to his chest, but Viridiana caught a spark of it, which made her look down quickly at her hands in her lap.

"If you could, you'd have talked this one already. Which means things are not going well, which means we get back to my initial question. Where's the money?"

"We can go in circles all evening if you want. But that won't get us anywhere. The money will wind its way down to us."

"Maybe we should pay a visit to Mr. Landry."

Viridiana glanced up at them again, cautiously.

"Henry," Daisy said, tossing her cigarette into the ashtray. "That's not how we do things. Give us a couple of weeks, it'll be dealt with. I'm no fool, you know that."

You had to give it to Daisy, she knew how to talk. She sounded very sure of herself, but there was also something sweet and charming about her words. Viridiana guessed that was part of the art of pulling cons. You had to have the charm. Daisy could deploy it in the right measure. Like right now, if she had been too cloying, it would have seemed desperate. Too little and you'd think she was being rude. Add the right dose and it comes out as a delightful tête-à-tête at a really nice party.

The thin man placed his glasses in his coat's pocket.

"Ten days," the thin man said and stood up. "What's the name of that one hotel in town?"

He looked at Viridiana and so she replied. "La Sirena."

"We'll be there. You better be here. Try to leave town and next time we meet I won't be so civil. Got it?"

"Yes," Daisy said.

The men left. The three of them remained in the living room, no one willing to start a conversation, each one of them wishing to say something.

She'd been wrong about Gregory and Daisy, both. Several times she'd compared them to sharks, but thinking it better, she decided scorpions were the better animal. Scorpions killed a lot more people than anything else in Baja California, lots more people than snakes and black widows. They'd sneak up on you, sneak into your camping tent or your bed roll, your shoes, and that would be the end of it.

Sharks were clean killers.

Scorpions were not. Scorpions were secretive little monsters.

"Who were they?" Viridiana asked, figuring they might as well get this over with.

"Who do you think they were?" Daisy said, chuckling. "God, you sound stupid."

"All right, I'll ask a better question. Who are *you*?"

"Another stupid question."

"Cut it out," Gregory said, placing a hand on Viridiana's knee. "It's a fair thing to ask."

"Why? I'm sure you've spilled your guts to junior here late at night. She probably knows your real name already," Daisy said. "She probably knows everything."

"No, he hasn't told me everything," Viridiana said. "But I know you're his girlfriend."

They seemed genuinely surprised by her words and she thought it was important that she use that surprise in her favor. They were usually firm, but the two men must have had an effect on them and this detail about their relationship had served to make them wobble even more.

"Did Ambrose figure it out too?" Viridiana asked. "Is that why you killed him?"

"Ambrose," Daisy said, and she let out a sound that was not quite a laugh. A bitter, brittle sound and she had a face like the townspeople before they head into the confession booth, that resigned face before meeting the priest. Perhaps this was her method of expiation. Viridiana had told her sins to the tape recorder, she spoke to a mechanical priest.

"This whole trip, it was the perfect setup. The perfect place. I said 'look, we'll have him drown.' There's strong undertows in this area, you said so yourself, didn't you? But then that day we went to the bay of Santa Caridad and you came with us. And you convinced him not to swim.

"I was upset. So when Ambrose fell asleep I went to Gregory's room, to tell him he shouldn't have invited you to the beach. To tell him that he didn't have to bring you to every god damn outing we had because he wanted to fuck you."

Daisy had sipped her drink while the men had been in the house, not truly drinking. She was not drinking now either. Not really. She held her glass with one hand, tracing small circles with her wrist. It was this little detail which alerted Viridiana of how irritated she really was, since her voice remained calm.

"And that's when I knew. He didn't only want to fuck you. He'd had enough of me and he was moving on. With you." Daisy concluded.

"We both had enough of each other long ago," Gregory said. "We agreed this was the last gig we were closing together."

"Yes. It doesn't mean I expected you to pick a whore as soon as we landed in Baja California."

Daisy's voice remained cool even as she spoke those words and stared at Gregory. They'd been more than lovers, they'd been partners, and now it had all gone down the drain.

"She started a fight," Gregory said, his eyes hard, returning Daisy's stare. "She said exactly that and more, and the problem is that Ambrose had woken up. He heard her talking, he rushed inside to yell at us both and tell us that we needed to get out of his house."

"He grabbed me by the hair," Daisy said and she grabbed her own hair, as if imitating Ambrose's gesture, "tried to drag me down the stairs."

"And you shoved him down instead," Viridiana said.

For the first time she could see the scene clearly, like in a film reel. She had made conjectures before but now it played as if on the big screen, in full color, with sound.

"Yes," Daisy said. "I did. He had his fucking hands on me and he wasn't letting go. I'm not even a little sorry that he's gone."

Daisy put her drink down on the coffee table, as if fed up with it. "Some men, they deserve a shove down the stairs. Or a bullet to the head," Daisy concluded.

"Maybe you've done that before," Viridiana said. "A bullet to the head."

The woman laughed. "What an imagination you have! You think that's what we do?"

"I don't know."

"Arson," Gregory said, his voice low. "What we normally do is arson. Claim the insurance, that sort of thing. But Daisy wanted bigger deals, bigger marks, wanted to try to score more and more."

"You wanted that too," Daisy insisted. "Don't be pretending modesty in front of the child."

"I wanted out long before this and you know it. I told you we shouldn't have picked Ambrose, he was all wrong. Wrong temper, wrong habits. Then this trip! To Mexico!" Gregory said.

"Aren't you glad we came to Mexico? So you could meet your new sweetheart?"

"Don't you start again with that. It's fucked. You and me, done and fucked," he said.

"I know, darling, I'm not even objecting to it, but I am objecting to the blame for this whole mess being piled solely on my feet. You had as much to do with it than I did."

It was obvious that this conversation, in slightly different configurations, had been repeated dozens of times before. Not that this diminished the vehemence of their words. Their voices had been rising and although Daisy had not lost her composure, when Gregory took out his pack of cigarettes from his trouser pocket, he could barely place the cigarette in his mouth, his hand was shaking.

"I used to be different, once."

"There he goes," Daisy said, grabbing her glass and shaking her head. "He used to be an innocent. Innocent my ass. A hustler, a petty criminal."

"It's true," Gregory said vehemently. "Damn it, it's true!"

Daisy walked to the other end of the room, looking up at the abstract painting that constituted the only decoration on the walls. It was huge, a monstrous yellow, like the yolk of an egg, and little bits of red. An egg with the blood of a chick smeared on it.

Daisy let out a sigh. "Forget about it, what matters now is the future. Our collective futures. Lawrence Landry needs to pay up so we can wind this thing down and go our separate ways," Daisy said. "You need to do your part, girlie."

Viridiana thought about protesting, but that had done her no good. She also knew that the more she remained in this room, the more likely she was to do their bidding. But she had to do their bidding. Daisy had that tape, there were those men after them, and there was Gregory.

An arsonist, hustler, God-knew-what-else, but hadn't she told him she loved him hours before?

Hadn't she meant it?

Viridiana shook her head. "I need to rest. I don't feel well," she said.

Gregory gave her a look, like he wanted to ask her something, but she hurried back to her room, slipped into the shower and got herself into a clean set of clothes. When she stepped out of the bathroom she found Gregory sitting on the chair.

"Fuck," Viridiana muttered. "What do you want? Stop chasing me."

"A minute with you."

"What for?" she asked, toweling her hair dry.

"I didn't say I was a good guy," he told her as he leaned forward, his fingertips touching her elbow.

Viridiana edged away from him. "That's obvious."

"I told you about the arsons, told you my real name and told you I used to have a girlfriend."

"But not that it was her."

"It's hard to explain."

"Is it now?" Viridiana whispered. Her comb was on the nightstand and she began running it through her hair. "Explain it."

He gave her a little shrug, as if the story didn't matter much, but even before he said a single word she could tell it mattered a lot. It was a big deal and it pained him, which is why he tried to appear nonchalant. That was good. It meant it was real.

"I met her when I was about your age. Daisy is older than me. Not too many years, but enough that she was an expert at the con game by the time we crossed paths. She was smart, pretty, bold. I was fascinated by her."

Viridiana looked at him through the tangle of her hair, she ran the comb slowly down. A big smile had spread across his face and she knew he was picturing Daisy in the past, like the flashback in a movie, tinted in black and white. Then the smile faded.

"I'm not saying my nose was all clean," Gregory said. "I knew a card trick or two, and I sold stolen goods. But Daisy did things at a totally different level. She scammed insurance companies out of a lot of dough. Scammed everyone."

Gregory chuckled. "One time she drove a Cadillac off the lot. Like that!" he snapped his fingers. "Drove away with it. I didn't dare to do that.

"There were a lot of men around her. Men who paid for her trinkets, her booze. Admirers. When we got together I was her shill and I was useful, but it's less useful to have a boyfriend when you're trying to convince another guy to buy you a Rolex. So we started pretending we were related."

He looked at the floor, thinking for a minute.

"Ambrose was the third guy she married. The first two, it was easy-peasy. She met them through lonely heart ads and in a bit they were swooning, married her, and a month later she was running off with whatever they had that we could sell.

"Ambrose was different, better. He had a lot more money and Daisy salivated at the thought of it. I couldn't stand him, but he was persistent. He came around with expensive trinkets and after a couple of months he proposed. I said 'look, millionaires don't part with their money that easily," but she didn't want to believe me."

"But you were right."

"I was, wasn't I?" Gregory said. "I told her I was leaving, but she said she needed help with this one last thing."

"Murdering him?" Viridiana asked.

"No! She came up with that later. Just help in general. And it's not like we didn't need the money. We got involved with Frank at one point, and we had to settle that."

"And like she said, you found a new lover pretty fast."

"I didn't expect it. I'll swear on that Virgin in your church."

He looked sincere again, his mouth curving a little, trying to make light of it. The smile trembling. Who was to say love didn't work like that? It's not like she had loved often. Could be it struck quick and fierce, cleaved you like a thunderbolt.

"On San Judas Tadeo," she said, remembering how she'd thought he looked like the saint. There was no point in ugly icons, she supposed. Who would venerate a Jesus with acne?

Oh glorious apostle Saint Judas, faithful servant and friend of Jesus, the name of the traitor who delivered thy beloved Master into the hands of His enemies has caused thee to be forgotten by many, but the Church honors and invokes thee universally as the patron of hopeless cases—of things despaired of.

Viridiana placed the comb down and stopped in front of him, pushing the hair out of her face so she could take a good look at him. Gregory looked back up at her, his eyes fixed on her own.

"It's like I told you. I'm twenty-nine and my life is slipping away."

She made an offhand gesture. "That's very sad."

He placed his hands on her waist, drawing her close.

"It's the whole story and you know it's true."

"I'm not going to be your shill," she said, but she was already dithering and he knew it.

"No, that's done," he said, shaking his head. "It's over and done. That's the whole reason why Daisy and I fought, that's why we grew apart. I wanted out. I *want* out."

That's what she desired, too. Out. Out of this town, this state, out into the world.

"So, then?" he asked, his voice smooth as silk. His left hand was splayed against her back but the right one had found her breast. "You believe me?"

"Of things despaired of," she whispered, a shiver running down her spine.

"What?"

"Yes, yes, alright."

"You mean it?"

She nodded and to prove it, she kissed him wholeheartedly, fiercely. She thought she'd drown without Gregory and clung to him tight. She couldn't let go now, she didn't want to. Her heart wouldn't take it. Without him, what did she have? Nothing but that damned and endless desert outside that wanted to eat her alive.

* * *

Two days they spent like that, between kisses and caresses and murmurings, moving between her room and his. Two days with the portable radio on, listening to music, dancing to slow songs, the same way people must dance in the big city discotheques. Or else, laying on the bed, his hands skimming her skin. There were a couple of things she wouldn't do, but in many ways she was willing to oblige, especially when his breath was hot against her ear telling her sweet words.

Two days she put off her trip into town, but the evening of the third day, Daisy opened Viridiana's door and waltzed in, not even a courtesy knock. Viridiana was sitting on the bed and she had the tape recorder on her lap. Viridiana tried to quickly stuff it away from sight.

"Don't worry. I don't want to listen to your silly tapes. There's nothing there that's valuable," Daisy said, leaning against Viridiana's desk.

"Then maybe you wouldn't mind giving mine back."

"No. That's the valuable part, silly."

Daisy looked out Viridiana's window but there was nothing to see there unless you liked staring at the generator.

"I want to make sure we are okay with each other, that we understand each other. I know you don't like me right now, but one day you will understand that what I am giving you is a good education," Daisy said.

Viridiana wondered exactly what kind of "education" Daisy had given Gregory. She didn't doubt it had happened as he said, that he had been the younger, more inexperienced party and then he'd met Daisy and he hadn't stood a chance. He'd been a tiny fly stumbling onto a great web and the jaws of a vicious spider.

"Seduction and manipulation are tools you should always have in your arsenal. Besides, Lawrence is an easy mark."

Daisy turned around and looked at Viridiana with this big smile on her face, like she expected they were fast friends again. Gregory had decamped for his own room, saying he needed a shower, and now Viridiana wondered if he'd timed it on purpose, so Daisy could have a go at her. She frowned.

"You should know. I bet you have a lot to say about marks," Viridiana replied.

Daisy did not seem put off by the curt response. In fact, her smile seemed to expand, to go from a placid imitation of a smile to the authentic item.

"You think we are very different, don't you? That I don't

understand you? You think you're the victim here, poor little thing. We're not so different," Daisy declared. "I know what it's like to claw your way up a steep cliff. It was a brutal, lonely climb."

"Not that lonely. How did you meet him?" Viridiana asked. "How long ago?"

"You really want to hear that old story? Ten years ago."

He'd said he had met Daisy when he was more or less Viridiana's age, meaning Gregory had spoken truthfully about that. He couldn't have been *that* jaded at nineteen. He couldn't have been *that* bad. Viridiana bet that much of Gregory's current predicament was due to Daisy and Daisy alone. She had ruined his life and now intended to ruin Viridiana's.

Viridiana stared at Daisy and Daisy sat down at the foot of the bed.

"He tried to pull a con on me. A little thing, an amateur's ploy. I saw through him immediately. And I wanted him immediately. I wanted him very badly. I don't think I've ever wanted someone quite as much as I wanted him. He wanted me back. It was thrilling."

Daisy traced a line across Viridiana's bedsheets, as if indicating the path Gregory had walked in his quest for her.

"Of course, I didn't relent immediately. I made him sweat for it, I made him guess. He ran in circles chasing me. He loves the chase. That's probably why he wants you. Because he doesn't quite have you *yet*. Once he does, he'll probably vanish in three seconds flat," Daisy said.

"He didn't vanish from your life, did he?"

"No. But it's not the same thing at all. We had a lot more gluing us together. Greed, for one."

"Now, you don't."

"You're right. But now I don't want him anymore."

"Maybe it's the other way around."

Daisy leaned forward and reached forward, catching Viridiana's face between her hands. "You're such a tiny girl. All you are missing is a pretty yellow bow in your hair and you'll be ripe for a picture book. Cinderella or Little Red Riding Hood? What do you think?"

"What's your point?" Viridiana asked, pushing her hands away, but Daisy caught Viridiana's hand in turn, clasping it tight. Too tight. She dug her nails into Viridiana's skin.

"Happy endings have a price, Viridiana. Hansel and Gretel don't get to escape the witch's house until they've pushed her in the oven, and you don't get to run off with him until you've paid the toll and the toll is Lawrence Landry."

"Let go."

"Your mark, Viridiana. Lawrence is *your* mark. Stop stalling and do it. Gregory can carry you to the fairyland you so desperately desire but I need to have what's mine," Daisy said, releasing Viridiana.

Chapter 19

Viridiana stood on the beach where the fishermen dragged the sharks. She had hoped to see their boats by the shore. They had left already, gone to find the day's catch. She was greeted instead by the boy she'd seen the last time. He was sitting under the shade of the shack. He raised his head when he spotted her and realizing it was no one of importance, he returned his attention to the net he was mending.

She needed time to think and she couldn't think inside the house. Either Daisy would ambush her, or Gregory would place bruising kisses down her neck, and it was the fourth day and Viridiana knew she couldn't put this off. So she'd gone to the seashore, to look at the shark meat laid out to dry like linen. The music from a little radio in the shack filled the air with the distorted voice of Camilo Sesto. The sea seemed to be painted with a brush, flat and lifeless.

What to do, now?

I'm going to lie.

I'm going to tell the truth.

Neither sentence had any meaning. The sea might have meaning, it might be the only thing left with meaning.

A fish had been left stranded by the tide between the crevice of a few rocks and a gull was pecking its eyes, even though the fish was still alive. It stirred and tried to flap its tail.

Another omen. No doubt a bad one. Viridiana turned away

from the sea. The sea didn't have answers. Neither did the desert.

When Viridiana did make it into town she veered towards her mother's store. It was near closing time and her mother lifted her head tiredly from behind the counter, her hands stilling on the cash register. She had her hair back in a bun, a few strands escaping it.

"Hey," Viridiana said.

"Hello," her mother said, counting change and carefully putting it back in the cash register, then turning to a notebook and writing down a figure.

"You need help with anything?"

"No."

Viridiana looked at the curtain behind the counter, which hid the back of the shop and its bathroom. With her eyes closed she could describe the pattern of the curtain, its exact shade of yellow, its texture. She could describe the soap in the bathroom or the plastic flowers placed under a tiny portrait of the Virgin of Guadalupe, which hanged by that bathroom.

Yet she felt like a stranger that evening, like this was the first time she'd walked into the shop.

She had gone to the beach for solace, for answers, for sympathy, and found none against the jagged rocks. Now she turned to her mother. She could tell her the whole thing, everything that had happened since she'd moved in with the tourists. She could tell her about Daisy and Gregory, and the men who'd paid them a visit. She could and maybe Marta would make it better.

She might. She really might.

Viridiana cleared her throat.

"Mom, I was thinking—"

"I've heard what you've been up to," Marta said.

"What do you mean?" she asked cautiously.

"Alejandro's been talking about you and that American. You're sleeping together, he says. And everyone in town has heard about it," her mother shook her head. "Alejandro says that's why the man fired him."

"Lawrence," Viridiana said. "He's told people I'm sleeping with Lawrence? He's lying. He's mad at me and he's lying. You believe him?"

Marta stared at Viridiana, and Viridiana couldn't help it, she thought of Gregory. Gregory's kisses on her lips, his hands on her thighs, his tongue exploring her. Guilty as charged, she thought, even though the man they had pointed at was the wrong one.

She blushed, but out of anger and not out of shame. That fucking bastard, talking about her behind her back.

"People have seen you," her mother said. "Walking around with him, eating with him."

"It's not a sin."

"Your stepfather is upset, our friends are gossiping. You shouldn't come by for dinner for a couple of weeks."

"You believe them!"

"I don't believe *them*," her mother said. "I believe my eyes. I know you and I know there's something going on with you. I can guess what it is."

Viridiana swallowed. People said her mother had been pretty when she'd been young, but Viridiana couldn't see how. Her face was narrow and her mouth was bracketed with lines. Her mother's eyes were hard as obsidian blades, ready to cut her into tiny pieces, but when she spoke Marta sounded tired. And she also sounded… indifferent. Like this discussion didn't even matter much. Or she'd expected it for a long time now.

Viridiana supposed it made sense. That her mother had prepared herself for disappointment a long time ago, that she had mapped the ways things would go wrong with Viridiana. *She'll fuck up because she's the daughter of a fuck up.* There it came, of course, the mention of her father, right on cue.

"I was like you, once," her mother said. "I wanted to have the whole wide world. What did it get me? It got me your father and he certainly didn't have the world in his pocket. This man, he's sweet talking you."

"I'm not in any relationship with Lawrence Landry," Viridiana said. She didn't even know if she was in a relationship with Gregory, for all the caresses he bestowed on her. When he was holding her, when he was right next to Viridiana, she was ready to believe the sky was green and the grass was blue, but when she had a chance to take a breath it all felt crooked. And there was Daisy. Was he really over her like he said? Even if he was, would Daisy let them go? What about the men who were trying to collect from Daisy and Gregory?

"Mama, I'm not with Lawrence," she repeated.

Marta looked right through Viridiana. Like grandma had done before she died, when she forgot people's names and confused Viridiana with her dead sister, when she sat in front of the TV set for hours, observing people in black and white musicals dancing to old tunes. The cloying scenes with Ginger Rogers, the melodramas with Dolores del Río.

Two years gone, her grandmother, and only now did Viridiana realize how much Marta looked like the dead woman.

Marta was silent.

"It doesn't matter if I am or not," Viridiana said, wanting to laugh. "You all want me to be guilty so you can punish me. You think I'm a brat, it serves me right."

Her younger brothers and sisters could do no wrong.

They were not tainted.

It was her, blighted plant. Born bad and twisted.

"I told you to stay in the shop, to work here during the summer, to—"

"I didn't."

Marta's face was a mixture of pity and contempt. Pity must have won because she sighed, pushing back a strand of hair behind her ear.

"I'll talk to your stepfather, I'll have a chat with—"

"Don't bother," Viridiana said, shrugging. "You're right. He's my lover. Big deal, huh?"

Her mother was old. She was not yet forty and she was old, like a washing cloth that has lost its colors. Rinsed and dried in the hot Baja California air. Viridiana wondered if she'd look like that one day, if she'd have a similar conversation with her own child.

But no, no. Not like this.

She wouldn't be like this.

A customer came in and Viridiana took the chance to get out quickly, heading to the hotel. Carmen was working the front desk. She was a nice enough lady with buck teeth and a big grin. She smiled when Viridiana approached her.

They exchanged pleasantries.

"Hey, Carmen, can you do me a favor? Can you ring Mr. Landry and tell him I'm down in the lobby?"

"Sure, alright, let me see," Carmen said. "Landry."

"Do we have any messages? Room 12," said a man

It was the slim man who had gone to visit Daisy and Gregory. Henry. He leaned against the front desk looking from Carmen to Viridiana. Carmen was distracted by a phone call and picked up the receiver and held up a finger indicating it would only take a minute.

Viridiana looked at the man and he returned the look.

He reached into his jacket.

She wondered if he had a gun with him. He must have. Would he wield it against her? Maybe it was a knife. Maybe he was about to take it out and stab her right there, in the lobby.

"Do you have a light?" he asked, as he took out a pack of cigarettes.

"I… I don't. Maybe, over at the bar," she said, gesturing in that direction, hoping he would go away. But he didn't move an inch.

"It's good to hear that. Young people, these days, they have such bad habits. They start drinking and smoking when they're still babies. And they keep such bad company. Such bad friends."

He spoke with the words of a concerned, fussy grandfather, but the guy was at most pushing forty. Besides, his tone was not that of a concerned relative. He had a cool, flat voice. The words didn't match the speaker at all, which gave them an unpleasant edge.

"You have good friends, don't you?"

"Yes."

"Trustworthy. They wouldn't lie. Or try to cheat someone would, they?"

Viridiana did not know what to say. She elected to stare at him. Every muscle in her body was tense and if Carmen got off the phone she might have noticed that Viridiana looked like she was about to collapse from the strain of standing.

Yet she stood and she nodded at the man. She must. She found inside of her not the courage, but the sheer willpower to do it.

I'm Liz Taylor when she first meets Rex Burton in Cleopatra, she told herself. *I stand upright. I stand strong.*

"Are you waiting for a friend?" he asked.

"Yes."

"A good friend."

"Not really."

"You think I pry, don't you? That I'm not a gentleman," the thin man said. "I assure you, I am a gentleman."

That's what he said. What she heard in her head, loud and clear, what she read in his eyes was entirely different. *Where's that money? The three of you better hurry. I am losing my patience.*

Maybe that's why the thin man worked for whoever he worked for. Because he could ask those questions without asking, because his circuitous phrases and his measured voice were more unnerving than a kick to the gut and open threats.

"I think you're a gentleman," she said.

She didn't even know what she was saying, but she must have telegraphed the right idea because he tucked away his pack of cigarettes and nodded at her.

Carmen was off the phone and had finally dipped into the tiny wooden bins on the wall behind her where all the messages were stacked.

"No, no messages," Carmen said.

"Too bad," said the man, but he didn't bother looking at Carmen. His eyes were fixed on Viridiana.

"Can I help you with anything else?"

"Make sure you are taking care of yourself," he said, still looking at Viridiana.

The man walked away without another word. Carmen grumbled something about rude people, then picked up the phone.

"Yes? Mr. Landry? There's someone for you in the lobby."

Carmen handed the phone to Viridiana. She pressed the receiver against her ear and exhaled. "Lawrence? It's Viridiana. I'm wondering if you had a minute."

"Sure. I'll be right down," he said.

Viridiana gently placed the receiver back in its cradle. She thought of how she was going to talk to him, how she could explain this whole thing. Funny, she hadn't figured that out yet although she should have. At the beach she thought nothing. She merely stood at the shore, dreamy and melancholic, which was not unusual for her. On the way to the hotel she had not paused to collect herself.

She kept telling herself, *maybe someone can save me*, and now that her mother had failed she turned to Lawrence Landry. Besides, she was jolted by her brief talk with the thin man. She needed at the very least some company, a sympathetic face.

He was in the lobby in a few minutes, asked her if she wanted to have a drink at the bar because it had opened and the restaurant was closing in turn. That's the way the owner of La Sirena handled the shifts, he didn't waste money on paying for extra servers when one could do the job.

The bar, which she'd only seen a couple of times before, was gloomy. Too much wood, too much furniture, and the décor was old, the golden wallpaper had been in fashion two decades before. The bartender looked bored as he did his crossword puzzle and the server seemed even more bored as he dropped a menu with a bent corner on their table.

She ordered a rum and coke, which was the only thing she knew how to order. She'd once chanced on a book about cocktails in Reynier's house, each cocktail described, with a little picture. The book said every city guy and gal most know how to make a few basic cocktails if they expect to have a good time, but Viridiana was not a city girl, and she had not paid attention.

Sherry, that's what the priest drank, and beer, that's what everyone else had during the game of dominoes Sunday nights. The game of dominoes she was no longer invited to. An exile in her own land. Then again, they had never wanted her, did they?

He ordered a whiskey sour. She had no idea what that was.

"I hope I didn't bother you," she said. "I ... I thought I'd stop by."

"No, it's fine. I was watching TV."

"Anything good?"

"*From Here to Eternity*," Lawrence said.

"I do mean it when I say I need you. 'Cause I'm lonely. You think I'm lying, don't you?" she said, repeating Donna Reed's line.

She thought he wouldn't get it, that he'd frown and be puzzled, like other people were often puzzled when a line stolen from a film made it into her mouth. Then she'd have to explain. But he nodded.

"Nobody ever lies about being lonely," he said, replying with Clift's line.

"Yeah."

"You're a film buff?"

"It's Montgomery Clift," Viridiana said. "My grandmother loved him. She was heartbroken when he died. We used to go over to the next town, where they have a movie theatre. They'd have the half price matinee certain days of the week and they'd show older movies. Clark Gable, Gary Cooper, Pedro Infante."

"And Montgomery Clift."

"Of course, Montgomery Clift," she said.

"The old movie theater is still open?"

"Yes. But I don't go that often now that she's passed away."

She had yet to take a sip of her drink. It sat upon a little napkin and she ran her finger around its rim.

"They have festivals and special screenings at the Cinematheque in Mexico City, over in Churubusco," he said. "They show a ton of art films. You should go to a screening, some time."

"Next time I refuel my invisible jet. Now, tell me the truth, have you only lived in Mexico City for a month or was that also a lie? Because I'm beginning to suspect you're a regular at the

Cinematheque."

"Two years, on and off. I came to watch after the family's business interests, after university."

"Next I'll learn you're married with four kids."

"No wife. One cat. You like cats?"

"Sharks and sea monkeys."

"My kind of gal."

She smiled and finally picked up her glass, drinking quick. He smiled too.

"It's Friday," he said. "I thought you'd be out with friends."

"I forget what day of the week it is, over at that house. But time has no meaning in Baja California, anyway."

"How so?"

"I don't know. It's a feeling. Like you're standing at the end of the world. It's the desert, probably. It gives you funny thoughts when you look at it, makes you try and figure out what 'forever' means."

"I should see more of it, although I can't say I'm much of a nature buff."

"The Cinematheque, then, and a few whiskeys for you," she said, pointing at his drink.

"Yes," he said. "A good dinner, that sort of thing."

She finished the rum and coke, and the server quickly brought another one. Slow night, it was the two of them at the bar. The bartender asked the server to take a look at his crossword puzzle and they both bent their heads over the piece of paper.

She drank.

The insistent pain in her stomach, the bezoar which was nothing but a knot of fear, pained her for a second, as if her body anticipated Lawrence's question.

"Why did you come to see me?" he asked. "It's not that I mind the company, I'm just surprised. You haven't been too thrilled to speak with me the last couple of times."

She had told Gregory that she wasn't going to be his shill, she had protested when Daisy talked about marks, but when Lawrence spoke, she realized conning him had been her plan all along. As much as she wanted to pretend she was going to reveal the truth about Ambrose's death to someone, she wasn't going to say a word. She was going to lie. Lawrence Landry wasn't going to save her. Viridiana was going to save herself, she was going to save Gregory, too. She was going to get them out of Desengaño and away from those angry men who wanted money. She was going to vanquish the evil witch called Daisy and break the spell that she'd put over Gregory.

Viridiana wasn't Little Red Riding Hood or Cinderella. Instead she would be the heroine freeing the prince from his enchantment. She'd make everything perfect.

Lawrence didn't know anything useful and he didn't have to know anything. Not if Viridiana played it right. He was a mark. That's what Daisy had told her and maybe she wasn't wrong. And Viridiana was in love, wasn't she? That justified it.

All she needed was to improvise a little. All she needed was bravado.

"Daisy has been talking about you, she's nervous. She's wondering what you're going to do next," Viridiana said, pushing an ice cube with her finger around the glass.

"And what? She sent you here to find out?" Lawrence replied.

"She's worried that you'll leave her without a penny because you don't like her, because you never did like her. You even talked Ambrose into changing his will."

"You make it sound like I've cooked this whole thing up in order to screw her over. That's nonsense."

"Is it?"

He leaned forward, his elbows on the table. He looked put off. Viridiana thought that if Daisy had been there she would have tried to sweet talk the guy, butter him up, but Viridiana wasn't going for that.

"I'm a fair man," he said. "I'm not trying to cheat her out of anything."

"But maybe you *did* talk him into changing the will."

"He talked himself into that," Lawrence muttered. "I agreed with him when we met in Mexico City."

"She doesn't like you, either," Viridiana said.

"And you don't like me, you're thinking I'm an asshole that's come to stir up trouble."

"I think you're sad. I'm sorry about your uncle. I am. But screwing her over isn't going to bring him back to life."

"What is it that you're not telling me?"

"Huh?"

"Every time I meet you I think you're going to tell me something and then you hold back."

She felt a bit sick and a bit stupid. Possibly because she didn't drink, possibly because of the non-existent bezoar, and quite likely because she didn't know what she was doing. She didn't know how to even begin playing this game.

Daisy made it seem easy but this wasn't quite going the way she wanted it to go.

Slowly he leaned back, he looked her over carefully. He sighed but didn't speak.

Half a dozen people walked in, laughing, happy, ready to begin their weekend. They sat around a circular table, loudly joking. She turned her head to look at them. It was a bunch of kids who'd gone to her high school, Manuel included. For a moment they hushed their voices, staring at her, before someone erupted in laughter. She saw their mouths moving, felt Manuel's eyes on her.

Damn it. Of all the nights for this. Manuel's crowd didn't even like drinking at the bar. But what did Viridiana know? She hadn't hung out with them in ages.

If God was good, they'd mind their own business. But God was not being good. Why should he be good to Viridiana? No, God wanted to teach her a lesson in fire and brimstone. And he'd sent Manuel over to do it. Her ex-boyfriend approached Viridiana's table.

I deserve this, all of this, she thought.

"You're too busy to go out but not too busy when it's not me," he said.

"Hello," she replied. Which sounded stupid, but what else was there to say?

"It's true, then," Manuel said, looking at Lawrence and shaking his head. "I told Alejandro it wasn't true, that you wouldn't be sleeping around with a tourist. I damn near broke his jaw today, Viridiana. And here you are, with the fucking guy."

Had he? That pleased her a bit—Alejandro needed to have several body parts mashed to a pulp—but she didn't like the way Manuel was looking at her at all, and she knew a conversation with him would lead to endless recriminations, the rehashing of things she didn't want to think about. Not now. She had other things to do, and Lawrence was looking at her in confusion while Manuel stared at her in anger and disgust.

His eyes reminded her of the gull which had been pecking the fish. Gasping, and dying, and flopping, that poor fish in the summer heat. It was dead by now. Dead and gone, to become nothing but bones on the rocks.

Fear and the taste of salt filled her mouth. The bezoar lodged in her throat.

"I should go," Viridiana said.

She grabbed her hat, which she'd placed on an empty chair, and headed outside.

As she stood in the lobby she wondered if the man she'd seen before might still be hanging around reception. But a quick perusal showed no one was there. That would have been the cherry on the sundae.

"Are you okay?" Lawrence asked. He'd followed her out of the bar.

"It's the folks in there... I know them," she said. "They're my friends. They *were* my friends."

"What was that guy going on about?"

"Alejandro told people around town that we're sleeping together. It's his way to get revenge on me. People around here love to talk, they're bored."

Fuck, she detested this town. She saw her face reflected in one of the hotel's mirrors and wanted to toss a rock at it. Instead, she pushed the front door open and stepped out into the night, which was warm and welcoming.

She coughed, bent down her head, pressed a palm against the hotel's wall. She felt very sick.

"Are you okay?" Lawrence asked.

She looked up at him, hair in her face, blinking. "I'm in a lot of trouble," she whispered. "You can't guess the amount of trouble."

She thought he would understand after that. That surely it was all tattooed on her face, that he would be able to discern the whole story: Daisy and Gregory's aliases, Ambrose's death, the men in the hotel. She thought he would straighten himself up and declare her guilty, right then and there.

She was sure of it. Which was fine. She wasn't going to fight it anymore.

She vacillated between the twin poles of victory and defeat. Defeat looked like the easiest path right now.

"I get it," he said, somberly.

Viridiana held her hat between her hands.

"I've been in Mexico for a while now, I get it. This is a small town… people are going to be more conservative. I didn't realize you'd get in trouble for talking to me. This is what you've been trying to tell me, isn't it?"

He didn't get it at all. He missed the obvious. She thought to correct him for a second, to say, *come on you fool, it's not about that.* She had been ready, a minute ago, to be dragged to the police station.

Now Viridiana straightened herself up and stared at him.

"I do feel bad. Is there someone I could talk to? Maybe that guy in there—"

"That's my ex-boyfriend," Viridiana said. "Talking to him is not going to help anyone."

"I guess not. But you're very upset."

I can do this, she thought. *He knows nothing.*

"I'm being silly," she brushed the hair away from her eyes. "You're right, I was trying to tell you but I thought it would sound silly. Small town and… everything else you said."

"Hey, look, maybe we can go somewhere else?" he asked. "Do you want me to take you somewhere else? We didn't even eat anything."

"You're hungry?"

"I did want dinner."

"There's a tortería," she said. "I can show you where it is. But you could go back in, you know. Order room service if you don't want them staring at you. Maybe catch the end of your movie."

"It's probably ended by now."

She'd left the bicycle by the hotel's entrance, propped next to a streetlamp. She grabbed it and they walked at a brisk pace. When they reached the eatery she saw that on the small TV screen they were showing *The Big Sleep*. Lawrence was right. His movie had ended.

The tortero didn't care who they were and there were no kids to laugh at them, no ex-boyfriend to stalk their table. Just a plastic table in a corner with two makeshift salt shakers and the tortas with two Cokes. Milanesa for her, ahogada for him. He could handle the chile de árbol, which she found amusing.

"What? You think I only eat cheese and crackers?"

"I don't know. I saw a picture of a 'Mexican' TV dinner in an American magazine and it looked terrifying. And a picture of aspic."

"I've had aspic," he said.

"It's disturbing."

"Come on, you don't want to try a slice of tomato aspic?"

"It even *sounds* wrong."

"The next fourth of July party at the American embassy, I'm taking you to have red, white and blue aspic there."

"No."

"Yes. Ring me up when you're in Mexico City, I'll take you out."

The tortero had strung a set of Christmas lights in the small eatery. They blinked on and off, like a poor man's neon sign. Viridiana grabbed a toothpick and rolled it between her thumb and her middle finger.

"Sure, I'll look you up in the phone book," she said.

"I mean it."

Lawrence smiled.

He is not immune to your charms. That's what Daisy had said.

Viridiana hadn't seen it before, but she could see it now, in the narrow space of the tortería, with Humphrey Bogart dubbed into Spanish speaking in the background.

She wondered what his life was like in Mexico City and she thought he was lonely. It was easy to spot, like a shabby suit. He wore the loneliness all around him. He didn't get along with the other expats, but he also didn't mesh with the locals. But he hadn't meshed back home, either.

"When do you leave?" she asked. "Do you know?"

"Soon," he said.

"I bet you can't wait to get back to the city."

Just as she thought, he shrugged, and in that tiny gesture she saw many evenings spent watching the exact same movie they were showing right now. She saw him lying on the couch in his tedium.

She did the same. She could recognize dissatisfaction and also the eagerness in his face, which he tried to disguise, turning his head towards the TV.

It was the same eagerness she had around Gregory.

Okay. She still didn't know how she was supposed to convince Lawrence Landry to give them the money, but now she was sure she could. Nothing too direct, nothing too obvious.

Viridiana dropped the toothpick on her plate and tilted her chair back.

"If you drop by tomorrow, I'll show you the lighthouse," she offered.

Chapter 20

Lawrence stopped by the next day. He looked like he hadn't slept, stubble on his cheeks. There was something sadder about him every time she saw him.

They went to the office. He shuffled a few papers, looked at a few things, but he gave up on all that shortly after noon.

"Where's that lighthouse?" he asked her.

It wasn't much of a lighthouse anymore. They'd stopped using it more than ten years before and the youths in the area had taken advantage of this to decorate it with crude drawings of penises, they spray-painted slurs and wrote nonsensical rhymes.

The lighthouse was square-shaped and at its top there still sat the Fresnel lens which had been used to light the way. It was always windy near it. Her grandmother used to say a strong wind could blow ghosts onto land. When she told Lawrence that, he asked her what types of ghosts she thought might walk around there.

"People from wreckages drifting up from the bottom of the sea," she said. "Sailors, fishermen, suicides who threw themselves off a cliff."

"I don't believe in ghosts."

"That's good," she said.

"How old is this?"

Viridiana looked up at the lighthouse. "It was built in 1892. There was an earthquake in Laguna Salada that year, they felt it all the way to San Diego. The land is not still here."

She pulled a rusted door open. It was never locked. "Would you like to go up?" she asked.

He did. When she chanced to bring tourists here, she didn't take them up, but she made an exception for him because he was truly paying attention to what she was saying. People were normally too busy taking photographs or chatting amongst themselves to listen.

"I didn't understand why my uncle would want to come here," Lawrence said. "I told him Puebla or Guadalajara were easier to reach. Or that he could head to San Miguel de Allende, where there are plenty of expats. He didn't come for the fishing, that's for sure. He never liked that."

Lawrence looked out a small, stone cut window towards the sea. "I feel like he came to die here. What you said about ghosts… I don't believe in them, but still I worry that I ought to take him home."

"A cremation can be arranged, if it makes it easier to move the remains."

"Yes, I know. The rest, though… I'm not even sure why I'm here," he said, laughing a dry little laugh. "It's like this trip has been for nothing. I have no more answers than I did before."

Viridiana leaned out the window next to him, nodding and he turned his head to look at her.

"I loved him. I had no father but him. No matter all his bad qualities, I loved him."

Viridiana thought about Daisy and Gregory, the two fraudsters, two murderers, two pale scorpions waiting for her at the house on the cliff. She liked the hint of adventure, of danger, that came with them. Like salt in the air. And she was still doing their bidding, wasn't she? That was love, maybe.

Despite it all, love.

"I need to know what happened," Lawrence said.

"You know as much as you'll ever know," she told him.

This was the truth. He wasn't going to find a secret note amongst Ambrose's papers, Daisy and Gregory weren't going to sign a confession, Viridiana wasn't about to tell him what she'd discovered. He had as much as he would ever have. In the end, isn't that true for everyone? Does a death have any more meaning if you tease out every single detail? A tombstone is a tombstone. Even ghosts seldom narrate their own demise. They go about, diaphanous, existing like pressed flowers caught in the pages of a book, but they are not the lines of ink on the page.

"You can't stay here forever," she added.

"Come on. You're telling me you wouldn't want to find out? That you wouldn't try and try?" he asked.

"I'd try," she admitted. "Are you afraid your uncle is going to be mad at you?"

"I told you I don't believe in ghosts."

"I don't believe in ghosts either. But sometimes they're here anyway."

She had prayed the rosary for Ambrose, but who knew if his spirit would come back to walk around the house one evening. Or even worse, who knew if it would follow them across land and water. Yet she was willing to accept this might happen. She thought now she understood her grandmother better, with her talk of omens and evil winds.

Certain things we must bear.

She'd bear a haunting if she had what she desired. City lights, city streets, a life altered.

Lawrence chuckled. "You're a curious girl."

"You can say eccentric. I won't mind."

"Eccentric. But I'll admit, maybe it's understandable. This landscape is strange," he said going from one window to another, looking from water to the desert.

"They said Baja California was an island, near the Terrestrial Paradise. They were wrong. It's not an island and it sits by the end of the world, but it's something to wonder at anyway. But the problem here is if you stay too long, you'll never leave."

She set a hand on his shoulder. "You've got to leave, Lawrence. Rehashing things will only make you more depressed."

"Who says I'm depressed?"

It was a laughable thing to tell her, not only because he had dark circles under his eyes but because he plain looked unhappy and lonely and melancholic. It was a poised sort of sorrow, one which he wore well, and which she suspected he'd been enacting for a long time. His uncle's death was but one more unhappy event in a chain of events.

Ambrose had possessed a hearty laugh and he could drag you with it, make you smile when he wanted. Maybe Lawrence had loved his uncle because of this.

"All right, all right," he said. He looked miserable and took a deep breath. "It doesn't add up. But if you knew anything you'd tell me, right? If anything was fishy?"

"Sure, I'd tell you," she lied, but when she'd said "sure" she'd thought of Gregory and the result was that she spoke with an intense earnestness that made Lawrence go mute. It was the earnestness of first love and he could tell.

Viridiana blushed and this made it all even better. Though unplanned, she'd hit the bullseye.

"Let's head downstairs?" she asked.

Because she wanted to cheer him, because she wanted to smooth things between them like ironing the best linens, she suggested that they visit a very small restaurant which was a bit farther down the coast, a half-hour ride from them. It was the kind of place tourists liked, with stuffed turtles hanging from the walls and puffer fish dangling from the ceiling. The furniture was rattan, and it was exactly the way tourist guides said Baja would be even though they always lied. Baja California was all small fondas, plastic tables, hardly any décor, and signs advertising Pepsi-Cola and Tecate.

This place was like an old Hollywood movie.

He thanked her for that, for the excursion.

She had made progress, that was for sure, although she couldn't pinpoint what exactly made her think this since he hadn't said anything in so many words. It had been Lawrence's eyes, Viridiana decided, which looked at her with a velvet softness and a promise. His distrust had melted. The Baja Californian sun could melt anything away, it seemed.

We're friends now, she told herself. *He trusts me and he likes me and friends do things for each other.*

Nothing as sordid as what Daisy had imagined. Not *those* things.

When she reached the house she hurried upstairs, to Gregory's room, to share the news. *We've got him.*

Music drifted down the hall and she slowed her steps. His door was closed, light filtering under it, the music seeping out, snatches of voices here and there. She could hear nothing until someone abruptly turned down the volume.

"Quiet that down, it's giving me a headache," Daisy said.

Gregory mumbled something. Viridiana pictured him sitting on the bed with a glass between his hands. She imagined Daisy moving around, a cigarette in her mouth, fiddling with Viridiana's radio. She stepped closer to the door.

"I'm telling you, she's got what it takes," Gregory said.

"Being young and having cute little breasts are not all that it takes," Daisy replied. "A three-dollar hooker is what she is."

"If we are going to South America we could use someone who actually speaks the language."

"Expats don't need to speak the damn language."

"It would help."

Gregory paused. He might be refiling his glass or maybe lighting a cigarette for himself. "If it doesn't work out, we ditch her quick," he said simply, without any care.

Something broke inside of her when he spoke. It was as if the coyote who was the moon descended and devoured her heart in one single, ferocious bite and all the little girl dreams that she'd been greedily clutching between her fingers spilled out.

Nyiew halah, black moon, the number zero and inside her there was the emptiness between stars.

It would have been kinder to shoot her down.

She pressed those fingers against her mouth to keep a single note of agony from escaping.

Quiet, quiet, she thought.

"You say that, now," Daisy replied.

"Honey, it's not like having a third player ever hurt anyone," he said.

"She's too fresh."

"All the better. Let's use her in South America. We'll cut her lose after that."

"No, we ditch her in Mexico, no sense in spending money on three plane tickets," Daisy insisted.

"What a tightwad you are. She comes through with Lawrence, then she's at least earned her plane ticket, hasn't she?"

"We don't want to be dragging an anchor. But maybe you want someone weighing you down, maybe you like this girl a bit too much. I told you at the beach—"

"You said *bring* her to the beach. You said we needed a witness. When Ambrose fell down the stairs, you said—"

"A *witness*. Not a lover."

"Don't start. You get jealous, then you get sour, then all the fun goes to hell. Three-dollar hooker, we both agree on that. I thought she'd come in useful down south, that's all."

Her eyes didn't water. She had no tears. Only that quiet cry which never slipped from her lips. It was stillborn, it was merely a shiver shaking her body and although she thought she'd hit the ground, she was able to stand up.

Turns out you don't need a heart to live, after all.

Someone—she thought Gregory—decided to change the station and turn up the volume again. It was okay. Viridiana didn't need to hear the rest. She walked quietly, quickly, down the stairs and into her room. Her radio wasn't there. Of course not, they had it upstairs. She sat on the bed in silence.

It was an impossible, absolute silence.

Viridiana lay down and pressed her hands against her stomach.

By now, she ought to have lost all the childish innocence she'd possessed, but it had lasted and held true until this very moment.

That is what pained her the most. Not the betrayal, but her steadfast devotion to her betrayers.

So they cheat, she thought furiously. *I cheat too.*

She did have what it takes. Fuck them both. They weren't going to take her chances away. Even as Paris dimmed inside her mind, even then she knew they couldn't take it all away. She'd figure something. *Improvise.* That's what Daisy said.

She thought of the men waiting back at La Sirena, and that scared her. They were dangerous. They might hurt her.

Then she thought about her family and her friends, and she wished they were all dead.

She pictured the men from La Sirena jumping through a window and smothering Daisy in her sleep, and then they smothered Viridiana.

She thought of smothering Daisy herself. She could clutch a pillow and murder her.

Viridiana pressed and pressed and the bezoar which she'd pictured so realistically dissolved under her fingertips. It went away and she closed her eyes. It didn't hurt anymore.

Nothing hurt. She pretended she was floating on the bed, the mattress melting beneath her. She thought of ghosts but was unafraid as she pictured their nacreous body. She pictured Ambrose. His ghost was made of blue and white wisps, like an oyster.

Lawrence stopped by in the morning and was admitted into the living room. Her instincts had been right, she could tell, with one look, that he'd capitulated.

Daisy and Gregory had been up late and were not expecting the visit. Daisy came downstairs hastily in a yellow wrap dress, smoothing her hair with both hands, and told Viridiana to empty the ashtray and bring coffee.

Viridiana put the kettle on and brought back a tray and three cups, the sugar in a dish, plus the empty ashtray. She thought Gregory and Daisy looked older that morning. Like they'd aged years during the night.

Maybe they'd always been this age. More jaded than she realized. Their smiles seemed terrifyingly artificial, the smiles of carnies trying to bilk an unwary customer. They were wax mannequins in a ludicrous horror movie.

"I don't understand," Daisy told Lawrence.

"It's held in a trust. That's the arrangement my uncle wanted. You will receive a lump sum now, of course. Two-hundred thousand dollars. But the rest is a lifelong trust. You will be able to draw upon it each month, up to a certain limit."

"A trust? That is for minors. For children," Daisy protested.

"As I said, it's what he had planned."

Daisy sat on the couch, ankles crossed, in a pose that Viridiana thought was supposed to evoke serenity. Gregory was a bit more nervous. When Viridiana set down the tray with the coffee he immediately leaned forward and grabbed a cup, tossing two sugar cubes in it, his spoon rattling against the rim.

"But you control this trust. You must be able to do something," Daisy said, carefully taking a cup for herself. She drank her coffee black.

"My uncle gave instructions that I could reduce the one million to a more modest amount or that I could eliminate it altogether. But a trust is what he wanted," Lawrence declared firmly. "I am following his instructions."

"Well," Daisy said, scoffing.

Lawrence picked up his cup, took a couple of sips, and set it down again. Now that he had finally made his choice, now that he'd come with his offer, he seemed to have acquired an obvious vitality. The Boy Scout was ready for a camping trip, checking maps and compasses.

"My lawyer is sending papers over. Would you be able to go to the notary public Friday, before noon? We can settle this then."

"I don't have much of a choice, do I? I must dance to your tune. I am defenseless."

Lawrence sighed. "I'm not taking a penny from you."

"No, you are treating me like a baby," Daisy said, leaning back and laughing with artificial delight. "I'll be tied to you."

"It's a trust, not a prison sentence, and it'll have very little to do with me. The lawyers can assist you if you have any questions or if you need anything."

"You must admit it feels a bit unorthodox," Gregory said. "This is not the way to dispose of an estate."

"I think it's very normal," Lawrence concluded.

Lawrence bid them goodbye and Daisy escorted him to the door, no doubt hoping to get a few more words in his ear, to plead her case for a couple of minutes longer. It must have done her no good because she soon returned to the living room and, eyeing Lawrence's abandoned cup, she tossed it across the room.

The sound of it smashing made Viridiana tremble. But the bezoar was gone and she composed herself faster than Gregory, who stood, wide-eyed, staring at the smashed cup, stammering, before he spoke.

"What's wrong with you?" he yelled.

"Clean that up," Daisy ordered Viridiana, then turned towards Gregory, arms crossed. "You heard him! Two-hundred thousand dollars. That will hardly cover the money we owe Frank."

Viridiana hurried to the kitchen, grabbed a couple of rags, and returned to find the volume of their voices had increased considerably.

"So, we give him what we have and—"

"And what? We are left with nothing! I didn't do all this to end up with nothing!" Daisy said.

"What choice do we have?"

Viridiana leaned down on the floor, drying the spilled coffee, collecting the bits of broken ceramic and placing them on one of the rags, which she wrapped tight.

"We leave. As soon as we sign those documents, as soon as everything is settled, we get into the car and drive away."

"Are you crazy?" Gregory said. "Do you know what they'll do to us?"

"We'll leave Friday afternoon. We'll leave immediately."

"And if they catch up with us? You know what'll happen then. They'll put a bullet in our heads."

"Friday. Afternoon." Daisy repeated.

"You are—"

"Friday night," Viridiana said, lifting her head and looking at them. "The air conditioning in the car is broken. If we drive out in the daytime it'll be very hot. And at night it'll be easier to pass unnoticed, less people on the roads"

Neither of them had expected Viridiana to speak, but now that she had spoken and tipped the balance in Daisy's direction, Daisy greedily latched on to this.

"She's right," Daisy said, giving Viridiana a smirk. "And *she* gets it. A little girl gets it better than you do."

"Then we'll do it, fine," Gregory said. He didn't sound pleased but it was obvious he did not wish to fight the combined attack of both women.

"Then it's settled."

"There's one thing," Viridiana said. "You owe me that tape."

"The tape will be yours once we are on the road," Daisy said.

"I'd like it now. I've done what you asked. He gave you the money."

"It doesn't mean you get the tape today."

Viridiana grabbed the bundle with the glass and headed to the kitchen. She tossed it inside the garbage. Damn fucking tape. Damn the both of them. Where could Daisy have stashed it? The house was large and if it was in Daisy's room, there was no chance for Viridiana to get in there. She now locked the door to her room.

It had to be in Daisy's room.

Gregory walked in and poured himself a glass of orange juice. He gave her a tired smile. Viridiana opened the kitchen tap, washed her hands and dried them using a pale blue washcloth which she carefully refolded and placed back on a hook.

"You did great. Thank you," he said.

Viridiana looked up at him. *Lying pig*, she thought, but she prided herself in the neutrality of her expression, even if she quietly clutched the kitchen counter with one hand, feeling she would not able to properly hold herself up together without a support.

And yet she must.

"The maid's not supposed to come over today, is she?" he asked.

"No," Viridiana said.

"Good. Then we can spend some time together."

Fuck you, she thought. But she also had another idea, an idea that had stretched itself quickly as she picked up the stray bits of cup. It was why she had suggested they drive out Friday night. If she wanted to see that idea come to fruition then she couldn't let him see anything was amiss.

Viridiana nodded.

He finished his juice and grabbed her by the hand. That morning, he went down on her and didn't even ask her to give him a blow job until the next day, which showed how generous he was feeling since blow jobs seemed to be one of Gregory's favorite pastimes.

Viridiana wondered if Daisy did the same thing for him, or if that was reserved to his flimsier conquests. She couldn't picture Daisy on her knees, perfectly-coiffed, with her nice makeup and nice nails, swallowing.

Cheap chicks did that, no doubt. Girls they picked up and used. Girls who didn't get tickets to any special destination. She wondered if they were planning on dumping her on the side of the road? Whether they thought they could leave her at a gas station, when she went to the bathroom.

She pictured herself standing by the gas pump, startled, clutching her hat, looking at the lonely highway, maybe even having to hitch a ride back home.

Or perhaps they'd be a smidgen classier. They'd creep out of a motel room while she slept, even fold a couple of bills in an envelope. *Sorry it didn't work out, sweetheart.*

It was her fault for thinking scorpions could be tamed, but Viridiana was nothing if not quick to learn. What she discovered in those days when the temperature soared and sweat clung to their bodies, the fan whirling slowly, was that there was an uncomfortable similarity between despair and desire; an agony of the flesh. She learned that she could loathe and want something, that his hands were repugnant and delicious. Most of all she learned to handle him with a brutal, quiet efficiency. It was not only the physical act of getting on her knees, more than that it was the dissimulation it took to do it with a smile.

"Baby, it's going to be so good you and me together," he told her, and she didn't contradict him, her body didn't tense as he spoke. His hand was splayed against her breasts and she nodded.

She felt very much alone as she lay on the bed with Gregory by her side. More alone than she'd ever been, but also considerably less afraid. There was a calm inside her now, a silence. She'd always been so afraid that the land would eat her, but it was obvious now that the answer was you had to eat it.

You have to be the carnivore, the devourer, the one who bites first.

A shark, enormous, majestic, unstoppable, rows and rows of teeth.

In mock play she bit into his hand, leaving the slightest indentation of teeth on his flesh. He thought it was funny.

"You're a cannibal," he said and she remembered that they said the Aztecs ate the hearts of men.

She bit his lips for good measure.

Chapter 21

It was easy to find an excuse to go into town. They were always needing things. Daisy was out of cigarettes—Viridiana had flushed the last two of them for good measure—and Gregory got cranky when the booze reserves were too low. No need to flush that, in their boredom they knew to do little more than drink and tan themselves. They were primeval creatures, despite their sleek appearance. They were the Nephilim in the first few pages of her family's Bible; golden-haired angels who had fallen low.

Viridiana went to town, parked her bicycle behind the hotel and walked in through a side door which was perpetually broken, avoiding the lobby and heading straight to the room she wanted. She knocked twice and the door opened wide.

The thin man, Henry, wore a different velvet jacket, this one blue, but looked at her with the same expression he'd employed before, like a man who is adding up numbers in a column.

"Can I come in?" she asked, calmly. She had rehearsed that line in front of the mirror half a dozen times until it sounded right, an actress preparing for the most important audition of her entire life.

"Please," he said.

She went in, stood in the middle of the room and saw that there was an interconnecting door and the other man, Scott, stood there, staring at her. Henry waved at the man, and Scott moved back out of sight. He was close enough. Close enough he could barge into the room in three seconds if he deemed it necessary, she'd understood the message.

Henry pointed to one of two plush chairs set next to a large framed photograph of the cave paintings in the Sierra de San Francisco. She'd never seen them up close, but the legends said they'd been painted by giants.

The giants had killed each other many years before, leaving behind only those paintings in black and red upon the walls of caves.

Every story in Baja California seems to end in death.

"What do you drink?" Henry asked, opening the mini bar.

"Water."

"Not with Lily and James you wouldn't."

Lily and James. Whoever they were. Their names had changed, but they must have started somewhere. Like this man, and the man in the adjoining room. They began somewhere.

Viridiana was beginning, too.

"They're not here," she said.

"Right. Why are *you* here, then?"

"You told me to make sure I was taking care of myself the other night."

He had filled a glass with mineral water and the other with whiskey, and handed Viridiana the one with water before sitting down in front of her.

"We all have to take care of ourselves," he said, smiling.

She did not smile back, although she thought that's what he expected. After all, we mirror people's expressions and emotions. But she thought there was no need for that now and that her face, impassive, would be taken seriously, while a smile would undermine her words. Besides, she had not practiced a smile.

"What story did they spin you?" Henry asked. "At one point Gregory told girls he was a photographer and he'd make them into famous models. Is that the line he threw you?"

"No," she said, although she could picture that all too easily. He probably hadn't bothered with that because there was no need, she was all too willing to cooperate, and Daisy had the cassette tape anyway. It was as good as anything else to force a girl's hand.

They'd forced a lot of people into a lot of things.

"Whatever it is, you don't really think you're their protégé, do you?"

"You've known them long?" she asked, instead of answering him. It still hurt, a little, the whole thing. It was like a discolored bruise.

"Some," he said. "They worked for my boss. Until they bungled that."

"Daisy and Gregory owe you a bunch of money, don't they?"

"Not me. My boss. But, yeah, they do," Henry said.

"You said you were a gentleman, you said that, too. The other night."

"I am."

"Then maybe I can talk to you."

"Talk away."

"Right. It may please you to know they'll be getting money from Lawrence Landry tomorrow. Two-hundred thousand dollars. They also intend to run off tomorrow night. Without paying you a single cent," she said.

Viridiana sipped her water. She had rehearsed this part but she was still surprised at how coolly she was able to speak. She was nervous. That hadn't disappeared. But she could also clutch that nervousness, clutch it tight and pin it in place so that it didn't radiate up and down her body. It stayed pinched in that single point.

"That would be very rude of them," Henry said. He didn't

sound angry. But his eyes fixed on the photograph on the wall in a way that was not at all pleasant. "Very rude, indeed. Are you sure they'll have the money tomorrow?"

"Not in coins and bills. They're headed to the notary public to sign papers. After that, Daisy will have access to two-hundred thousand dollars."

Henry fixed his eyes on Viridiana now. "How do you know this?"

"Lawrence Landry told them that's the way things would go. Tomorrow they'll conclude their business, then they'll go to the house, have a few celebratory drinks and then some more, and late at night they'll head out of town."

"And you are telling me all this, why?"

"They're shortchanging me, too," Viridiana said. "And also because I intend to have a very long, very happy life."

"Don't we all?"

"It's very hard to live happily ever after when you don't settle your affairs properly. I want to settle mine. I'm not sure how Daisy and Gregory got involved with you, or why they even call themselves that, or what they've done before getting here. I don't care whether your name really is Henry and what you do for a living. I care only to be left out of this situation, and to go on with my life as it was before I met them."

Henry had finished his drink, he stood up and set his glass on top of the mini bar.

"I see."

He turned to her, pulled her up from her seat, one quick motion which almost caused her to spill her drink and she opened her mouth to protest, but managed to shut it quick.

"If you're lying to me, you'll be sorry," the man said. "I walk in there tomorrow and if they're ready for us, if it's an ambush, I'll tear you apart."

"It's not. I'm not an idiot."

"Could be you're feeling suicidal."

"I feel like living."

He let go of her and Viridiana straightened herself. "You'll come by tomorrow night, then. I can expect you?" she asked. Despite her composure she bit her lips for a moment, the slightest hint of the anxiety she was managing to control.

He smiled again. "Aren't you scared, kid, to invite us like this?"

What did he want her to say? She didn't reply, placed her glass next to his.

She left, rode her bike to the liquor store and made sure to buy cigarettes while she was in town.

The next day they marched into the notary public. Lawrence and Daisy signed a bunch of papers. There were polite handshakes and when Lawrence approached Viridiana she leaned forward, whispering to him.

"Maybe we can hang out tonight?" she asked. "I'll stop by."

He blinked at her and nodded, and then he whipped his face away so quick that she knew Daisy had been right all along. He had it bad for her. Until that moment she hadn't wanted to admit it, because admitting it meant she was using him. The same way Gregory had used her. But there was also something surgical and clean about the words inside her head. About the truth.

He wants you, plain and simple.

She turned her head, too, looking at the ugly church by the square.

Delfina was heading out by the time they reached the house, but she had left a bounty of food as she always did. Fish and potatoes and fresh bread from the bakery, and the cold cuts and cheeses Daisy liked to nibble on.

Rather than eating right away, Viridiana suggested they walk down to the beach. Daisy and Gregory were jubilant, and readily agreed. Viridiana spent most of the time under the umbrella, watching them frolic in the water while she traced letters in the sand.

When they got back inside it was time to gobble the food, to drink and smoke and lay on the couches, blasting music and idling around. Viridiana sat with a fashion magazine in her lap and considered the many times she had done this with them, the evenings spent in a haze of indolence.

Gregory lay on the floor with a hand behind his head, popping smoke rings out of his mouth. How impressive that had been a few weeks ago. Now Viridiana looked down at him, at his tight shirt, first two buttons open, the expanse of visible skin, and felt incredibly foolish for thinking him Prince Charming.

Daisy, sitting in front of Viridiana, her arms resting on the back of the couch, a glass in her hand, with her bangles and her rings, was still regal. But even her appeal had diminished. She was like a plaster figurine of the Virgin of Guadalupe which has been scraped of bits of its paint. The plaster was showing.

The night was long in coming. It took a thousand years for it to come because that's the way it was here, with clocks that did not mark the right time. Time stalled and they sat in that living room, listening to the same tunes, for years and years. So long, that when Viridiana raised her eyes and saw that the two men had walked into the room, she had almost completely forgotten she'd left the front door open for them.

Viridiana slowly put aside the magazine she had been reading and regarded them in silence. Henry was wearing a black velvet jacket with wide lapels and metal buttons down the center front. This was his uniform, then.

She supposed it was important to know who and what you were. To pick a uniform.

Daisy and Gregory hadn't seen them. They continued chatting, the music played, until a hand lifted the needle from the record and the two of them turned their heads.

"Good evening."

"Henry," Gregory said, jumping to his feet. "Why, Henry, you should have told us you were coming over. We would have tidied up a bit."

"Celebrating something?" Henry asked stepping forward and looking down at the empty bottles on the floor, the full ashtray, the plundered plate of cold cuts.

"You know us. Killing time."

"Really? I thought you were doing business today. I heard you were at the notary public. After that, you went to the bank. Bought some travellers checks, I think."

Henry stepped forward, pushing aside an ashtray with his foot, clearing himself a path towards Gregory and Daisy. The big guy, Scott, remained by the stereo, looking through the LPs stacked there. He flipped an album over, checking out the liner notes, like he didn't care what Henry and the others talked about. He was a guest at a party admiring the host's record collection.

"Do you think I haven't been watching you?" Henry asked.

Viridiana remembered how he had popped up next to her at the hotel, nonchalant. He had probably been following her. He might have been following her when she went to the lighthouse or the restaurant.

"Henry," Gregory said. "Look, man—"

"You two must think I'm a fool," he said pausing in his trajectory, pausing right in front of Gregory.

"Sit down, let's chat," Gregory said, pretending friendliness.

Everyone was pretending.

"I'll sit down in a minute, and we'll chat alright."

"Let me get you a drink."

"No, not you," Henry said. "Kid, get me a glass of whiskey. Neat."

There were bottles on the other side of the room, on a table, along with a few glasses. She poured him half a glass and handed it to him. He nodded at her.

"Where's the money? And don't you dare give me that song and dance number that you don't have it." Henry said, casually, as though he was in a bar and they were all having a friendly chat during cocktail hour.

"It's... it's in... *she* would know. She handles that," Gregory said.

Henry walked behind the couch Daisy was occupying, leaning forward, glass between his hands, turning his head to stare at her. She looked at him, unblinking.

"Help me here, or I'm going to have to be unpleasant."

"You're going to be unpleasant anyway," she replied.

"No. Not me. You know me. I don't like unnecessary messes. Maybe we can square this."

Viridiana figured Daisy spent her life squaring out a lot of things, but this time it was going to be difficult to settle the score. Daisy nodded, anyway.

"I transferred it to an account. And then it'll need to be transferred again," Daisy said. "You know how it is. I have a few thousand in travelers checks, but that's only to tide us up for the next few days. You can't put that kind of cash in a purse."

"I know how it is. I suppose you have all the necessary documentation to execute these transfers and get ahold of this money."

Daisy tucked a strand of hair behind her ear and nodded again.

"Bring the documents down," he ordered Daisy. "Scott, keep her company."

Scott and Daisy went up the stairs together. Gregory did not seem to know what to do with himself. He thrust his hands into his pockets, looked down at his feet. Henry concentrated on his drink, turning the glass between his hands.

Daisy and Scott came down. Henry handed Scott the glass and Daisy handed Henry the papers. He looked them over, turning the pages, pausing over a certain section, his finger on it.

"Two-hundred thousand," Henry said.

"That's right," Daisy said. She stood next to Gregory. Her fingers grazed his arm.

Viridiana remained with her arms crossed, by the big yellow painting. She fixed her eyes on Daisy's long fingers, the bangle on her wrist, the movement of that wrist as it touched Gregory as if to reassure him.

She must do that often. She reaffirmed his courage, or gave him courage where there was none.

"Just about what you owe Frank."

"Then we're square, right?" Daisy said. "Like you said, we're square."

"I said just about."

"Be good, Henry."

"I am being good, Lillian."

Henry handed Scott the papers and he took back his glass. He finished his drink.

"I've always liked you both," Henry said, shaking his head. "Always did. And maybe, if you hadn't tried to run from us a second time, I would have left it at that. But you gave us the slip the first time and then you tried to give us the slip here. That's not right."

"I mean, Christ, Henry, we didn't go anywhere," Gregory said.

"You were planning on going somewhere. It's the principle. Whose idea was it to run off tonight?"

"Hers."

Gregory spoke lightning quick. He couldn't have spoken any faster. Daisy's fingers stilled on his arm and she looked up at him, a smirk across her face.

"And it was you who pushed for Mexico," she replied.

"Come on now," Gregory said raising his hands, palms in the air, stepping back from her. "That wasn't me, either."

"It was someone," Henry said. "Who pushed for it, kid? Chatter in my ear a little more, tell me the whole thing."

He was talking to *her*.

It took Viridiana a few seconds to realize he was talking to her. She had been able to keep her nerves at bay so far. Mostly because she had been prepared for everything, she'd rehearsed her conversation with him and had pictured a similar scene as this in her head. However, she had not thought he'd speak to her again. He'd be too busy with them.

It made it all worse if he spoke to her. Because she had to speak back and she knew that they knew. They were staring at her, and they knew she'd gone to the hotel, they knew she'd done this. The way Daisy stared at her and Gregory's ghostly face, it was right there, that terrible knowledge.

Fuck it. Fuck them both. They'd have done the same thing. They were going to fucking dump her like garbage on the side of the road and she'd clawed back.

Viridiana looked at the man in the velvet jacket.

"It was Daisy who pushed for it."

"It figures," Henry said, but rather than approach Daisy he

pointed at Gregory, who stepped back, a scared wild animal trying to find a burrow. "Scott. Teach him a lesson."

The big man took out a knife, as casually as if he was taking out a cigarette, and went towards Gregory. Gregory tried to put up a fight, he yelled and raised his arms. But the man was big and fast and tough. Gregory landed a couple of punches, but Scott took it all in stride. Give him half a minute and he was slashing at Gregory's face and give him another at the belly, once, twice. Then he tossed him on the floor like a clump of wet tissue. Gregory rolled on his back, mouth open wide, looking very much like the sharks when they drag them onto the hot sand. He tried to roll away and let out a pitiful groan, pressing a hand against his belly.

Henry approached him and kicked Gregory in the face. He groaned again.

"Don't ever say I wasn't nice to you," Henry said, looking down at Gregory. "Scott, get Lily to the car. I'll be over in a minute."

The big man motioned to Daisy and Daisy lifted her head. Her eyes were not on her lover, who was whimpering on the floor, they were set on Viridiana. If a ghost rose from the waters off the coast to haunt Viridiana, she knew that ghost would have those eyes. But she was ready to be haunted. Ready to pay the coin.

She had been ready for a while now.

Scott and Daisy walked out. It was the three of them now.

"One for the road," Henry said, pouring himself more whiskey. "You sure you don't drink?"

"Not on a night like this," she said, her voice a whisper, but he must have heard her because he smiled at her. Or could be it didn't matter what she said.

"I told you I was a gentleman," he said, downing his drink and setting it down. "I'm going to prove it now. You better listen carefully, kid."

The Prince of Darkness is a gentleman, too, she thought. Funny how that quip had not occurred to her before, how she'd forgotten that in the lobby of the hotel and now it was in her head. *Oh, the devil is quite a gentleman. He's called Modo and Mahu.*

"He's not dead yet. You can get him a doctor if you want. But you've done me a favor tonight so I'll do one back for you. He's trouble. He stays alive, I bet trouble follows you around. You don't want trouble, do you?"

She wanted city lights and city fun and money and Gregory, but Gregory was on the ground with blood on his face and blood seeping from his gut.

Viridiana did not reply.

"Up to you," he said. "Give me your hand."

She stretched out a hand and he shook it with a firm grip and leaned forward a little.

"Don't be telling anyone about me, will you?" he whispered in her ear.

"No. Wouldn't want trouble following me around," she said.

The man smiled at her. A smile that was all teeth. Then he was gone. Gregory had managed to quiet his moans, but as soon as Henry left he began to complain.

"That motherfucker," he said, rubbing a hand against his face, smearing blood on his forehead in the process. "Get me bandages, some… some alcohol. I'll need the doctor."

"Okay," she said. "But first, where's the cassette?"

"What?"

"The cassette," she repeated. "Where did Daisy put it?"

"What are you worrying on about that!"

"Tell me and I'll help get you patched up. Come on, you don't want to waste time, do you?"

He stared at her and let out a dry chuckle. "You're a fast learner.

Try the toilet upstairs and then hurry the fuck down."

Chapter 22

The door was still unlocked from when Daisy had gone to fetch the papers, so Viridiana didn't have to smash her way inside, which would have been a hassle. And the tape was where Gregory said it would be: wrapped in a plastic bag and taped to the inside of the toilet tank. Viridiana tucked it in the back of her jeans.

A half-packed suitcase lay on Daisy's bed. Viridiana rummaged inside of it, then opened the drawers on the night tables. A purse contained traveller's checks and a makeup compact and nothing else. They were of no use to her – cops might be able to trace them, it was too risky – so she tucked them back inside the purse.

She went downstairs.

Gregory had not moved nor attempted to sit up. When she walked into the room he turned his head to look at her.

"I said…I said get bandages."

"There are no bandages," she informed him.

"Fuck. Cut a bed sheet. Get me rubbing alcohol. Get me a doctor."

"There is no doctor," she said.

"A doctor…that doctor you know."

Viridiana looked down at him. It was like he hadn't heard her or didn't care what she said. He had both of his hands pressed against his stomach and he was licking his lips. He tried to sit up and when he did the crimson stain on his shirt seemed to grow bigger. He winced.

"Help me up, help me to the couch," he said. "Come on. I told you were the cassette was, didn't I?"

She did not approach him, contemplating him from across the room.

"You were going to leave me behind."

He managed to sit up, grunted and looked down at his wound, but he snapped up his head when she spoke.

"I don't know what you're saying. Come on Viridiana, what are you saying? That guy stabbed me in the fucking liver, stabbed me in the fucking… God…go get the doctor."

He managed to stand and stumble onto the white couch, smearing it with his hands, smearing it red. He sat down. She didn't think he could walk more than a few steps.

"Viridiana," he said. "You've got to help me."

"I'll go into town and come back," she told him. "If you say you love me, I swear I'll come back."

"Of course, I love you. I do."

"Loved me the moment you saw me," she whispered.

"I loved you *before* I saw you," he said, eagerly spitting out the words, in a cheap imitation of dear Montgomery Clift.

But now she could admit she was no Liz Taylor. She wasn't living in one of those matinee movies her grandma used to watch, no romance, no musical, none of that. No black and white photography. It was bright red, the blood on Gregory's face, wide eyed his pain.

The space where her heart used to rest had been torn raw and she looked at him but all she felt was a heavy blankness.

She nodded. "I'll come back," she promised.

The men had taken both cars, but she still had her bicycle. She rode with ease into town, stopping to crush the tape in her back pocket, stomping on it twice, then tossing it away. It fell near a lonely cactus, upsetting a lizard or small animal, which scurried away.

No one saw her do it, no one but the moon. The Coyote moon, hungry and eager, keeping her secrets.

She went straight to the pharmacy. There were a few men gathered near it. Not Alejandro's crowd, but the same type of men. Doing nothing, wasting time.

Daisy said improvisation was the key to success, and Viridiana wouldn't deny improvisation was a good skill, but you also need good planning.

You need to have thought things through.

"Can I get a pack of condoms?" she asked the pharmacist and he gave her a disapproving look, but sold them to her all the same.

She'd thought this through, she'd had days to go over the whole sequence of events in her head. After the first reel, there comes the second one and so forth. She had to follow through, one foot after another.

She stopped at the front desk of the hotel and asked the clerk to ring Mr. Landry.

"Can I see you? What room are you staying in?" she asked, twisting the cord between her fingers.

"Uh, Twenty-one," he said.

"I'll be up."

She gave the handset back to the front desk clerk who looked at her curiously.

Twenty-one was twelve inverted. There's some symmetry there, she thought, since that was Henry's room number. Might be an omen, but this time, she wagered it was a good one.

She traced the door numbers with her index finger before knocking.

"Come in," Lawrence said.

His room was like Henry's, except the painting on the wall was a view of the Sea of Cortez. The TV was on, but he'd turned down the volume. A black and white movie was playing and she recognized it immediately, even without hearing a line of dialogue.

"Not a big night on the town, huh?" she said. He'd had room service, the tray was still sitting on the table along with a glass bottle of Coca-Cola.

"Not exactly," he said, sliding his hands into his pajama's pockets.

"*Creature from the Black Lagoon?*"

The woman in her pale bathing suit had jumped into the water. She was swimming on her back and the creature peeked at her from behind a clump of algae. There she went and there he went, following her.

"You're a romantic, then," she said.

"What?" he said with a chuckle.

"It's a love story," she replied. "A lot of the monster movies are love stories, too. *Bride of Frankenstein* and *The Mummy* work like that. It's all unrequited, of course."

Her eyes were fixed on him, black, like peering into abyssal depths.

"I guess you could see it that way. Did you want… I mean, I could get dressed and—"

"I asked you if we could hang out tonight."

"Do you want to go out? I'll get changed," he offered.

"I suppose they couldn't be happy together. He's a scaly monster, she's a pretty lady without gills," she said, turning her head and looking at the TV set.

"She'd have to buy a gigantic fish bowl to keep him in it," he said. "Cleaning an aquarium is no easy thing when it's that big."

"Someone once told me a goldfish will grow as big as its bowl."

Gregory told her. That's who. Gregory who was James who was someone else, who was a liar and a cheat. Who was dying all alone. Back in the house on the cliff, with no one but the moon watching over him. She could save him if she wanted, pull him from the jaws of the hungry Coyote moon.

"I've never been much for fish," Lawrence said.

"Try a shark," she said, for the sake of saying something and slid a hand into the back pocket of her jeans, checking that she still had the condoms.

It's important to know who you are, she thought. *It's important to know how far you'll go. It's important I do this now.*

It's the only way it worked. She needed an alibi or they'd get suspicious. What better alibi. Custom made.

Viridiana turned to him and lifting herself on her tiptoes wrapped her arms around his neck and kissed him. There were no swelling violins, nothing like that, it was a brief kiss, but still she borrowed a line from that old movie.

"Do I make you nervous?" she asked, in a pitch-perfect imitation of Taylor.

She didn't care about the answer and kissed him again, this time with all the passion and skill Gregory had taught her. He pressed a hand behind her neck, a lock of hair snagging between his fingers.

He probably wouldn't have cared to answer even if she'd had given him the chance, because despite whatever Boy Scout instincts he possessed, he took off his clothes quick enough, though not as quick as Viridiana.

Here's the reason why they didn't show sex scenes in the old Hollywood movies, she thought. It's not because they were prudes scared of hiding breasts—although she knew there were censors and codes—but really, in the end, when you reduce it all to its basic elements one body is like another body, and a fuck is a fuck.

The way things worked between Viridiana and Gregory was that he initiated everything. He asked for caresses, kisses, blow jobs. She let him have them. With Lawrence, it was the reverse: she asked, she coaxed; he responded, dizzy with feeling. But it was still a body next to her body, it was still lips on her breasts and a hand touching her thigh. It was her head resting on the curve of a neck and the frantic, ragged breathing in her ear.

This is a movie, she thought. *It's not the movie I started watching but it's the movie that it's become.*

When she went to the bathroom and dragged her hand across her thighs, looking at the blood on her fingertips, blood on her nails, and she looked up at the mirror, she thought it was such a big fuss over *this*? Everyone in her family always insisting on Catholic virtues, talking about the danger of being "easy", and the priest from the pulpit shaking his head at women in tight shirts. But it was such a little thing. No big deal at all.

There's worse sins, she thought. *It's not even a sin.*

No, a sin was the man waiting back at the house, bloodied and injured and scared. Waiting for her to return with the doctor. She hadn't lied about that. She'd head back.

Later.

If there's something she had learned, it was that in order to deceive you should speak the truth.

She had not told a single lie that day.

"I see you've had a misspent youth," she told the mirror and then she smiled, the way Liz Taylor smiled, lips curling a little.

She washed her hands and leaned forward, drawing a line across her reflection from the bridge of her nose to her chin.

"Do I make you nervous?" she asked the mirror.

She didn't sleep much, that's true. She'd learned that nerves are no good, you've got to approach each situation with a firm resolution and a cold head, but she still couldn't make herself sleep.

When it was morning and they had showered, and she was combing her hair with his comb, Lawrence looked appropriately embarrassed, he even blushed as if he had been the virgin.

"You should have told me," he said. "I thought you'd done it before."

It. Like a kid in high school, this was exactly the way her friends had talked, whispering as they fixed their makeup and their hair in the school's bathroom. Have you done it with Manuel? Have you gone all the way? How far, then?

Nothing, nothing, we are only fooling around. That had been her stock response.

Viridiana shrugged. She sat next to him on the bed.

"It doesn't matter."

"It could have been nicer."

"You're a nice guy, Stanley Lawrence Landry."

He really was a nice guy. The sort of man who would help little old ladies cross the street, who would take in stray puppies and inform a shopkeeper that they'd given him too much change.

"Besides, I didn't want you chickening out," she added, flopping back onto the bed and looking at the ceiling.

"I like your high opinion of me. Or is it low?"

"Low. Make it up to me."

He ran a hand through his hair and laughed, like an awkward kid. "Want to have breakfast? And maybe there's a matinee at that old movie theater in the next town."

"Sure," she said. "But I should get into a change of clothes and tell Daisy and Gregory that I'm hanging out with you."

As they drove back to the house she felt her heart accelerating— *boom, boom, boom* it went beneath her fingertips—and Viridiana reminded herself that she shouldn't be nervous. After all, she didn't really have a heart anymore. It was a blank space.

They got out of the car.

The front door was open and the living room was the same mess she'd left behind: bottles and glasses and cigarettes in an ash tray testifying to an interrupted celebration. And a puddle of blood on the floor, blood stains on the couch, a trail of blood which led them down the hallway, to the downstairs bathroom.

Gregory had dragged himself there and lay half slumped next to the bathtub. He must have tried to stand up and grabbed on to the shower curtain, because it half-covered him like a mockery of a shroud.

She couldn't see his face properly from where she was standing, but it jolted her all the same and she had to step aside and turn away, a hand pressed against her mouth, despite all her plans to remain calm.

"Dear God," Lawrence said. He tried to hold her, but she brushed his hands aside and rushed outside the house.

She stared up at the sky. The sun was up high, blazing and cruel, like the unblinking eye of a god and she crossed her arms, grasped her shoulders, feeling the bones beneath. She hurled near the entrance and then Lawrence came out, helped her up. Now she let him hold her, cheek pressed against his chest, her eyes wide open.

"Come on," he whispered. "Let's get the police."

They got back in the car and drove into town and thankfully Lawrence was also rattled, so he didn't speak to her because the taste of bile in her mouth made her want to tell him everything. But she clamped her mouth shut.

Chapter 23

It proved a little difficult to find the policeman because he had gone out on a bender the night before and wasn't home. Eventually the doctor came over and the policeman, and they began asking questions.

The questions were easy to answer, but a murder is not the same as an old man falling down the stairs. A murder *and* the disappearance of an American tourist is an even stranger, more pressing category, meaning that the judicial police was summoned. Three officers waltzed into town, much to the amazement of everyone.

The man who questioned her wore large sunglasses, and when he began talking to her he took them off and slowly set them on the desk. They were sitting at the police station and it ought to have been the same drill, but this guy seemed more menacing than Homero. She knew Homero. He was a kid like her.

The judicial took out a tape recorder, much like her own, and placed it on the desk. He also took out a notebook and a pen.

He asked her to tell him how she knew the American. The he asked her what she had done the day Gregory died and Daisy went missing, beginning in the morning. Viridiana explained that they had gone to the notary public, then she had helped Daisy pack her clothes. She said this in case they dusted fingerprints from the room and found hers.

"Did they say where they were going?" the man asked.

"No."

"They didn't mention it at all?"

"No, when we got back to the house Daisy asked that I pack her suitcase. She said they would leave during the weekend."

"But they didn't say how long?"

"I thought it might be a permanent move."

"You didn't think this was unusual? That they'd leave from one day to another?"

"Not really," Viridiana said. "Daisy didn't like the town much."

"Why didn't she leave before, then?"

"She had unresolved business with Mr. Landry."

"But that business had been resolved, after the visit to the notary public."

"Yes, that was my impression."

The man wasn't really writing anything down. Viridiana could write in shorthand and take dictation. He was idly scribbling a single word here and there, like it didn't much matter what she said. That's what the recorder was for, she supposed. And still, she thought this detail mattered. That it wasn't good.

"What kind of business did Daisy have with Landry?"

"Her husband died here in town. Ambrose—he fell down a staircase. Mr. Landry came to settle her husband's will. He is heir to Ambrose's estate and he gets to control it. That's all I know."

"What did you do after you packed Daisy's clothes?"

"We did some other packing, but then Gregory said he wanted to go to the beach, so Daisy and Gregory went."

"Alone?"

"They asked me to tag along. To bring the beach umbrella, their sun tan lotion. It's the kind of work I did for them. Like I said before, I was their personal assistant."

"Then what?"

"Daisy and Gregory asked me to fix them drinks, and I talked with them for a little and had a drink too," she said, because they might have also dusted for fingerprints in the living room or they might count the glasses, or who knew. She needed to hew as close to the truth as possible. "Then, I went to my room to nap, and when it was dark, and since it was Friday, I decided to come into town."

"What did you do in town?"

"I came to see Mr. Landry."

"How long were you with him?"

"I spent the night with him."

"The whole night?"

"That's what I said."

The police officer nodded. He slowly drummed his pen against the notebook and leaned forward, staring at Viridiana. Whack, went the pen against the notebook. Whack. A little louder each time, until he set the notebook and the pen down.

"That's mighty convenient."

Viridiana felt her breath hot in her mouth. She wanted to cough. "What?"

She had gone over every question they might ask her but she hadn't expected that. This man was inflexible and you could tell he wasn't the type that drew his paycheck and let things go by.

"I said it's mighty convenient. Mr. Landry had been going around town for days, asking if the death of his uncle looked suspicious, questioning people. He was convinced there had been foul play. He probably didn't feel very friendly towards Daisy and Gregory and suddenly one is dead, the other disappears into thin air."

He stood up as he spoke. Rounded the desk. When he was done talking he let a hand land on her shoulder. He let it lay there, unmoving, like an ugly tarantula creeping out of its burrow.

"That's ridiculous. We were together."

"I'm sure you made it to the hotel. The front desk clerk remembers seeing you."

"Then?"

"He could have slipped out sometime during the night."

He was beginning to spook her. His tone of voice was outright hostile and his hand was still resting heavily against her shoulder. "Are you covering for him? You better tell me now."

"No."

"Think harder," he said, giving her shoulder a painful squeeze. "Because there are bits and pieces that are not aligning. I hate it when things don't align," he said.

Viridiana decided she was not going to reply to that. After a couple of minutes the man lifted his hand and sat down again, staring at her.

Shit, she thought.

* * *

"What did they ask you?"

She had gone up to Lawrence's room because no peace could be had anywhere else. If they sat at a restaurant, people would stare at them or eavesdrop. Thus, they'd kept their distance from each other but that day Lawrence was fed up and he'd waited for her outside the police station and brought her to the hotel.

"A bunch of things," she said. "The cop told me maybe you'd killed them and I was covering for you."

"That's nonsense! If they start with that, why... why, I'll have to get my lawyer out here immediately. They said it was only routine questions but it's been two days of that now," Lawrence declared.

He took off his jacket it and tossed it on the back of a chair. He also removed his shoes and sat at the edge of the bed, shaking his head.

It was odd being in the same room with him.

She did not feel much like talking to anyone. The police already asked her to talk too much, and at home her mother demanded answers. At home she had become a stone and her silence had extended to him.

This had not been her plan

"As if I had anything to gain from their deaths."

"Revenge," she said. She thought then of Gregory's unseeing eyes, his body crumpled by the bathtub.

"Garbage," he muttered, steadying himself. He opened the newspaper he'd bought in the lobby and looked for the news item he knew would be there. In the capital, no doubt everyone, including *Alarma!* would have reported on the case. It would have been a huge deal. But there were only a couple of reporters who'd come into town. It was a pain in the ass having to send someone to Baja California and they probably were feeling cautious. Maybe those Mexico City lawyers had phoned certain editors real quick, too, because the article in the paper was not very long.

"Christ, right there, my damn name," Lawrence said, nevertheless, smacking his hand against the newspaper.

There were two photos. Daisy and Gregory. It must have been their passport photos because they were staring right at the camera, right at Viridiana.

"Could be worse," she said, looking away.

"My picture isn't there, but it's no picnic. Look at that, right there, 'Stanley Lawrence Landry, 24, a resident of Mexico City.'"

"My name's there, too."

Viridiana snatched the newspaper from his hands and crumpled it, tossing it away. She didn't mind her name there, she didn't want to look at Daisy and Gregory's faces. The officer had flung pictures of them in front of her already, and she remembered perfectly what Gregory looked like.

"I'm an idiot," he said soberly. "I'm sorry, it must be very bad for you, too."

He tried to grab her hand in sympathy but she had the sudden, ridiculous notion that if he did, he might read her thoughts. That a simple caress alone would reveal her every secret and she took a step back.

"You shouldn't touch me," she said, rubbing shaky fingers against her arm. "It's not right."

"I'm sorry, Viridiana," he repeated. "But you haven't done anything wrong."

"You have no idea," she whispered, despite herself. The talk with the police investigator must have rattled her more than she thought. That damn bulldog, sniffing and sniffing and going at her again and again, waiting for her to make a mistake. And the cop knew she'd make a mistake at one point, he was absolutely certain. Maybe you developed an instinct for these things if you conducted enough interrogations.

Lawrence leaned forward, looking serious.

"Okay, look, it's not wrong."

She closed her eyes and pressed a hand against her face and she thought about Daisy, somewhere, with those men. Dead, perhaps, or held prisoner. Gregory's blood on the floor, tinting the bathroom red.

No, it had been wrong.

It had been terribly, horribly, wrong.

She'd be found out. Surely she'd be found out and—

"Making love, I mean, I know there's the whole Catholic thing, but you won't burn in hell, I swear."

"Sorry?" she said, blinking and moving her hand away from her face.

"Sex. That's what's bothering you. Isn't it? I won't touch you, I swear. But it's what it is. It's done, I mean."

She nodded, realizing how much of an idiot she was. One quick interview with a police officer and she was ready to fall to pieces. Why, that judicial didn't know anything! He thought Lawrence was guilty which meant he didn't think *she* was guilty. She was tying herself into knots over *nothing*. And he'd said it himself: his lawyer could jump onto a plane and start pushing them away real quick if they pushed back too hard against Lawrence.

Lawrence was her best card, her shield—not an alibi, but a pristine exit.

Gregory was dead, Daisy was missing. It was very simple. All she needed to do was calm down.

"It is what it is," she said slowly. "It's all over and done with."

He must have taken this to mean there wasn't anything between them because he nodded sadly.

Viridiana sat on the bed and rested her chin on Lawrence's shoulder, hiding her face against his neck. She heard him inhale in surprise.

"Don't be blue. There's no reason to be blue," she said. "I can stick around for a bit if you want."

"A bit" turned out to be three hours, which she honestly had not expected. They played cards since he had a pack in his suitcase.

She was tired and she was irritated, and she wanted to be with someone who liked her. At home everyone was mad at her, in the streets they stared, the cops were relentless.

She'd suddenly think, *I let him die*, and feel a chill go down her spine.

She wondered if Gregory's ghost would slip under the sheets late at night while she slept.

She played cards with Lawrence Landry and tried not to chew her nails. Card by card, minute by minute, she relaxed. They watched TV. It was nice to discover he was like this in private, tranquil and sort of sweet.

When she left she kissed him on the lips, quickly, and he grabbed her hand. "Come back tomorrow?" he asked.

She nodded.

* * *

"How well did you know Daisy and Gregory?" the man asked. His sunglasses rested on the desk. This time he had dispensed with the notebook and merely clasped his hands together and stared at her. He knew something was up, alright.

"I'm not sure I understand the question," she replied.

"Were you good friends?"

"They employed me."

"But working for them, living with them, it must have been easy to get to know them."

"I guess."

"We found a few interesting things around the house," he said, opening a drawer and taking out an envelope. He dumped its contents on the desk. Gregory's IDs. She thought they would have found those long ago, but he must have moved them, made them more difficult to find. Or had the cops simply kept this discovery a secret? There were also several passports she did not recognize. Daisy's?

If they dusted for prints, wouldn't they know she had touched the IDs? What to say, then? How much could he know? Viridiana decided to say nothing.

"You haven't seen these before?"

"I'm not sure what that is."

"A driver's license. And another," the cop said. "One, two, three, four passports. An address book."

He shoved the passports toward Viridiana. She looked down at them and struggled to keep her face impassive.

"You tipped him off, didn't you?"

She clenched her left hand closed and rested the right on it. At the tip of her tongue there were words she wanted to start yelling, but she could not speak them. The cop must have thought her silence was as good as any answer because he grinned at her and jabbed his finger against the desk.

"You told Landry those were criminals, didn't you? That you'd seen their fake papers. And he went and he killed them. Where's the woman's body?"

Viridiana didn't parse what he was telling her at first. *Landry?* He was still going on about that? She recalled what Daisy had said about improvising. All right, she hadn't exactly imagined she'd be having this sort of conversation, but she might as well go with it. Let the cop say whatever he wanted.

Skew as close to the truth as possible. Skew close and he'll miss, she thought. *Please, God, let him miss.*

"Landry killed them," he said sharply, pointing a finger at her. "Tell me now. He killed them."

"He didn't kill anyone," she said.

"He had a reason. He thought they offed his uncle. They demanded money and he didn't want to give it to them. Didn't want to part with his cash."

"Lawrence Landry has money. You think he couldn't part with a tiny bit of it?"

"Okay," the cop conceded. "Maybe it wasn't money. But he didn't like those people. A crime of passion. Maybe jealousy?"

"What?"

"We found the tapes. We played a few. You go on an awful lot about that fellow, Gregory. Maybe Lawrence Landry didn't want any competition."

Those *stupid* tapes! She ought to have destroyed all of them, but she didn't think they'd matter. Damn it. Viridiana didn't recall everything she had said in them. She hadn't spoken explicitly about Gregory and her. She would have been too embarrassed to discuss her sexual relationship with him. But she had said things. That he was good looking. That he was interesting. That he'd given her a camera.

She'd destroyed one measly tape and left the others around. Since she didn't recall the details of those tapes she wasn't even sure what she should admit and what she should deny.

"Lawrence Landry already disliked Gregory and Daisy. You picking Gregory over him could have sent him over the edge."

"You're making things up," she said and she knew how she sounded: a little breathless, a little desperate. He kept coming closer and closer, a shark sniffing blood.

"You don't talk about Lawrence Landry in these tapes and you sound very interested in Gregory. Let me show you," he said, giving her one long, steady look.

The cop took out her tape recorder and stuffed a tape into it. He pressed a button. Viridiana's voice sounded strange to her ears. It was her, though. No doubt about that.

"He reminds me of Montgomery Clift. No, not Clift. I can't even decide if he's more Errol Flynn or not. It doesn't matter. What matters is that I can't stop thinking about him. God, Gregory."

The man gave her a satisfied smile. The tape kept going on with more inane words. What a ridiculous idea. At the same time, it was uncomfortably close to the truth and if this cop started thinking this way, he might start thinking she had something to do with Gregory, and then that led to questions she didn't want asked.

But what to say? How to deny it?

The cop was now toying with his sunglasses, smirking at her like fucking Alejandro smirked at her, that smile that spelled "you little hussy". And then it occurred to her, quite suddenly, that she didn't have to deny it at all.

"Sure, I started thinking about Gregory, but Gregory had no cash. Lawrence did."

The cop frowned. "So what? You decided you weren't interested in him all of a sudden?"

"There's no point in chasing a guy who admits his bank account is almost empty."

Viridiana leaned forward, resting her elbows on the desk. She wasn't Liz Taylor in a *Place in the Sun*. No, no. A pretty socialite? Impossible. She had to be Liz in *Butterfield 8*. She had to be the gold-digger.

"I change my mind all the time. You can ask around town. I dumped my boyfriend because he wasn't good enough. Then I stopped paying attention to Gregory because he wasn't much better. Now there's Lawrence Landry. I'm a regular Goldilocks trying all the beds," she said, and she said it like Liz would have said the line, imperious. "Is that a crime? I don't think it is."

The cop was frowning, trying to reconstruct his theory in his mind, making it fit. But it wasn't, and the picture he was getting was of something very prosaic. A girl trying to get trinkets from the rich tourist, cavorting with him, and they both come back to the place where she works to find a corpse. Nothing to do with them. A coincidence.

"Look, I don't know what happened to Daisy and Gregory. Neither does Lawrence Landry," Viridiana said.

The cop stopped the tape. He was silent. No blood in the water, after all.

* * *

The investigation fizzled out. The cops couldn't find much more than what they already had, which was two American nationals who were wanted for fraud and other crimes in their country, and one of them had turned up dead and the other was missing.

Lawrence Landry's lawyer phoned a few people who phoned other people who told the judiciales to stop inconveniencing the young man.

There had been a third story in the papers about the case, but it was short, Daisy and Gregory's photographs reduced in size. The fourth story was a mere stub. The cops decamped back to wherever they came from, and that was the end of that.

There were no ghosts chasing Viridiana, either, and she was beginning to forget the color of Gregory's eyes.

"Did you have any idea who they were?" Lawrence asked her after he read the stub in the paper, which mentioned some of the aliases Gregory and Daisy had used.

She was seeing a lot of Lawrence— there were no other people to see. It was impossible to spend any time at home. She went to visit Reynier, who asked her no questions, quiet and solemn as he'd always been. Then she stopped by Lawrence's hotel.

Viridiana looked out the window, which had no proper view. But the moon was out. She could look at the moon and think of the coyote in the sky.

"I had no idea who they were," Viridiana said. This wasn't a lie.

Because she'd thought Gregory was Montgomery Clift taking her in his arms and dancing with her, he in his tux, and she in a white dress which bared her shoulders.

It turned out she was wrong.

So, no, she hadn't known who they were, she hadn't known what movie she was in, hadn't known the ending or the sort of music that would play over the credits.

Viridiana sat back on the bed and he put away the newspaper and wrapped an arm around her, so that she might better rest her head against his chest. She rubbed her foot against his leg.

"What day are you leaving?" she asked. She knew he had stretched his departure for a while now and she knew why. He was fond of her.

"Thursday," he said. "I'm thinking of buying Reynier's car."

"You're going to drive back?"

"I don't like to drive, but the bus was a mess. Plus, the car is beautiful. You like it too, right?"

"Yes," Viridiana said.

"I was thinking you might need one in Mexico City. I can't handle the traffic, but you might not mind."

She glanced up at him. He'd made no promises to her, which was fine with Viridiana. Gregory had promised her the stars and that turned out to be a crock of shit. It was better to avoid big pronouncements.

"You talked about going to Mexico City," he said. "Why not go with me? I have a big place in a nice area. You wouldn't have to worry about a thing."

"Except you tiring of me," she said simply.

"Could be the other way around."

"Could be," she conceded.

"The odds are in your favour. I'm bad with women."

"That's terribly romantic."

She meant it as a joke, but he looked bashful and shook his head. "I'm saying it all wrong. I know it. But you... how about it? How about you give the capital a try with me?"

"They don't need you in Boston?"

"No. I never did like it, anyway."

To reply too quickly, too eagerly, might make him think she was desperate for this. Maybe she was, but she didn't want him thinking she was a cheap souvenir he'd picked on the side of the road, like the shells of turtles and the shark jaws they sold to tourists. She decided to push back, rather than accept him with a smile.

She was silent and serious and he was forced to explain himself more.

"You said something to me one time: do I make you nervous? You do, if I have to be honest. But I like that feeling," he said. "It feels unlike me."

How odd. She felt unlike herself these days, and she wasn't sure she'd ever go back to being herself at all. Which was fine, because there had been a girl who had arranged the murder of her lover, left him to bleed out in a house by the seaside, but she was ready to be an entirely different girl. One who lived not in Desengaño, but in Polanco. Who rested her hand on Mr. Landry's arm and drove that sleek car he'd promised and who laughed a full laugh, with no regrets and no worries.

Viridiana sat on Lawrence's lap and wrapped her arms around his neck, looking at him in the eye, but still she didn't speak. He ran his hands down her back, pulling her even closer to him. She decided not to give him an answer now, to leave him waiting and tremulous. To drag all the desire and the tension, until early in the morning hours when she said a simple *yes*.

She had learned to put on a performance and realized it would serve her in the future.

Epilogue

The night before their departure she dreamt a man in a yellow jacket was tossing food to the sharks. He tossed them a human foot, an arm, a leg. This was not a nightmare because it didn't unsettle her. She surveyed the scene calmly, and in the morning she decided to stop by the beach.

The sharks were gone, they would not return until the next summer. It was only the sea and the jaws of the great monsters, still dangling from a wooden rack.

She ran her fingers along one of the huge jaws. You'd think them tough as iron. They were so delicate. So is a lump of coal, before the titanic forces under the Earth transform it into a diamond which can be faceted.

The kid from the shack had dragged out a mounted turtle and was trying to sell it to Lawrence, who kept saying no. The kid kept saying, "bargain". Two fishermen sat in plastic chairs by the shack and chuckled, looking at Lawrence, then at Viridiana.

It didn't bother her. She was used to being a celebrity in town. One more reason to be leaving, even if her stepfather had made a weak argument about how she should remain with them.

You didn't leave home unless you were married. You certainly didn't leave home unmarried and on the arm of a foreigner.

She had to go somewhere, and Mexico City was fine with her.

"Don't you come back," her mother had told her, quietly, while they stood next to the birdcages on the patio. Viridiana realized that she wasn't being cruel by saying this. That the way she said it, with tears in her eyes, it was almost like a prayer. *Don't you ever come back.*

She wondered if someone had told her mother the same thing, and what it must have been to return, but it didn't matter. Viridiana was no salmon who'd trace its course back to its birthplace. She had the money she had earned during the summer, and she had a ride out of town. She even had an apartment in Polanco, because Lawrence Landry was a crazy fool who was taking her to live with him.

And even if the Boy Scout reneged on that, Viridiana had no doubt she could find her way around the city, that she was born to ride its subway, cross its streets and sit at its restaurants, wearing a fashionable coat, with her nails done and her lipstick very red.

Lawrence was still talking to the boy, while she turned her head and looked toward the mound of dead sharks in the distance. You couldn't tell what it was from where she was standing.

She remembered coming here with Gregory and looking at those carcasses. For a moment, her hands went to the camera dangling from her neck and she had the strong desire to dash it against the ground, as if to appease her guilt.

But that would have been silly. He was dead, and Daisy was likely dead, too.

If she wasn't, Viridiana doubted she was anywhere nearby. The police wanted her for questioning. If she had half a brain, she had fled the country.

"Then this is the shark beach," Lawrence said, finally extricating himself from the boy and standing next to her, sunglasses in hand. "It looks peaceful."

"For now. A storm's coming," she said.

He looked up at the sky, surprised. It was pure and unblemished, but you could smell it, like the salt in the air.

"It doesn't look like it," he said.

"Trust me," she said.

She took a picture of that sleepy seashore and watched it develop before her eyes. When the rains come, that's when the waters are stirred and the dead haunt the shores, but they'd have to walk a long way to find Viridiana. How many kilometers? It would take them years to find her if they moved in the slow way ghosts always move.

Whatever happened, she'd endure the haunting.

Not that it was that difficult to endure. It seemed to her that the summer had been nothing but a cheap B-movie she'd watched late at night on the battered TV set. Had that been her? It had been a Viridiana before Viridiana.

"Let me see," Lawrence said and she showed him the picture. "Would you look at that. As pretty as a postcard."

She tucked the picture away and pulled his head down for a kiss. He complied happily.

The boy in the shack was making a bracelet and stared at them when they walked by, hand in hand. She'd never bought anything from the kid. She paused, because this was different. This time she was leaving and she was taking the picture as a reminder. She might as well take something else as a trophy.

"How much?" she asked, pointing at a shark's tooth dangling from a cord.

The boy smiled, a gap-toothed smile that showed he knew all along that she'd buy his wares.

She handed him the money and put on the necklace.

"Want me to take a picture of the two of you?" the kid asked.

Viridiana took off her hat. Lawrence placed his arm around her and they smiled. The kid pressed a button and the camera spit out a picture.

They went back to the car. It was Reynier's fine old car. Lawrence had come to town with a single suitcase, riding the bus, but he was leaving with two suitcases and a girl.

They got into the car and Lawrence placed the camera on the dashboard. The tape recorder was at her side and the map was in the glove compartment, but she didn't need it. Even with her eyes closed she could have directed him to La Paz, onto the ferry, and back to Mexico City.

"Not too shabby, I think," Lawrence said holding up the picture of them together and handing it to her.

Viridiana examined it. She thought she looked different. That her hair was black and her eyes were as dark as they'd always been, but it was as if she had reassembled herself.

She had found herself that summer and peeled off that first skin she wore to become someone new. An ambia ago, a world before, she had met three strangers and they'd died. The desert swallowed them but it did not devour Viridiana.

She would not apologize for that, because here she was, at the beginning.

Her beginning, the beginning of everything.

"Wait," Lawrence said, grabbing the tape recorder and holding up the microphone. "You've got to say something."

"What am I supposed to say?"

"Anything. You're always talking to this thing, and you were the one who told me you wanted to document the trip back."

"It doesn't mean I have anything to say," she protested.

He smiled at her and Viridiana leaned forward, took a breath and spoke.

"Day one," she said and then pressed the stop button.

That was enough for now.

Acknowledgments

Many thanks to my husband for always reading my work. Thanks to my agent, Eddie, and to the publishing team at Polis, including my editor Chantelle. And thanks to Lavie, who read an early draft of this book and said it was good.

About the Author

Silvia Moreno-Garcia is the author of the acclaimed *New York Times* bestseller *Mexican Gothic*, as well as the critically acclaimed speculative novels *Gods of Jade and Shadow* (named one of the best books of the year by NPR, Tordotcom, The New York Public Library, BookRiot and LitHub), *Signal to Noise*, *Certain Dark Things*, and *The Beautiful Ones*. She has edited several anthologies, including the World Fantasy Award–winning *She Walks in Shadows* (aka *Cthulhu's Daughters*). She lives in Vancouver, British Columbia. Untamed Shore is her first thriller.

CPSIA information can be obtained
at www.ICGtesting.com
Printed in the USA
LVHW032122080121
675922LV00005B/5